EVOLUTION

DR WHO – THE MISSING ADVENTURES

Also available:

GOTH OPERA by Paul Cornell

EVOLUTION

John Peel

THE MISSING ADVENTURES

First published in Great Britain in 1994 by
Doctor Who Books
an imprint of Virgin Publishing Ltd
332 Ladbroke Grove
London W10 5AH

ISBN 0 426 20422 0

Cover illustration by Alister Pearson

Typeset by Galleon Typesetting, Ipswich
Printed and bound in Great Britain by
Cox & Wyman Ltd, Reading, Berks

This is for everyone who has helped make VISIONS the best conventions:

Organizers: Bob McLaughlin, Dennis Light and especially Debi Smolinske – not forgetting Jeff and Dana (cousin Dashiell says *Woof!*)

Staff members: Lisa Albergo, Dee Dee Aquino, Tasha Avon, Jeanna Bloom, Patti Duke, George Fergus, Louis Galvez III, Morn Geiger, John Golkosky, Jennifer Adams Kelley, Sandy Kinnard, Nancy Kolar, John Lavalie, Anne Macko, Kate Raymond, Cherry Steffey, Ruth Ann Stern, Dave Thomas and Charlie Thomson.

Attendees: Emma Abraham, Jean Airey, Paul Scott Aldred, Lee Bahan, Tom Beck, Jane Dietz, Chrissy Carr and Martin Hunger, Lee Darrow, Jan Fennick, Jenn Fletcher, Alex Franges, David Gee, Bob and Lorie Kessler (thanks for the photos!) and Bekki Wolf (and for the tie!), Bill Massey, Jr, Kelly McDonough, Grace Meisel and Scott Tefoe, Dan and Katherynn Murphy, Bea Owens, Kevin Parker, Howard and Carol 'Mac' Rubin, Dean Shewring and Teri White.

As well as all of the wonderful guests.

You all deserve a book dedication of your own, but that would take forever! Thanks, everyone: every year so far has been terrific – and I'm certain that the best is yet to be.

1

Childhood's End

He had been human once. He had to remember that. But it was so hard. When the blood-lust came over him, he could almost taste the kill in his fangs, feel the small bodies crunching, become intoxicated by the fresh blood that would dribble down his throat. He tried to fight it again, as he tried to fight it each and every time.

And, as always, he failed.

Night had fallen, burying the humans who lived here in their small houses, huddled together for companionship and warmth. He had no one. There was nobody to keep him company, no companion to offer him warmth. His only warmth came from the thrill of the hunt, his only companionship from the prey he ran down and then devoured. He was alone, unique, the sole member of his kind.

But he had been human once.

Long, long ago. He could barely remember those days. In his new state, time had little meaning. His mind wasn't working as it had once. Days and weeks blurred together. The only times were night or day, feast or famine. By day he hid, knowing that if anyone saw him, he'd be killed. Nights he hunted. If it was a good night, he ate: crunching the fresh bones, draining the delectable marrow, chewing on the tough sinews. If it was a poor night, he fasted, waiting for the following day, his belly growling and complaining. That always made the blood-lust worse.

1

Rabbits were good prey, but they were fast. He had to be faster to catch them. But with rabbits one bite from his massive jaws was more than sufficient to kill. Foxes were good too, with their rich, predatory taste and hunter's blood. Foxes he admired. They were almost as good at killing as he was. But he could kill them, and they avoided him.

The small ponies were a feast, but much harder to take down. They were wiry and tough, fighting with their hoofs and teeth, kicking and snorting. And he couldn't kill them with a single bite, as he did with the rabbits and foxes. For the ponies, he'd developed a trick of biting their throats and then hanging on until they died choking in their own blood or until one of his paws could break their necks. If he took a pony, then he could drag it to his lair and eat for a week without having to venture out to hunt and to risk being seen.

Not many people came out onto the moors, and virtually no one was foolish enough to try the trip at night. But humans were tricky, and they were curious, and they were lethal. There was no animal that could hurt him out here. Even the ponies could only bruise him through his thick fur. Humans could do more, with their guns. He'd been shot at once, and in the stormy weather he could still feel the ache from the shot.

They wouldn't ever get another chance to shoot him.

The clouds covered the crescent moon, and he was satisfied. Sniffing the air cautiously, he could tell that there were no humans around. They were not smart enough to be able to hide from his heightened senses. He could detect the faint trail of rabbits, and the merest hint of a fox. The main scent this night was badger.

Badgers had claws, and they fought hard and long. But his fur warded off their worst slashes, and they were good eating. He could almost taste the hot, delicious blood in

2

his mouth, and the blood-lust came down over his senses like a curtain at the end of a play.

He had been human once.

But now he was only a killer beast.

Howling his happiness, his anger, his hunger, his hatred for what he had become, he sprang out onto Dartmoor. With long, loping strides, he began to cover the distance to his prey.

Tonight would be a good night. Tonight, he would feast.

Tonight, something would die.

Ben Tolliver loved the sea as he had never loved any human being. He'd been married twice and fathered eight children, but he loved none of them as much as he adored his silvery mistress. He'd loved these waters as long as he could remember. He'd been born beside them, and he knew he'd die beside them – or in them, as his father and grandfather had done, and as his brother and two sons had done.

The sea was a fickle mistress, Tolliver knew. She could be sweet and serene, romantic and flirtatious. She could coyly beckon you down to her cold embraces, then turn violent and murderous in an instant. She was his only mistress, but he wasn't foolish enough to ever think of trusting her capricious moods. He was content simply to be with her, sharing the same night breezes that stirred the dark surface of the waters. He felt an empathy with the sea. When she was calm, he felt rested. When the waters raged, he felt helpless and imprisoned.

He'd spent more than sixty years here, either floating in his small boat in these waters, or else in his small cabin where he could look down on the sea. It had been a rough life, and a poor one – no question at all about that. No Tolliver had ever grown wealthy from the sea. But he

3

was content. Even with the loss of both wives and his sons, he wouldn't have wanted anything to have been different. Then he chuckled to himself. Well, maybe that saucy lass at the Dog and Pony. Now, if she'd agreed to some of those romps he'd often suggested . . . But aside from that, he was content. It had been a hard life, true, but a fair one. He'd been able to live as he'd wished.

And here he was as always, floating gently on the sea in his old boat. It was a lot like him: grizzled, getting no younger, and maybe a slight achy in places, but overall a good, stout craft that had many a year left to it. And, like him, his boat was built for the sea and would be at home nowhere else.

Tolliver sighed and straightened up from his nets. He'd checked them thoroughly, as he always did. One small tear in the mesh could ruin a night's fishing. He'd seen plenty of foolish fisherfolk lose their entire catch like that, but it had never happened to him. Nor would it. The day he lost a single fish was the day he'd retire from the sea; the day he'd lie down and die. The sea was his mistress, and he knew that if he treated her right, showed her the proper respect and care, why then she'd be flattered and give generously of her bounty.

He heaved the net into place, ready to cast it over the side and into the dark, nocturnal waters.

Then he paused, astounded.

There'd been talk in the taverns recently from some of the younger men about mermaids and fairy fires under the sea, but he'd always dismissed it as the foolishness of poor men in their cups. He'd believed it was the beer talking, not the youngsters. Why, he'd fished these waters sixty years and never seen any sights such as they had claimed.

Until tonight.

The moon had hidden itself behind the clouds, and the

4

silvery reflections on the waves were gone. But the sea wasn't dark and impenetrable as it should have been. Far below the surface, Tolliver could see light. The fairy fires, then, were real! With the surface breaking and shivering as the waves lapped past his small craft, it was impossible to make out much. Just that there were lights down there, lots of them. Small, pinprick lights shivering and shaking with the movement of the waters, but real.

Moving to the bows, Tolliver discovered that he had a better view of them. As he stared downwards, a pattern started to become clear. It was as if the fires were on the spokes of some immense wheel, maybe two hundred feet across. The pattern was quite regular, the lights all lined up, neat as you please. The centre of the wheel lay about a quarter of a mile to starboard of him. As he watched, utterly wrapped up in this beautiful mystery, Tolliver realized that the wheel analogy was very appropriate.

The lights were moving, turning about their hub, just like some immense wheel in motion. The procession of light was slow and ponderous, but it was nevertheless quite real.

Tolliver was captivated. He'd loved the sea in all her strange and often terrifying moods for six decades, but he had never been a witness to a sight like this. Just like a woman to keep all her best secrets hidden till it was too late for you to take advantage of them! Tolliver couldn't tear his eyes from the sight. What could be causing this? He had no idea.

He'd heard enough foolish talk in his years as a fisherman to know plenty of legends of Davy Jones and his ilk. He knew for a fact, though, that such talk was utter nonsense. There was plenty of life in the sea, but it was all victim to line or net or harpoon. None of it was intelligent, none capable of building the sight he was seeing now.

5

But neither could man. In this year of grace eighteen hundred and eighty there were many marvels about that Tolliver had never dreamed of seeing in his simple life, but there wasn't a man alive who could have built this wheel of light he was watching. That engineer, Isambard Kingdom Brunel – now there had been a genius! Building ships the like of which this world had never seen before. Many folks had laughed at him, but Brunel had been proven right time after time. A man with vision, Brunel had been. But even he could never have dreamed of constructing anything like this. Besides, he'd been dead for twenty years now, and there wasn't a man alive that could hold a match to his candle.

Then what was he seeing? What could be the explanation for this strange wheel of lights, turning with grim relentlessness off his starboard bow? Tolliver had heard from some of his colleagues about fish that had their own light, a bit like those fireflies whose bums burned bright on nights they were looking for love. So Tolliver could believe those stories. Still, even granted that there were fish whose backsides were filled with fire, he couldn't imagine anything that would induce them to line themselves up as if they were ready for a dance and then slowly turn around a common centre. It went against everything Tolliver knew.

So, then, what –

A shape flickered past barely under the surface of the water, blocking the lights for a second, and it was then gone. It must have been a fish. What else could it have been? It couldn't have been what he had thought. It couldn't have been –

It rippled past the boat again, and Tolliver shivered in shock. Cartwheels of fire were bad enough. Maybe he was going senile. Or maybe his old mistress was having fun with him.

He had seen a human face, and then the flicker of a fish's tail.

A mermaid?

Tolliver wished he could laugh at this stupidity. Mermaids were seen more often in the bottom of a jar of ale than in the bottom of the sea. But he hadn't been drinking this night. And he had seen something that looked like a woman's face. A bit of a body, and then there had been the fish's tail, grey and smooth. Not at all like the legends suggested. No green scales or over-ripe breasts. Just a face, slim form and tail.

He *had* to have imagined that! There were no such things as merfolk who farmed the pastures of the sea. They were just legend and tall tales.

On the other hand, if there were some kind of folk who were – God alone knew how! – able to live under the sea, then perhaps they had made that monster wheel below him. It went against his experiences and all he knew about the world. But it did make a sort of off-kilter sense of its own.

Tolliver leaned over to get a better look. Maybe that whatever-it-was would pass this way again and he'd get a better look at it on its next pass. Maybe –

In a sudden explosion of spume and cold water, something shot up from the sea. Tolliver reeled back, horrified and screaming, but he was not fast enough to escape this thing. In the last half-second of his life Tolliver made out sleek skin, the thrashing tail that had propelled this creature out of the black waters, and the huge mouth filled with pointed teeth.

And then the thing bit his face entirely off.

Sir Edward Fulbright knew precisely what he liked and didn't like. He liked, for example, Fulbright Hall, the ancestral home. Portions of it dated back to the fifteenth

7

century, when it had been founded by William Fulbright, but the majority of it had been either constructed or restored by his grandfather, Augustus Fulbright, in 1842. There was absolutely no question that the Hall was not merely an elegant and spacious domicile, but also the most architecturally interesting home within the boundaries of Devon.

He liked even more the Great Hall. This spacious room had been constructed by old William for those grand medieval feasts, with a huge stone fireplace in the centre of one wall, the family crest carved in the stones above the immense mantel. In the old days whole hogs had been roasted within that fireplace; nowadays, of course, the cooking was all accomplished in the Hall's capacious kitchens. A huge, cheery fire blazed instead in the grate. The wall opposite the fireplace had been one of Grandfather Augustus's main achievements. The old, small windows of the house had been removed and large glass doors – in the French style, but still very attractive – had replaced them. This allowed easier access to the large grounds of the Hall, and gave a superb view across the moors in all seasons. There was, at the far end of the Great Hall, a minstrels' gallery that had been carefully rebuilt, and for this occasion held the small orchestra that had been engaged for these festivities.

He liked parties, and this was one of the best he'd ever hosted. His wife had outdone herself this time, and everyone who was anyone in the region – and quite a few from London – was here. Still, it wasn't every day that one's only daughter announced her engagement. Fulbright watched her whirling one of those new-fashioned dances – he never could recall their silly names – with affection. He liked Alice a great deal. She was a dutiful and beautiful girl of nineteen, who brought him much pleasure.

8

And he liked her fiancé, young Lieutenant Roger Bridewell. He was a handsome figure of a man, with the prospect of a fine military career. He was smart, well bred and quick to understand and follow orders. He was just the kind of son that Fulbright had always wished for. One day, of course, he would inherit Fulbright Hall. Pity that the family name would be gone, but at least Fulbright could rest easy that the Hall would be retained by good blood. Bridewell's father had served in the Crimea with Fulbright and had died bravely at Sebastopol, having never seen his new-born son. Fulbright had always felt as if Bridewell's son were a member of the family, and he was most gratified that he was finally to become precisely that.

What he didn't like was that friend of Bridewell's. His eyes scanned the room and the many guests dancing, drinking or chattering. Eventually he saw the man again, and he frowned. The disturbing young man was engaged in conversation with Sir Alexander Cromwell, the local Justice of the Peace. What the deuce was he up to now? Fulbright had known this Colonel Edmund Ross for barely a week, but he knew that the man had a quiet intensity and some hidden purpose for being here. If he hadn't been Bridewell's guest, Fulbright would have asked the man to leave.

There were a number of small matters that disturbed him about Ross. Individually they were almost insignificant, but together they painted a very puzzling portrait of the young man. For example, he wasn't even thirty yet but had managed to acquire the rank of colonel. He was terribly vague about the regiment he actually served in, and had in the course of conversations admitted to serving in three different places at the same time! Fulbright would have assumed that the man was a simple blackguard and confidence man, but Bridewell had, rather unusually, gotten rather prickly when Fulbright had raised the possibility.

'Sir,' Bridewell had replied stiffly, 'Colonel Ross has impeccable credentials and is in a position of utmost trust. I would appreciate it if you would not attempt to besmirch his reputation.'

Fulbright had agreed, but his suspicions still lingered. And, just before the commencement of this ball, his butler had mentioned a fresh problem which was still troubling Fulbright. As he watched Ross, he saw Sir Alexander laugh at some witticism and move off. Seizing the opportunity, Fulbright crossed the crowded room to his most troublesome guest.

'Sir Edward,' Ross said, bowing slightly. 'Allow me to congratulate you on a most entertaining evening.'

'Thank you,' Fulbright replied gruffly. He stared at the young man. Ross was a handsome scoundrel, no doubt of that – tall, well built, with saturnine dark looks and grey eyes that hid his thoughts but not the intelligence behind them. He dressed impeccably and had the manners – if not the breeding – of a gentleman. Fulbright again sensed the feeling that there was far more going on with Ross than he ever allowed anyone to know. 'I'm sorry that I have to speak to you about that manservant of yours.'

'Abercrombie?' Ross barely hid his smile. 'And what has the poor fellow done now?'

'He's been scaring the serving maids half out of their wits,' Fulbright complained.

'Dear me,' Ross said. His sympathy seemed quite feigned. 'He hasn't been making unwanted advances, I trust?'

'Nothing like that,' snapped Fulbright. 'He's been lurking in the bushes.'

Ross raised an eyebrow. 'Lurking? In the bushes?' He shook his head. 'Dear me. Perhaps the maids have simply mistaken his interests in nature for other less polite activities? Abercrombie is quite an avid bird-watcher, you know.'

Fulbright almost laughed at the thought. He'd seen Ross's man a few times during the past several days. He was a small, shiftless-looking individual with a prominent nose and one of those horrible low-class London accents. If the man looked at birds, it would be only ones that were on his dinner plate. 'At night?' he asked sceptically.

Ross shrugged. 'I understand that many birds are nocturnal. Owls, perhaps. But I quite understand your concern, Sir Edward. I shall instruct Abercrombie to confine his avian interests to the daylight hours in future.'

Fulbright realized that this was probably the most he could expect. 'I should appreciate that,' he agreed.

Bridewell and Alice moved to join them. 'Hello, Papa,' Alice said, her eyes sparkling with delight. 'Isn't this a marvellous affair?' She nodded to Ross. 'Edmund, are you enjoying yourself?'

Ross bowed to her. 'How could I not?' he asked. 'Your father is a most gracious host and provides excellent entertainment.' He smiled slightly. 'Though I fear the activities of my man Abercrombie are somewhat taxing his patience.'

Bridewell laughed. 'What's the old scoundrel been up to now?'

'Upsetting the servants, I'm afraid,' Ross replied.

'Really, Edmund,' Alice said, 'I don't know why you tolerate the man. I'd have dismissed him long ago. He's positively creepy.'

Ross didn't seem at all upset by the remark. 'He has his uses,' he answered. 'He's not the best manservant in the world, perhaps, but he's absolutely devoted to me.' Ross smiled. 'I'm afraid that all the dancing has tired me.

11

I feel the need for a breath of fresh air.'

'Dancing?' Fulbright snorted. Perhaps Bridewell and even Alice liked this fake, but he didn't. 'I haven't seen you dance a step.'

'I haven't,' Ross agreed cheerily. 'But watching everyone else has quite exhausted me.'

'I could do with a little air myself,' Bridewell offered. 'Alice?'

She laughed happily. 'I feel as though I'm floating on it.' She took her father's arm and smiled at him affectionately. 'Why don't we all step outside?'

Fulbright didn't really want to socialize further with Ross, but he couldn't deny his daughter's whim. 'As you wish,' he said.

The music was still almost as loud outside, and there were a few knots of other guests out on the terrace. Alice led the three men toward the Italianate fountain that dominated the small walk down toward the formal gardens. From here in the daytime was the best view of the moors. Now, of course, it was simply darkness. Clouds hid the moon, and beyond the angelic dispenser of water lay only black night.

'Isn't it glorious?' she asked.

'If you like it,' Bridewell replied, 'it must be glorious. You have such exquisite taste.'

Alice laughed. 'That must be why I'm marrying you,' then,' she said happily.

Fulbright was pleased to see his daughter so happy. Marriages weren't necessarily an impediment to love — his own had always made him content — but neither were they exactly conducive to it, either. It was good to see that Alice and Bridewell were not merely marrying, but looking forward to the estate. The only dark spot on his pleasure was that damnably secretive Ross. What was he really after? Perhaps he was indeed a friend of Bridewell's,

12

but there was more to it than that. Ross had the air of a man with many secrets, the sort of person who let no one into his thoughts if he could avoid it.

So why was he here?

Fulbright was not impolite enough to come right out and ask the man directly, but it was a close thing. And he suspected that Ross knew this – and that it amused the younger man for some unfathomable reason.

Ross smiled at the couple. 'It does the heart good to see a couple so in love,' he said.

'Then why don't you try it for yourself?' asked Alice, bantering. 'Don't think I haven't seen the looks you've been getting from some of my friends.'

'And most flattered I am, too,' Ross replied with a laugh. 'But I'm not prepared to settle down with any woman yet. On the other hand, if Roger hadn't snatched you up at the first opportunity, perhaps you could have persuaded me to change my opinion.'

Alice laughed, but Fulbright was appalled. It was bad enough having to tolerate this man as a guest. The thought of his courting Alice was too much to bear.

'See here, Ross,' he began roughly. But he never finished.

Despite the strains of music from inside the Great Hall, there was un unmistakable sound of a howl in the air. The cry rose and fell, the ululation of some weird, wild hunting beast. It struck through to Fulbright's soul, the cry of some terrible creature in pain and anger.

'Dear Lord!' gasped Alice. 'What in the name of heaven was that?'

Bridewell clutched her to his side protectively. 'Some creature on the moors,' he said, looking almost as pale as the girl. 'But I've never heard a sound like that before.'

'I have,' Fulbright snapped, glad to have something other than Ross to vent his anger against. 'The day before

13

you arrived. We found one of the ponies ripped to shreds the following day. Some monstrous travesty of nature had torn the poor beast to shreds. The servants tell me that this wasn't the first such slaughter.'

There was a stir of movement in the darkness beyond the fountain as the unearthly howl rent the night a second time. The figure that slid out of the shadows was revealed to be none other than Ross's strange manservant.

'It's that blinking hound,' he announced, ignoring everyone but Ross. 'Two, perhaps three miles out on the moors.'

'I had gathered as much,' Ross said drily. 'It seems to be a fine night for a ride, Sir Edward,' he commented, turning to his host. 'With your permission, I'll have Abercrombie saddle a couple of horses.'

Bridewell gasped. 'You're not thinking of going out after that creature alone?'

'Not alone,' agreed Ross. 'Abercrombie's coming with me.'

'What?' Abercrombie shuddered. 'Begging your pardon, sir, but I'd rather stay right where I am. I don't like the sound of that thing.'

'You never like the sound of anything like work,' Ross said without concern. 'Sir Edward?'

'I'll be damned if I allow you out on the moors at night,' Fulbright snapped. 'It's dangerous enough out there if you don't know your way, let alone with whatever made that terrible cry out there hunting.'

'Then perhaps you would be good enough to loan me a guide?' Ross asked. 'I assure you, this is no frivolous whim.'

'I'll do better than that,' Fulbright growled. 'I'll accompany you. Nobody knows the trails better than I do.'

'Papa!' exclaimed Alice. 'I don't think anyone should venture out there tonight. I don't know what that thing

14

was, but it sounded monstrous.'

'By tomorrow it will have vanished, just like last time,' Fulbright answered. 'I want to stop whatever is killing those ponies.'

'Then I'll go along with you,' Bridewell stated, brooking no argument. 'The more of us there are, the safer we'll be.'

'Blooming Ada,' muttered Abercrombie. 'It'll be a ruddy circus out there.' Then, as a thought struck him: 'Here, with all this help, you won't be needing me, will you?'

'Nice attempt,' Ross told him. 'But you're still coming along.' He turned back to Fulbright. 'I'd be grateful for your help, Sir Edward. But you are coming to catch the beast, not to keep an eye on me, I take it?'

You almost had to admire the impudence of the man. 'A little of both, perhaps,' Fulbright replied frankly.

Ross smiled and nodded. 'Thank you. It's nice to know where one stands. Well – shall we go?'

Fulbright turned to Alice. 'I'm sorry for the interruption, my dear, but we probably shan't be very long. Keep the guests happy, please.'

'Take care, Papa,' Alice said. She was obviously very worried. 'You, too, Roger.' She turned to Ross. 'And also you, Colonel.'

Fulbright led the way, and found to his disgust that Ross's man Abercrombie was walking almost next to him. Didn't the disgusting creature know his place? Ross had fallen back slightly, conversing with Bridewell in low tones. Fulbright glared at the ugly little man beside him. 'Perhaps you, at least, will have something to show for this night,' he said coldly. 'You could indulge in a spot of ornithology.'

'What?' Abercrombie stared at him blankly.

'Bird-watching, man,' Fulbright snapped. 'I understood it was a hobby of yours.'

Abercrombie guffawed. 'Watch birds? Me? Stone the crows, whatever gave you that idea?'

'I don't recall,' Fulbright answered icily. So . . . as he had suspected, Ross had lied about his man's activities. What was Ross's real purpose here, then? And why did he tolerate this obnoxious low-life? Perhaps it was time that this so-called colonel's secrets were revealed.

The TARDIS gave up its secrets rather sparingly. Sarah Jane Smith lay on her back in what the Doctor had dismissively referred to as 'the bath' and lazily stirred her hands and feet. She couldn't remember the last time she'd been able to wear a swimsuit – let alone inside the TARDIS. It felt good to be able to simply relax and enjoy herself for once, particularly after the series of harrowing adventures she'd experienced.

The Doctor had been very moody of late. Well, he was always moody; Sarah imagined it was because of his alien nature and incredibly lengthy life-span. He claimed at various times to be anything from four hundred to a shade over a thousand years old. For a being who travelled in time as much as the Doctor did, he seemed to be very shoddy about keeping note of his personal time. Either he wasn't certain how to calculate his age due to all the varying times he had stepped into and out from, or – which Sarah personally believed – he had virtually no interest in it.

She couldn't blame him, really. Imagine the size of the cake he'd need to fit on several hundred (or a thousand) candles! You'd need a flame-thrower just to light them, and even the Doctor could never blow them all out with a single breath.

Which all meant that the reason the Doctor seemed unsure of his age was because it wasn't simple to work out. But he was showing all the signs of some sort of mid-life crisis. If, of course, four hundred to a thousand years old was mid-life for a Time Lord. The Doctor was always pretty vague about that, too. He'd once claimed to be 'immortal, give or take a few years' and at another time had said he was as mortal as the next man. Consistency was not a virtue he believed in or practised.

Something was clearly bothering him, and it was a something that their recent encounter with the renegade Time Lord Morbius on that nightmarish world of Karn had exacerbated. The Doctor had been broody enough before that, but now he was positively grim. He had taken to prowling the corridors of the TARDIS, hands rammed firmly into his capacious trouser pockets, his battered felt hat perched precariously atop his mop of thick, dark curls. His sombre face looked more inscrutable than ever, and his tooth-filled grins had virtually vanished. Even his long multi-coloured scarf seemed to have become more subdued to match his mood.

Sarah had tried her best to tease him into talking, but that had been no use. When he wanted to, the Doctor could talk the hind legs off a donkey, and probably the front ones, too. But when he was in a mood you couldn't even get the time of day out of him. Assuming he either knew or cared what time it was.

Sarah had always been rather wary about exploring the TARDIS too far from the main control room. The ship had so many corridors and rooms that it made a labyrinth seem positively simple. You needed either a guide or a long ball of string to find your way around. She had been reading in the room she'd taken over for herself when the Doctor had wandered past her open door, lost in his morose thoughts again. Tagging along, she had attempted to cheer him up without any noticeable success. Finally,

17

she'd asked him what some of the rooms they were passing were.

'Bathroom,' he'd growled, and then ignored her.

'Which one?'

'All of them.'

This hadn't made much sense to her until she'd opened the first door. She'd been expecting almost anything from a small closet with a toilet to a whirlpool bath. So she simply stared in amazement at the room within.

It was the size of several football fields, and held an Olympic-size swimming pool. Surrounding this were recliners and huge potted ferns and other plants she couldn't even begin to classify. The ceiling was a glowing panel stretching into the distance.

'That's a bathroom?' she gasped.

'Yes,' the Doctor answered, looking at her as if she were some kind of idiot. 'Can't you see the rubber duck in the tub?' There was indeed a small yellow plastic duck bobbing up and down in the water. He rolled his eyes and strode on.

Since she clearly wasn't going to get any further by talking to him, Sarah had rushed back to her room, and into the closet. Like the rest of the TARDIS, her closet seemed to expand to accommodate the clothing she placed in it. The room had clearly belonged to at least two other people before her, because she'd discovered outfits in two distinct styles and sizes already in the closet. One set had been pastel-shaded Victorian outfits; the other had been all silver and leather. Presumably at least two of the Doctor's previous companions had stayed in here. Sarah had simply pushed their stuff to the back and added her own closer to the door. Now she shuffled through the spacy-looking clothes, searching for something she could recall seeing once. Finally she found it: a one-piece bathing suit of some kind of opalescent material. It shimmered with pinks and silvers as she held it up to see if it might fit her. She'd never thought to bring along a swimsuit of her own. Most of the seas they had landed beside turned out to be filled with acid or monsters. Or both.

The suit had moulded itself to her body when she'd tried it on. It was perhaps a trifle daring, being very low-cut in several places, but for the TARDIS's bath-room it was fine. And here she was, lazing in a huge pool, inside a time and space machine taking her who-knew-where in the cosmos. It was something that anyone else might have found utterly bizarre, but which Sarah simply accepted. One thing you had to take into your stride with the Doctor was the unexpected. And at least this was pleasantly unexpected, unlike the usual turn of events.

Eventually, though, she tired of lazily swimming around and returned to her room to dry off and dress. She considered returning to her book again, but she was getting a trifle hungry. That meant a trip to the food machine. Since that was in the room next to the control room, she supposed she ought to take a look in there as well, in case the TARDIS had landed or the Doctor had decided to do more of his running repairs.

Munching on a Mars-bar-like meal of calimari in clam sauce, she wandered into the control room. She wasn't too surprised to discover the Doctor already there, brooding over the time rotor. The lights from the spin-ning vanes within the rotor cast weird shadows across his gloomy face.

'Is it Halloween already?' she asked lightly. Sometimes that helped drag the Doctor from his introspections.

The Time Lord gave a sudden jerk, as though he hadn't noticed her arrival. It was quite possible that he hadn't. As he straightened up, a dismal cloud seemed to lift from within his eyes. There was a sudden flash of teeth, and he brushed back his tangled hair. 'Hello, Sarah Jane,' he said brightly. 'I'm afraid I've been neglecting you, haven't I?'

'Uh-huh,' she agreed, crossing the large room to join him at the central console. She was relieved that he seemed to have cast off his depressing introspection.

'I'm sorry.' His eyes sparkled with the old humour once again. 'I was lost in my thoughts. I have so many, it's easy to get lost.'

Sarah grinned and wolfed down the last of her meal. 'Do you have two brains as well as two hearts?' she asked.

'No. Perhaps I should, though. I'll have to put in a request. Or would that make me a dinosaur?' He started to study the instrument panel. 'Ah, we're still in flight.'

'Where are we going?' asked Sarah. Most of the instruments on the panels weren't labelled, and they didn't seem to be measuring anything that was at all familiar. The few dials and meters that did have labels were generally named in the kind of scrawl that a drunken chicken with its head chopped off might have made.

'Nowhere. Anywhere.' An idea seemed to strike him. 'I'll tell you what – why don't you pick our destination?'

'Are you joking?' Sarah gave a snort. 'You know that the TARDIS never gets us where you aim for.'

'That's not true!' the Doctor exclaimed. His innate honesty compelled him to add: 'Well, not always true. And the old girl is in a good mood right now. Aren't you?' he asked the mushroom-shaped control console, patting it fondly. He often spoke as if the TARDIS were alive and understood every word they said. For all Sarah knew, that might well be true. The TARDIS was at the very least an incredibly sophisticated machine. That it might be aware and intelligent wouldn't surprise her too much.

'Do you really think you might be able to get where you're aiming?' asked Sarah.

'Probably. Let's try, shall we?' He gave another of his grins. 'So where in all of time and space would you like to go? Metabelis? Tarbethon Beta? Argolis?'

Sarah shrugged. 'I don't know,' she confessed. 'I've never really thought about aiming to go anywhere. I've got rather used to simply wandering.'

'My moods must be infectious,' he replied. 'Well, is there anybody you've always wanted to meet? Anyone at all? Plato? Genghis Khan? Llandro Cabot? Charlie Chaplin?'

Laughing, Sarah considered the idea. To be able to meet anyone, anyone at all, from any world or time . . . 'Are you really serious?'

'Cross my hearts.'

Sarah shook her head in wonder. 'You mean you could really control the TARDIS if you want to?'

He shrugged. 'Only when it's very important.' He gave her another of his engaging smiles. 'To be honest, Sarah Jane, I usually don't bother. It's much more fun to let the old girl take me where she wills. After all, I've got nothing but time, and my appointment book is almost empty this millennium. So – who'll it be?'

'Well,' Sarah began, her mind having finally focused, 'you'll probably think this is silly.'

'Oh, I doubt it,' he replied airily. 'After all, once you've met Marie Antoinette almost anyone after that seems to be very serious.'

'I'd like to meet Rudyard Kipling.'

'Kipling?' he asked, raising an eyebrow. 'That's very unusual.'

'It's just that he was a journalist who became an absolutely marvellous writer,' Sarah explained quickly, afraid he did think her choice was rather frivolous. 'And I grew up on his stuff.'

'I'm not complaining,' the Doctor assured her. 'Quite the contrary. I'm rather fond of Kipling myself.

> *Far-called, our navies melt away —*
> *On dune and headland sinks the fire —*
> *Lo, all our pomp of yesterday*
> *Is one with Nineveh and Tyre!*
> *Judge of the nations, spare us yet,*
> *Lest we forget — lest we forget!*

'Stirring, eh?' The Doctor grinned again. 'It's just that he's one of the people I've never met and always wanted to. That means that this will be a doubly interesting trip.' He stared at the panels and began resetting the controls. 'Hang on to your hat, Sarah Jane.'

'Are you sure you can get us to meet Kipling?' she asked.

'Trust me,' he replied. 'When have I ever let you down?'

'Too many times.'

'That was in the past. And we've already passed through those times. This time we'll definitely get there. Now, where and when exactly?'

Sarah wasn't sure she could really believe him. Still, maybe it was worth the risk. If he messed up as usual, at least she wouldn't be too disappointed. 'Lahore, India. February 1889, when he was just getting established as a writer.' She watched him enter figures into the TARDIS's controls. 'I'd feel a lot happier if this thing came with an owner's manual.'

'It does,' he said, dancing around the console to another panel. 'I think I still have it somewhere.' He frowned. 'You know, I think I may be a trifle overdue for her three-thousand-year check-up.'

'There *is* a handbook for this thing?' Sarah could hardly believe her ears. 'Then why don't you use it?'

'She didn't mean to be rude,' the Doctor whispered to the panel, and patted it consolingly. To Sarah he said, 'That would be so boring. It's much more fun to experiment, don't you think? Besides, I can't remember where I put it. Or who I was when I put it there.' He shrugged. 'If it's needed, it'll turn up.'

Sarah didn't know what to say, so she settled for an exasperated sigh. It was extremely difficult to believe that the Doctor would actually manage to get them where and when he had promised.

He looked up at her. 'Better get changed,' he advised her. 'It's very hot in India. Something white would be best.'

'If we get to India,' she retorted. She remembered one of those Victorian dresses in her closet that she'd worn before. It had been that time they'd had the run-in with Sutekh. The Doctor had mentioned that it had belonged to a former companion of his, called Victoria. Leaving the Doctor to fiddle with the controls, she went to put it on.

The night was cold, chilling the marrow in Fulbright's bones. The wind howled mournfully around the bare rocks and craggy outcroppings which rose like grey ghosts from the blackness of the moor. The moon was gone and clouds scurried like rats across the sky. It was a night, the locals would say, when Satan himself was known to walk upon the moor.

Fulbright remembered with a shudder some of the tales he'd been told as a child, growing up out here in the bleak wilds before being sent to the boarding school that had beaten the child out of him to make him the man he was today. Tales of the devil striding across the snow-strewn hills, or of giant, fiery hounds from hell running down their terrified human prey. Tales of monsters that lived within the bogs, reaching out with twiggy fingers to grip the ankles of unwary travellers and drag them down to the murky depths where they would be devoured.

On nights like these, it was hard to completely dismiss such tales as rank superstition. He knew, with the intellectual part of his mind, that such legends were fancies born in drinks and fears. But in the darker, deeper, colder portions of his mind the fears were still there and still as potent as they had been when they had induced nightmares and bed-wetting in a four-year-old boy. But he was no longer that boy; he was a man, and this was a task for a man. Burying the terrors that wanted to seize and shake him, he hunkered down in the saddle and pressed his nervous steed onward, into the jumble of rocks.

Behind him he could hear the other horses nervously picking their own paths. Both Bridewell and Ross were superb horsemen, having no trouble keeping up the pace. Abercrombie, on the other hand, was merely adequate, and Fulbright suspected that the reason he seemed to lag behind had more to do with fear than lack of riding ability.

Since the initial sounds that had drawn them out onto the moor this dismal night, there had been no further indication that their quarry was still around. Then again, if it were hunting, it was hardly likely to advertise its presence, was it? And what were they hunting? Some wild beast escaped from the menagerie of a collector, perhaps? During his days in India, Fulbright had seen both cheetahs and tigers make their kills. Both were powerful, silent hunters and quite capable of disembowelling the ponies that roamed the hills here. But neither was capable of producing the terrible sounds they had heard earlier. The beast had sounded more like a hound of some kind.

But what kind of dog ever known to man could have produced a howl such as they had heard? None that Fulbright knew, and anyone in the county would have admitted that if ever a man knew his hounds, that man was Edward Fulbright. The memories of the local boys telling tales of a spectral hound that haunted the moors flooded back to him. The beast was supposed to possess eyes of fire, teeth of pure flame and an insatiable appetite for wicked children. Nothing more than a horror tale told to terrify the young. And yet . . .

And yet there were children missing. Cromwell had mentioned it earlier in the day. As a Justice of the Peace, Cromwell was perforce privy to police reports. Several local children seemed to have vanished without trace recently, including one from a boarding school in the area. Most disappearances could be laid easily to any number of factors, but the schoolchild had been the son of a minor Indian official and there had been an investigation. It had turned up nothing, but there were many questions unanswered.

Was it even barely possible that there was something out here that stalked the night and was preying on human beings?

Even as the thought fastened hold on his imagination, Fulbright gave a start of shock. Out of the blackness ahead came a scream such as he'd never heard in all his days. He'd seen action on three continents, and seen and heard men die in terrible pain. Never outside the pits of hell would he expect to hear such a scream. It was a high-pitched howl, throaty and filled with horror. It didn't sound even remotely human, and it set fire to every nerve in his body.

And not his alone. As his mount shied in terror, he fought to control the horrified steed. His companions faced similar struggles as the other horses were equally unnerved.

'Bloody Nora!' exclaimed Abercrombie, his voice trembling. 'What the bleeding hell was that?'

'Whatever it was,' Bridewell exclaimed, his own voice shaking, 'it can't have been human.'

'It wasn't,' Ross announced with certainty. He alone didn't sound on the verge of panic. Was it because he knew something that the rest of them didn't? 'It was one of the local ponies. Our target must have just slaughtered it. Come along!' Ross kneed his steed hard, urging it forward. The beast – perhaps wiser than its rider – fought and bucked to retreat instead. Ross wore it down, however, and pressed ahead.

Fulbright would just as soon have returned home, but he couldn't back down now. Instead he managed to control his own rebellious, terrified mount and forced it after Ross. Bridewell fell in behind him.

'Lummee,' Abercrombie announced, 'I ain't staying around here alone.' He brought up the rear as they moved through the rocks.

The cry had certainly been close. As they threaded the minimal pathways, Fulbright hit what was almost a wall of such an overpowering stench that he almost vomited on the spot. Blood, bile and other noisome odours gripped his throat and lungs. Then, as they rounded a rocky pinnacle, they saw the unfortunate prey.

It probably had been one of the local ponies, as Ross had claimed. It was almost impossible to be certain, so little of it remained intact. The stocky little body had been ripped apart by a creature of massive power. What remained of the poor beast's hide was torn by the tracks of savage claws. The pony had not merely been disembowelled but shredded. Globs of flesh, dripping and steaming, were scattered across some twenty feet of the pathway. Even in the poor light, Fulbright could make out far too many details. Even if he could have seen nothing, the stench alone would have told him more than enough.

'Dear God,' he muttered, fighting back the urge to be sick. 'What monster could have done such a thing?'

'Whatever it is,' Ross told him, his face strained and grim, 'it is only a short distance ahead of us. It must be carrying the missing portions of this unfortunate creature to devour at its leisure. Perhaps it will be unable to outrun us.'

'You want us to chase a creature capable of doing this?' Bridewell waved his arm at the grisly remains.

'You and Sir Edward have done more than enough, Roger,' Ross replied. 'No one could fault you for returning home.'

'I could,' Fulbright snapped. 'This monster roams where I make my home. I'll be damned if I allow it to escape me.'

Ross gave him an appraising glance. 'Good for you, Sir Edward,' he replied. 'Then stay close to me. We may need one another's aid before this hunt is over.' With a sly smile he pressed his horse onward again.

Fulbright fell in slightly behind Ross. This man might be an enigma but he seemed to be brave enough. Or . . . Was the situation something he knew more about than he was letting on? It was impossible to dismiss the feeling he had that Ross was more than he claimed.

The night was broken once again by another unearthly noise. This one didn't sound like any they had heard yet, nor did it sound entirely natural. It was a booming noise about a mile or so ahead of them, rising and falling like the pounding of some immense steam-hammer or an off-key hurdy-gurdy of immense size and power. Before Fulbright could make out more, the noise had ceased. All he knew for certain was that it was ahead of them, and that the quarry they were hunting must have been heading in its direction.

* * *

'India?' Sarah Jane shivered with cold as she stepped out of the TARDIS's doors and into the bleak night. 'This doesn't feel like a tropical country to me.'

The Doctor shrugged. 'It gets very cold at night in the Indian foothills,' he told her.

'These aren't foothills,' she answered as something squelched under her feet. 'It feels more like a swamp. Are you absolutely certain this is India?'

'Absolutely.'

'Then it's probably the Isle of Ely. Or another weird alien planet.'

The Doctor half-turned. He was hardly more than a shape in the gloom. 'Do I detect a note of cynicism?'

'A note?' Sarah laughed bitterly. How could she even have fantasized that he would get this right? 'More like a whole ruddy symphony!'

'Well,' he said, sounding hurt, 'I may be out by a little – '

'A little?' she cried. 'If this is anywhere near Lahore, I'm a Dutchman. I'd be very surprised if we're even on the same planet!'

'This is definitely Earth,' he said, sounding miffed. 'Its smell is unmistakable. I'll agree I may have strayed a few miles, but that's all.' His foot squelched down in something. 'We're most likely in the vicinity of some river. Probably the monsoon season.'

'Then you've missed the right time, too,' Sarah snapped. 'Honestly, I don't know why I ever listen to you.'

'Because I'm such a wonderful conversationalist,' he answered. 'Well, let's just find a native, and then we can – '

Before he could finish his thought, there was a noise ahead in the darkness. Sarah tried to make out what was making it, but saw nothing. It sounded like some animal running hard. Something large and –

It sprang out of the blackness, and seemed to be almost as startled to see her as Sarah was to see it. The beast paused in mid-stride, then opened its mouth. Something it had been carrying in its huge jaws fell to the ground, spraying fresh blood as it bounced. The monster bared massive fangs and growled deep within its immense throat.

Sarah staggered back, terrified.

The beast was a dog of some kind — in the same way that a great white shark was a fish of some kind. This apparition was immense; over five feet at the shoulder, the size of a horse. Its body was powerfully muscled, its jaw overcrowded with four-inch fangs that dripped saliva and blood as it growled at her. Great eyes glared at her in shock and hatred, and four massive paws clawed at the ground.

Sarah felt her strength and sanity giving out. Her heart seemed to be trying to hammer itself free from her ribs, and she was in danger of fainting. As she stared at the monster, it gave a challenging roar and leaped straight toward her.

2

Predators

For a second, Sarah was certain that she was dead. The powerful body hurled toward her, lips drawn back from the vicious teeth in a furious snarl, the claws of the powerful limbs spread ready to rip the flesh from her bones. There wasn't time to move, to scream, to do anything.

And then the monster passed over her, the claws barely touching her hair. She heard the beast slam into the ground quite a way behind her, and keep on going.

Giddily, Sarah spun about and stared into the gloom. Her heart was still hammering away at the inside of her rib-cage, but her adrenalin high was starting to evaporate. Reaction to the close passage of death made her weak.

'Did you see that?' exclaimed the Doctor, excitement making him almost hop up and down.

'See it?' Sarah yelled. 'That monster almost killed me!'

'Oh, don't exaggerate,' he replied, scuttling along the ground and then bending to examine the spoor where it had landed. The creature had managed a running leap of some twenty-five feet, Sarah realized. He glanced up at her. 'I could see the poor thing was simply running away, not attacking you. It was scared.'

'It was scared?' she exclaimed. 'What about me? I almost had a heart attack!'

'You're too tough for that,' the Doctor answered dismissively. He whipped a magnifying lens from one of his overstuffed pockets and started to crawl about on the

30

ground. 'Fascinating, utterly fascinating.'

'You can't tell me that we're on Earth,' Sarah complained as she joined him. 'Nothing like that beast ever lived in India.'

He gave her a thoughtful look. 'No, Sarah Jane,' he agreed. 'That was no animal native to your world. But – ' He broke off and pointed back down the faint trail in the direction that the creature had come. 'Company.'

Sarah heard the sound of riders, and an instant later four horsemen emerged from the darkness. Startled, they reined in their steeds.

'Good grief!' exclaimed the leader, a grizzled and dignified man in his fifties. 'What on earth are you doing here?'

'Good evening,' the Doctor replied, politely raising his hat. 'Nice weather for the time of year, isn't it? Incidentally, what time of the year is it?'

'What year is it?' growled Sarah under her breath.

'Stone the crows,' a tubby little man with a prominent nose and shifty features said.

'Well,' the Doctor commented, giving Sarah an I-told-you-so glare, 'I think that proves we're on Earth, at least.'

A third rider, darkly handsome, stared at them. 'You must be lost, I assume?'

'You wouldn't believe how lost,' Sarah told him, glaring back at the Doctor.

'Did you see anything running past here?' asked the elderly man.

'Only a monster hound,' Sarah replied. 'It almost killed me.'

'We'd better get moving,' the fourth man snapped.

The Doctor moved to block their way. 'It was terrified,' he said quietly. 'And now I know why. Let it be.'

'What?' the leader spluttered. 'That beast is a mad killer, sir! I aim to destroy it!'

31

'Do you indeed?' asked the Doctor. For a moment Sarah thought he was about to drag the man from his horse, but then he shrugged. 'I doubt you'll even be able to catch it. It has a considerable head start by now, and it's not a good night for tracking.'

'Perhaps not,' the handsome rider replied. 'But we have to try.'

'I can't stop you,' the Doctor agreed. 'But is there perhaps somewhere around here where we might be able to get shelter? The night's getting a trifle chilly.'

The elderly rider thought for a moment, and then nodded. 'Follow this trail back about two miles,' he said. 'Don't stray from the path. There are bogs out there that will suck you to your doom before anyone can help. You'll come to Fulbright Hall. Tell the servants there that Sir Edward directed you.' Then he glowered. 'Wait for me there. I wish to have words with you when I return.'

Despite the fact that this was a not-too-veiled threat, the Doctor grinned as if it were a compliment. 'And I with you,' he answered. 'My thanks. Come along, Sarah.'

'I could show them the way,' offered the Cockney rider. 'Or offer the lady me horse.'

'Come along, Abercrombie,' the handsome rider snapped. Spurring on his horse, he led the four riders off into the night.

The Doctor turned to Sarah. 'And what do you make of that?' he asked her. There was a twinkle in his eyes.

'A hunting party,' she replied. 'After that monster we saw.' She frowned. 'They were definitely English.'

'So we are on Earth,' he chided her. 'And in about the right period, judging from their dress.'

'But not in India,' Sarah retorted. 'I remember Fulbright Hall from a story I did. It's in Devon.' Why wasn't she surprised to discover the Doctor had made a mistake again?' 'I don't suppose you'd consider just going back to the TARDIS and trying again?'

'Sarah,' he said reprovingly. 'There's a mystery here. I can smell it.'

'That's just doggie doo-doo you can smell,' Sarah complained. But she knew that there was no point in arguing. Once the Doctor had made up his mind, a planet was easier to deflect than his intentions. With a sigh, she started back down the pathway that Sir Edward had indicated. 'Just what I wanted,' she said. 'A two-mile hike over the moors.'

'Exercise is good for you,' the Doctor informed her. 'It gets the blood flowing.'

'That monster almost got my blood flowing,' Sarah snapped.

'It wasn't attacking you,' the Doctor insisted. 'It was just trying to escape. I don't think Sir Edward and his merry men will catch it.'

Something in his voice made Sarah wince. 'You're not thinking of looking for that thing tomorrow, are you?'

He simply grinned in reply.

Bernard Faversham generally liked his job as Bodham's sole representative of law enforcement. Bodham, on the whole, was a quiet little town where the worst crime was normally a spot of drunk and disorderly behaviour on a Saturday night. Faversham lived in a small cottage on the edge of town, which doubled as his police station. There was no jail here, and there had never been the need for one. It was usually a quiet little post, which suited Faversham fine.

Until recently.

Then there had been the problem of missing children. And now . . .

He was a trifle overweight, he knew, but it wasn't

just the unexpected exertion at this time of night that was making his heart pound and his nerves jangle. Jim Brackley had roused him from his bed with the news that Ben Tolliver was dead.

Tolliver had been a fixture in the village for more than sixty years. Faversham had grown up here, and Tolliver had always been one of the local characters. He flirted with the barmaids, joked with the other fishermen and had been pretty tolerant of even the most unruly of children. Faversham had many memories of the old man. It was hard to think of him being dead. And even harder to picture what the shocked Brackley had described.

As they arrived on the small wharf, Faversham slowed down. There was already a small crowd gathered near the end of the wooden structure. News travelled fast in Bodham, and Tolliver had been well liked. Most of the crowd were women. The men would still be out at sea for another few hours, making their living. Only the old, like Tolliver, or the injured, like Brackley — whose right sleeve flapped as he moved — were home.

'Stand aside,' Faversham ordered, panting. The crowd melted slowly. Faversham saw shocked expressions on several faces, and traces of vomit staining clothes and chins. Brackley had warned him that Tolliver's body was mutilated. Faversham tried to steel himself for the sight.

Even so, he almost contributed to the stench on the boards. Holding down the bile with difficulty, he drew closer to the old man's corpse.

Tolliver had been dead only a couple of hours, that was clear. And the cause of death was more than apparent. Something had bitten through half of the old man's head. The face was completely gone, and only grisly remnants of his brain and other organs were left. Bone showed through, stained and scored. The left arm was also missing, ripped from the battered body.

Brackley moved close. 'We found his boat,' he said quietly. 'Poor old Ben was in it, just as you see him.'

'Has – ' Faversham began. Then he had to fight back nausea before he could continue. 'Has anyone gone for the doctor?'

'Doctor Martinson is up at the Hall,' one of the women offered. 'At Sir Edward's big do.'

'Someone had better fetch him,' Faversham decided. 'There'll have to be an autopsy. We have to find out what did this to old Ben.'

'I'll go,' Brackley offered. 'I can borrow a horse from Marlowe.'

'Good.' Faversham nodded his approval. 'You'd best alert Sir Alexander to the news, too.' As the local Justice, Sir Alexander would have to be notified and make a ruling on the cause of death. Brackley grunted and moved off. He looked relieved that he didn't have to stay with the body. Faversham took one of the lanterns that were burning beside the body and turned to the villagers. 'You'd best all go home,' he said, trying to sound like the pillar of the law that he was. 'I'll take care of things now.'

Millicent Chadwick shuddered. 'What do you think it was?'

'It's too soon to say,' Faverham replied. 'Rest assured, though, that as soon as we know, steps will be taken.'

'To the Devil with steps!' Millicent yelled, pale and angry. 'My Ronnie is out there at sea this night! All our husbands are! Will whatever did this – ' she gestured at the ravaged corpse ' – go after them next?' There was a mutter of agreement with this view from the others.

'Please, Millie,' Faversham said gently. 'Go on home. I'm sure that Ronnie and the others will be fine. Old Ben always went out alone, and just into the bay here. The menfolk are further out, and all together. They'll be fine, just you see.'

35

This seemed to calm the women down. As he knew, half the battle was sounding like you knew what you were talking about, even when you didn't. Especially when you didn't.

'But,' he added, 'it might be best to keep the young ones away from the water for now. Until we're certain that whatever did this isn't still about.'

The women started to drift away, save for Jen Walker, the barmaid from the Pig and Thistle. She moved to join Faversham. 'There's a doctor on that ship that docked this morning,' she offered. 'A young man, but he might be able to help.'

'The whaler?' Faversham had forgotten about that recent arrival. It was rare to get the whalers in here. They generally made for the larger ports, but the captain of this one had business with Breckinridge at the factory, and the ship was stopping over for a couple of days. 'Do you think you could ask the gentleman to step down here, Jen?'

She nodded and faded into the night. In a few moments, Faversham was alone with the body. He gave it another quick glance, then looked away. Poor old Ben must have died swiftly, but it had been a gruesome death. Moving to a pile of supplies, Faversham dragged out an old tarpaulin. He settled it over the corpse, which made him feel a little better. Then he gathered his courage and sat on a bollard to await the first of the arrivals.

Doctor Doyle shuffled through his notes in the small cabin he had been assigned as ship's surgeon to the *Hope*. The vessel was a stout three-master that had weathered a seven-month stay in the Arctic Circle well. The holds were filled with seal skins, whale bones and vats of oil, and the crew was anxious to return to their home port of Peterhead as soon as possible. Aside from wishing to see his family again, Doyle was interested in the money that this voyage would bring him. His share of the profits was a handsome three shillings a ton of the oil money.

Thankfully there had been little call for his services during the voyage. He'd spent considerable time aiding in the hunting of seal and whale, in fact. The captain, John Gray, had even offered him a double berth for the next voyage as both surgeon and harpooner. Flattered – and tempted by the money he could make – Doyle had nonetheless turned down the offer. He was longing to get his feet back on solid land for a while. He had been hoping to be back in Edinburgh by now, but Captain Gray had made an unexpected and unannounced detour to this small Devonshire fishing village instead. The only reason he had given for the lengthy detour was 'business'. While Gray was a fair and able captain, he was not inclined to explain his actions.

So, faced with a few extra days on the ship and with little to occupy his time, Doyle worked on the notes he had taken during the voyage. He was trying to work out some way to turn them into a story, but the threads of plotting eluded him. *Chamber's Journal* had bought and printed his fledgling attempt at fiction the previous year, and he was rather proud of 'The Mystery Of Sassassa Valley'. It had taken him a good deal of work, but had fetched him the sum of three guineas. The idea of following this tale with others appealed to Doyle, but it was a matter of finding the right storylines. Mysteries were always sought after, and –

There came a rap at the cabin door. With a sigh, Doyle replaced his journal. 'Yes?' he called. It was typical that after an uneventful voyage his services should be required while the ship was calmly docked.

'Doctor?' came the voice of Jack Lamb. The wiry little fellow was the ship's steward, and a staunch supporter of

Doyle's skills with both medicinal and boxing dispensations. They had sparred any number of times together these past few months. 'There's a woman from the village to see you. Claims it's very urgent.'

'Thank you, Jack.' Doyle rose to his feet and picked up his medical bag. Bodham had its own medical practitioner, but Doyle supposed that the man was unavailable for some reason. Oh well, perhaps he'd earn himself a fee while he was here. More likely, though, he'd end up with an unpaid bill. Still, if there was a need for his services he could hardly turn down the call.

He went up onto the deck, where a young woman, attractive in a rustic sort of way, stood waiting for him. The way that she stood on the gently swaying deck confirmed that she was no sailor. 'I'm Ship's Surgeon Doyle,' he informed the woman. 'I take it you are not the patient?'

'I'm Jen Walker,' the woman replied, the Devonshire burr prominent in her voice. 'And there's no patient, Doctor.'

Doyle frowned. 'Then what is the meaning of this call?'

'It's a dead man, sir,' she replied. 'The local constable would appreciate it if you'd have a look-see at the body.'

'Ah.' Doyle began to understand. 'Drowned, has he?'

'I doubt it.' The woman gave him a dour look. 'He were on his boat when the men found it drifting.'

'Hmm.' That sounded more promising. Perhaps a small autopsy fee . . . 'Well, lead on, miss.' Jen Walker nodded, and started down the gangplank. Clutching his bag, Doyle followed along.

Sarah had been walking for almost twenty minutes now, following the Doctor as best she could. He had long legs and seemed never to tire. Hands thrust deep into his

38

pockets, he simply strode along. She, on the other hand, was feeling the effects of this night tramp. 'Oi!' she called. 'Can we take a breather?'

The Doctor halted. 'Five minutes,' he agreed, without looking around.

Collapsing onto a convenient rock, Sarah didn't much care that the cold stone numbed her behind. It felt so good to get the weight off her feet. 'What a dismal place,' she complained.

'Dartmoor,' the Doctor answered. 'It's not hard to see why it's reputed to be haunted, is it?' He stared all around.

'It doesn't need any legends,' Sarah commented. 'There really is something running around out here, and it certainly wasn't any ghost.' She shuddered at the memory of the monstrous beast. 'Do you have any idea what that thing was?'

'I always have ideas,' he replied enigmatically. 'What do you think it was?'

'I asked first,' Sarah objected. Then she shrugged. 'Off hand, I'd say it was some prehistoric ancestor of a rottweiler or something.'

The Doctor shook his head. 'No dog on Earth has ever looked like that,' he told her. 'It's very, very wrong. And there were definite signs of intelligence.'

'What?' Sarah stared at him in astonishment. 'Look, I like dogs as much as the next person, but I wouldn't call them intelligent. Personable, yes. Clever, maybe. But that's about it.'

'That was no dog, Sarah,' he said softly. 'I examined the pawprint, remember? The foot structure was all wrong. And it had a semi-opposable thumb.'

'Come again?'

'It was almost able to use its paw as a hand.' The Doctor shook his head. 'We must be somewhere around the turn of the twentieth century, but that creature was

39

more like a dog from twenty million years in the future.'

Cold sweat started to trickle down Sarah's spine. 'You mean that it's from the future somehow?'

'No, I don't think so.' The Doctor frowned. 'The TARDIS may be a trifle grouchy, but the old girl would have detected a temporal disturbance of that order.'

'Then would you kindly explain what you mean?' snapped Sarah.

He wrinkled his nose as he stared out into the darkness. 'It's as if something has somehow accelerated that poor creature's evolutionary trends,' he replied. 'That paw is all wrong.'

'That *dog* is all wrong,' Sarah retorted.

'Yes,' agreed the Doctor thoughtfully. 'That dog is definitely all wrong.' He gave her a smile. 'Come on, time to get going again.'

'Do we have to?' complained Sarah. 'My feet are killing me.'

His eyes twinkled. 'You want to stay out here on the moor with that creature? Besides, I'll wager that Sir Edward has a well-stocked cellar. A nip of Madeira would hit the spot right now, wouldn't it?'

'You talked me into it.' Sarah slowly clambered to her feet. 'Let's get on with it, then.'

Doyle hurried along the wharf to the lonely pool of light cast by several fitfully burning storm lanterns. The local constable, a slightly rotund man in his forties, sat hunched on a bollard, guarding what appeared to be a pile of tarpaulin. It was obviously where the victim lay. Doyle felt a surge of almost excitement, and then a twinge of guilt. This was at least out of the ordinary, but it was a shame that a man had to perish to break the day's monotony. As he approached, the constable glanced up, then slowly rose to his feet.

'Ship's Surgeon Doyle,' the doctor introduced himself. 'I understand you have need of my services.'

'That we do,' agreed the policeman. 'I'm Faversham.' He nodded at the bundle on the planks. 'Old Ben Tolliver was killed tonight.'

Killed? Then this was no simple accident, or some unfortunate old man whose heart had picked an inopportune time to stop working. The excitement began to rise within Doyle again. A murder, with him helping out the police! This would be something to remember for future stories. A doctor who helped to solve crimes . . . it had possibilities. 'So you're talking murder, then?' he asked.

'Maybe,' the constable agreed guardedly. 'That's what I want a professional opinion on.' He reached down to remove one corner of the tarpaulin, then halted. 'It's not a pretty sight,' he warned.

'Neither is watching a man dragged to his maker by a dying whale,' Doyle replied. 'But I've seen that.'

Faversham nodded, then drew back the covering.

Doyle had to fight the urge to throw up his meagre supper onto the dock. Judging by the smell, others had failed at this task. It was no easy thing for Doyle to retain control of his stomach. He'd seen bodies dissected as part of his anatomy classes, but nothing to match this. The dead man was missing most of his head and one arm. God alone knew what else the rubber sheet prevented him from seeing.

'What could have done this?' he gasped.

'I was hoping you could tell me, Doctor,' the policeman answered drily. 'That's why you're here.'

Doyle nodded, then stopped the motion, afraid it would make him sick. 'It appears to have been some violent action,' he said. Trying to wipe from his appalled mind the fact that this had been a human being who lived

41

and loved and laughed just hours earlier, Doyle bent slowly to study the mangled corpse. Once his nausea was under control, his curiosity came to the fore. 'This is most unusual,' he finally announced.

'Aye,' agreed Faversham, with sardonic humour. 'It's the first body I've come across that's missing its face. But can you tell me anything of help?'

'Several things, I think,' Doyle told him. One of his professors at Edinburgh, Joseph Bell, had astounded people by his inferences and deductions based on small facts. Doyle knew he couldn't emulate the master fully, but he could do so in some small measure. 'First, obviously, the man died recently – within the past three or four hours, I think.'

'That's most likely true,' agreed the constable, 'seeing as how I had a drink with Ben myself late this afternoon.'

'His death was clearly caused by the facial wound,' Doyle plunged ahead. 'If it had been inflicted after the man was dead by some sort of means, there would have been less bleeding. And it was performed by some animal with rather large and incredibly strong teeth.' He gestured at what remained of the sphenoidal and frontal bones. 'You can see the scoring of the bones where the teeth clamped together.'

The constable frowned. 'You mean he was attacked by a shark or something?'

'Not a shark,' Doyle said firmly. 'For one thing, no shark's teeth I've ever seen or read about could score the bones in that way. And sharks attack limbs, not the head. Besides which, he would have had to have been in the water to have attracted a shark's attention. There is no sign of dampness on the clothes, and I perceive a pouch of tobacco in his pocket which appears to be still very dry. Therefore whatever attacked this benighted soul was on the boat and not in the water.'

Faversham shook his head in puzzlement. 'Well, it certainly beats me, sir.'

Doyle nodded. This was a most intriguing mystery indeed! 'I could tell you more if there were some well-lit place to perform an autopsy,' he offered. 'Would that be possible, do you suppose?'

'I reckon,' the policeman agreed. 'I could speak with the landlord of the Pig and Thistle. He has an old stable that might be of use.' He glanced down at the body again. 'Would you mind staying here, sir? I can't leave poor Ben unattended.'

'Oh, I understand perfectly,' Doyle replied. 'I'd be happy to stay and await your return.' There was no way anyone could drag him away from here at the moment: this was far too intriguing to pass up. He reached down to cover the face of the body, though. It was one thing to wait here, but quite another to stare at that sight alone as he did so.

'Thank you, sir,' Faversham said. 'I don't know what this world is coming to. This used to be such a quiet little town.' He shook his head sadly. 'I've already had to send to London about the missing children. I'd hate to have to write to them again. They might think I'm not up to this work. Still, you don't need to hear about my troubles, do you, sir?' He managed a small smile. 'I'll be as quick as I can. I promise.'

'Take your time,' Doyle answered airily. Then he sat on the bollard, and was lost in his thoughts before Faversham had gone five steps.

A medical man helping the police to solve their crimes. Yes, it had distinct possibilities for story-telling.

'Bear up, Sarah,' the Doctor said, irritatingly cheerful. 'We're almost there now.'

'You've been saying that for the past fifteen minutes,' Sarah objected.

43

'Then we're at least fifteen minutes closer to our destination, aren't we?' he rejoined.

Sarah sighed. No matter how often he was proven wrong, the Doctor always managed to end up thinking he was somehow right all along. Before she could object to his latest load of cheek, he held up a warning hand. Mindful that the monster was still at large on the moors somewhere, Sarah promptly stood still, peering into the darkness nervously. 'Is it that monster back again?' she whispered.

'Worse,' the Doctor answered in his normal, velvet tones.

'Worse?' Sarah tried to imagine what could possibly be worse than that giant hound. She doubted her imagination was warped enough. Shivering, she stared fruitlessly around. 'What?'

'Boys.'

'What?' Sarah felt like punching him for scaring her further.

'Young boys,' the Doctor said, striding across to a bush that was barely more than a shadow in the gloom. 'You know,' he remarked pleasantly, 'if you really want to hide, you'll have to switch to a less pungent brand of tobacco.'

There was a rustle of movement and three smallish shapes emerged from their hiding place. One, tall and thin, turned to one of his companions. 'I told you that weed was noxious, Gigger.'

'Lay off, Duns,' his target complained. 'I'll wager it was your socks he could smell anyway. Or McBee's bad temper.'

Sarah stared at the three apparitions with some surprise. It was not quite so much their unexpected appearance from the night that astonished her, but that she knew who they were. The tall, gloomy looking lad was

44

L. C. Dunsterville; the smaller, darker youth was George Beresford. And as for Gigger . . .

He was a strange-looking boy, of that there was little doubt. On the stout side and shorter than his friends, he wore steel-rimmed glasses with pebble lenses – his nickname came from these, derived from 'Giglamps' – and there was the faint but unmistakable trace of a moustache on his upper lip. He possessed penetrating blue eyes and a strong, blunt manner.

Sarah punched the Doctor on the arm. 'You're a decade early,' she complained. 'He's still a schoolboy.'

'I may only be fifteen,' Gigger said with as much dignity as he could muster in the circumstances, 'but I'm a man.'

'Ah,' said the Doctor, with understanding. He held out a hand. 'Rudyard Kipling, I presume.'

Kipling took his hand and shook it seriously. 'Do I know you, sir?' he asked.

'No,' the Doctor replied. 'But we know of you. My friend here wanted to meet you. This is Sarah Jane Smith, and I'm the Doctor.'

Turning to Sarah, Kipling took her hand and bowed over it, planting a kiss. 'Enchanted.'

'Don't hog her, Gigger,' Beresford complained. 'Let us have a go, too, you beast.'

'Quit your jawing, McBee,' Kipling snapped. 'She came to meet me, remember.'

Sarah was not at all sure she wanted three overly active fifteen-year-old boys fighting for her attention. Trust the Doctor to miss their target by several continents and a decade! Still, he had managed to get to the right planet, at least. 'Okay, enough,' she announced, pulling her hand free of Kipling's surprisingly strong grip. 'What are you doing on the moors at night? Shouldn't you be in school?'

Dunsterville snorted. 'There? They don't much care where we go, as long as we're back for morning prayers.'

'Don't you know that the moors are dangerous at night?' Sarah asked.

'We scoff at danger,' Beresford replied airily.

'How remarkably foolish,' the Doctor muttered. He glared at the boys. 'Didn't you hear the hound out hunting?'

'That thing?' Kipling shrugged. 'It's often out. It doesn't hurt anyone. Just animals.'

'You've seen it, then?' asked Sarah.

'Not as such, no,' Kipling admitted. 'We've heard it and found its tracks, though.'

'But we're not afraid of it,' Beresford added quickly.

'You should be,' the Doctor snapped. 'Three heads, and not a brain between you. What possessed you to come out here?'

Kipling scowled, obviously not keen on being lectured. 'We were looking for Anders. He went missing a couple of weeks back, and there's been a frightful stink about the whole thing.'

'It was Gigger's idea,' Beresford explained. 'He thought we might find some clues the local policeman missed.'

'At night?' Sarah asked incredulously. 'What do you think you'll find at night?'

'A pretty woman, for one thing,' Kipling answered.

'Suck-up,' the Doctor muttered. In a louder voice, he added, 'And to get a chance to smoke in peace, eh?'

'That too,' agreed Dunsterville, not at all embarrassed. 'Two birds with one stone and all that rot.'

'Speaking of rot,' Sarah said, 'don't you know smoking's bad for you?'

Kipling stared at her in amusement. 'Now *that's* rot. Smoking is an art-form. And it makes a man out of you.'

The Doctor shook his head. 'You're a century too

early,' he informed Sarah.

Staring at the Doctor, Kipling announced, 'You're an odd fellow.'

'And you're an impudent wretch,' the Doctor replied, grinning. 'Does that make us even?'

'What are you a doctor of?' asked Kipling.

'This and that. That and this. Mostly that.' The Doctor grinned again. 'Why don't you go back to school tonight? You'll have much better luck if you search for clues in the morning.'

Kipling shrugged. 'I suppose we could do that,' he agreed.

'Besides,' added Beresford, 'we've smoked all we brought with us.'

'That's the spirit,' the Doctor approved. 'By the by, where is this local constable located?'

'Bodham,' Kipling said. 'You do know where that is, I take it?'

Sarah scowled at him. The youngster was definitely on the cheeky side. 'I imagine we can find it if we want,' she replied.

'Anyway,' Dunsterville asked, 'what are you two doing on the moors at night?'

Kipling poked him in the ribs. 'Don't be so naïve, Duns,' he said in severe tones. 'What else would they be doing out here alone?'

Sarah felt herself blushing. 'You've got smutty minds,' she informed him.

'And smutty bodies, too,' Beresford piped up.

'At the moment,' the Doctor interrupted them, 'we're heading for Fulbright Hall. It's just ahead, I take it?'

'About a ten-minute walk,' agreed Kipling, not bothering to hide his grin. 'Got lost in the night, eh?'

'Maybe we should show Miss Smith the way next time,' added Beresford, snickering.

Sarah had almost forgotten how obnoxious teenage boys could be — even if one of them was to become one of England's greatest writers. 'Grow up,' she advised them.

'Show us how,' suggested Dunsterville, which reduced all three of them to a fit of giggles.

'If you want to live to grow up,' Sarah said firmly, 'you'll knock it off right now. And you'll go back to Westward Ho! Now move it.'

Kipling threw her a mocking salute, and the three boys faded back into the night. Sarah could still hear them giggling as they moved away. She glowered at the Doctor. 'You were a lot of help.'

'You were doing fine,' he replied. 'Anyway, the Hall's just ahead, like I told you. Come along.' He strode off into the night. Sarah rolled her eyes, but followed.

Sir Edward reined in his steed, holding up a hand to halt his companions. 'It's no use,' he announced. 'The beast has gone too far into the marshes. We can't possibly follow it further on a night like this. We need torches, at the very least. It's not safe in this gloom.'

Ross slapped his fist into the palm of the other hand. 'Damnation.' Then he glanced across at the leader. 'You're right, of course. Further pursuit would be pointless — and most likely dangerous to boot. However, if you'll permit me a moment?' Without waiting for a reply, Ross slipped down from his mount and examined the ground. 'Abercrombie,' he called, 'bring me the dark lantern.'

'Fetch me this, fetch me that, ' grumbled Abercrombie. Fishing under his clothes, he pulled out a compact metallic lantern and opened the lens. Striking a match, he lit the wick inside, then dismounted and brought the light to his master.

Taking the lantern, Ross examined the ground at the edge of the bog. He seemed absorbed by the task.

'What the devil are you up to?' asked Fulbright a few moments later.

'Looking for prints,' Ross replied without getting up. 'There are numerous.'

'So?' Fulbright couldn't restrain his impatience.

Ross clambered to his feet, blew out the light and handed the lantern back to Abercrombie. 'So it proves that the beast we were chasing traverses this path often. Animals, as I'm sure a keen sportsman such as yourself knows full well, tend to keep to the same paths. I suspect that we've discovered one of our quarry's home trails.'

'Capital!' exclaimed Bridewell. 'So all we need do tomorrow is to return here and take up the trail once again in the daylight.'

'Or simply await the monster's emergence tomorrow evening,' Ross suggested. 'Either way, we have it. Provided Sir Edward can return us to this spot.' He glanced up at his host as he remounted.

'I can indeed,' Fulbright replied.

'Splendid,' said Ross. 'Then I suspect we shall be able to clear up at least one aspect of this intriguing mystery before another day has passed. For the moment, however, I am certain that a glass of your excellent Jerez would be more than welcome to us all, Sir Edward.'

Fulbright nodded. Whatever else this man was, he was neither a fool nor did he lack discrimination. The sherry was a particularly fine batch. 'Then let us return to the Hall,' he agreed.

The sight of lights suddenly appearing from the darkness cheered Sarah up immensely. She had begun wondering if Fulbright Hall was some sort of mythical place, like Brigadoon or Shangri-La, and it was comforting to have proof that something physical existed at the end of their journey.

'The end is nigh,' she muttered happily. 'I wonder if I can get a footbath there?'

'We're Sir Edward's guests,' the Doctor pointed out. 'I should imagine you can get whatever you want.'

'I don't recall him using the word "guests",' Sarah objected. 'In fact I got the impression that we were to be held to account.'

'Semantics,' the Doctor replied dismissively. 'I'm sure he meant us to think of ourselves as guests. Hello!' He grinned again. 'Do you hear what I hear?'

Sarah listened carefully. She could just make out the strains of violins. 'Music?'

'Right.' His teeth flashed. 'I do so love a party, don't you? Fancy a dance?'

'After this slog?' Sarah snorted. 'Besides, I don't imagine they know the twist or anything else I can do.'

'We are a bit before the Beatles,' the Doctor agreed. 'Pity.'

They had come to a pair of wrought-iron gates that stood some fifteen feet high. Lanterns blazed on either side of the gates, showing tall walls stretching off into the night. The gates had been flung open, and the gravel driveway showed evidence of the passage of a number of carriages. Without hesitation the Doctor marched along the lawn on the side of the drive. Sarah followed his lead, dodging around patches of flowers and shrubs. Their way was illuminated by lanterns on small pedestals that stretched up to the main doors of the Hall. To reach these doors, they had to ascend a flight of wide steps. The Doctor rapped on the door, and then bent to examine the knocker.

'Fine workmanship,' he observed. 'Sir Edward's family obviously has taste.' The door opened, and he was staring at the midriff of a portly butler. 'Hello, I'm the Doctor and this is Miss Smith.'

'Quite, sir,' agreed the functionary. His face was absolutely impassive. 'And you are here for the affair?'

'Naturally,' agreed the Doctor, giving Sarah a big wink. Sarah simply grimaced and followed him inside.

The hallway showed taste and money in about equal amounts. Sarah's knowledge of art was spotty at best, but she was fairly sure that the portraits of various personages on the walls included a Gainsborough and a Holbein. Suits of armour stood guard at the base of the main stairs, and guests and servants circulated about the pedestals which held vases and busts.

A lovely young woman broke through the throng, her pretty face flushed and eager. 'Roger? Papa?' she began. Then, seeing the two arrivals, her face fell. 'Oh. Your pardon. I had hoped – '

'Quite,' agreed the Doctor amiably. '"Papa", I take it, is Sir Edward?'

'Yes,' the young lady replied. She offered her gloved hand, which the Doctor solemnly touched to his lips. 'I'm Alice Fulbright.'

'Charmed,' the Doctor assured her. 'I am the Doctor, and this is Sarah Jane Smith. Say hello, Sarah.'

'Hello,' said Sarah obediently. 'We did meet your father and three other people out on the moors.'

'Were they all right?' asked Alice, concern in her voice.

'They were when we left them,' Sarah answered. She decided against mentioning the beast they had been pursuing, afraid the young woman might faint or something. 'Your father suggested that we meet him here when he returned.'

'Oh. How rude of me.' Alice blushed at her lack of manners. 'Would you care for a glass of something?'

'A glass of anything,' Sarah admitted. 'My throat's parched.'

'Of course.' Alice led them into the main hall. This was still quite active, despite the lateness of the hour. It had to be at least one in the morning, Sarah judged, but the ball was in full swing. She felt a little under-dressed amid all the military uniforms, dress uniforms and bejewelled dresses. The Doctor, naturally, seemed to feel he was perfectly attired, despite his ratty appearance. He managed to snaffle two glasses of champagne from a passing waiter and handed one to Sarah.

It was, of course, first class. Sarah had to fight the urge to down it in a single gulp. It felt good to get something to soothe her throat at last.

'I don't know if you know anyone,' Alice said.

'I know a lot of people,' the Doctor admitted, 'though I doubt any of them are here.'

Alice smiled. 'I'm sure you do, Doctor. You have the air of a man of the world. Do you travel much?'

'You wouldn't believe how much,' Sarah assured her. 'It's our first time in Devon, though.'

'At least this century,' agreed the Doctor.

Alice laughed, delighted at what she clearly thought was politely silly conversation. 'Come along, then,' she said. 'I'll introduce you around.' She took them to the closest knot of people. 'This is Sir Alexander Cromwell, Lady Burnwell and Captain Kevin Parker,' she announced. To the trio, she explained, 'This is the Doctor and Miss Sarah Jane Smith.'

'Charmed,' replied Parker, a tall, neatly bearded military man. He kissed Sarah's hand. 'A pretty lady always lightens up the room.' Sarah curtsied, smiling at the compliment.

'Doctor?' asked Sir Alexander. 'Of what field of studies, sir?'

'All that I've found,' the Doctor replied modestly. 'I dabble a lot.'

'Are you interested in astronomy, by any chance?'

'By every chance,' agreed the Doctor. 'It's a special study of mine.'

'Capital!' exclaimed Sir Alexander. 'Mine also. I've my own telescope set up at home, you know. I've been cataloguing nebulae.'

'Really?' The Doctor gave him an engaging grin. 'Perhaps I could have a peek sometime? I've always been awfully fond of a good nebula myself.'

There was a slight motion in the surrounding crowd, and one of the liveried footmen approached. 'Begging pardon, sir,' he said to Sir Alexander, 'but there's a man from the village come to see you. Says it's very important.' The servant lowered his voice. 'There's been a death.'

'A death?' Alice gasped. She went pale. 'Is it . . . ?' She couldn't finish the sentence.

'One of the villagers, my lady,' the footman assured her. 'No one important.'

'Thank goodness for small mercies,' said Sarah sarcastically. 'It's just a villager.'

The footman flushed and looked away.

'I suppose I'd better speak with the man,' Sir Alexander apologized to the group. 'If you'll excuse me?'

'Allow me to accompany you, Sir Alexander,' the Doctor said quickly. 'Perhaps I may be of some small help.'

'Thank you.' Sir Alexander moved across the room, the Doctor in his wake.

Sarah eyed her empty glass and sighed. She'd have liked another, but she couldn't let the Doctor out of her sight. 'Oi,' she said to the footman. When he looked at her, she stuck the glass in his hand. 'Thanks.' Then she made off after the Doctor.

Sir Alexander stopped at the front door, where a

one-armed man was hovering nervously, clearly out of his depth at this posh function. 'What is it, my man?'

'My name's Brackley, sir,' the man replied, tugging at his forelock. Sarah had never seen anyone do that before. 'Constable Faversham sent me to tell you that there's been a death in the village. Old Ben Tolliver.'

'Tolliver?' Sir Alexander thought for a moment. 'Isn't he that old fisherman whose wife died several years ago?'

'The same, sir,' Brackley agreed. 'We found his boat adrift earlier tonight, and him dead on the deck.'

'Natural causes?' asked the Doctor.

Brackley snorted. 'Not unless you count having half his head missing as natural, sir.'

'I see,' Sir Alexander said. 'Very well, tell Faversham I shall be with him first thing in the morning.'

'Aye, sir.' Brackley tugged his forelock again. 'Will you tell Doctor Martinson as well, please, as he'll be needed, too.' He then slipped out of the front door. Sir Alexander sighed and pulled out a large gold pocket watch.

'I suppose I had better retire now,' he said. 'I will have to rise early. One of the drawbacks of being the local Justice of the Peace, I'm afraid. I have to sit on the Coroner's Court for every death. And I'll break the news to Doctor Martinson as well. He'll have to examine the body for the report.'

'Perhaps I could come along?' offered the Doctor. 'I may be of some use.'

'That's awfully decent of you,' Sir Alexander said. 'Eight sharp, then?'

'Absolutely.' The Doctor watched him leave and then turned to Sarah, his eyes sparkling with excitement. 'Isn't this intriguing?'

'Oh, yes,' gushed Sarah sarcastically. 'I've spent the evening being attacked by a mutant chihuahua with an attitude and I get to spend tomorrow looking at mutilated

54

corpses. It's the perfect holiday, isn't it?'

'Sarah, Sarah,' the Doctor chided her. 'Where's your sense of adventure?'

'I think it's still out there on the moors. That monster scared it out of me.' She scowled. 'Let me guess: you think this death might be connected to that thing we encountered?'

He gave her a big smile. 'It would have to be a rather large coincidence otherwise, wouldn't it?'

Sarah sighed. She knew when she was beaten. 'You think we could get a room for the night here?' she asked. 'If there's more walking to be done, I've got to rest my feet.'

'Let's ask Alice,' the Doctor suggested. 'She seems to be a kindly soul. I'm sure she'll take pity on your feet.'

'I'm glad somebody will,' muttered Sarah. Following the Doctor around seemed to be a habit she'd acquired and she dutifully wandered along, ignoring her protesting metatarsals. She snagged a sandwich, a slice of meat pie and another drink as they moved about the main hall, looking for their hostess. The food and drink helped to mellow Sarah's mood a little, but she was still in desperate need of a rest and was starting to suspect that the party would never wind down. It was like something from Dante's *Inferno*, where the giddy socialites might be doomed to spend eternity in one long round of dull social soirées. That would be hell, all right.

Finally, though, they stumbled across Alice again. Naturally, before Sarah could ask about a bed for the night, there was another commotion at the door. This time it heralded the return of the hunting party. Sir Edward strode into the room, followed by Ross, Bridewell and Abercrombie.

'How was the hunt, Sir Edward?' called Captain Parker cheerily.

'Damned pointless,' the host growled. 'I think it's high time we wound this blessed evening down, don't you?'

Alice had run across the room to hug her fiancé, and to smile happily at her father. 'Of course, Papa,' she agreed. 'I'm so happy that you're all safe.'

'Safe?' her father barked. 'Of course we're safe. It was just a wild goose chase, when all is said and done.'

'Hardly that, Sir Edward,' Ross put in mildly. 'We've tracked the creature almost to its lair, and tomorrow we can finish it off.'

'What?' exclaimed the Doctor, catapulting out of the chair where he'd thrown himself. 'You'll do no such thing!'

Sir Edward appeared taken aback, and then he turned crimson. 'You again!' he thundered. 'What are you doing here?'

'You told us to meet you here,' the Doctor replied. 'So here we are.'

Their host glared at him again. 'I do not appreciate your questioning my decisions continually,' he said.

'Then stop making them without thinking,' suggested the Doctor blithely. 'This creature you're hunting is not some monster to be slaughtered, you know, and you're not Saint George spearing a dragon.'

'How dare you, sir?' thundered Sir Edward.

'It's about time someone told you the truth,' the Doctor snapped. 'I don't suppose you get a lot of that around here.'

Sir Edward was clearly not appreciating the Doctor's candour. 'That monster is slaughtering ponies and other wildlife in this area,' he said, struggling to keep his temper. 'It is a menace and must be killed.'

'It's just hunting for food,' the Doctor countered. 'You should attempt to capture it and study it. There's something unnatural about it.'

'You may study it as much as you wish,' Sir Edward countered, 'after I've made good and certain that the beast is dead.' He poked a finger in the Doctor's face. 'The trouble with you scientific types is that you're too keen on studying from the ivory towers of your universities, and loath to get to grips with the real world.'

'And you're a typical military man,' retorted the Doctor. 'Anything you don't comprehend must be killed first and studied later.'

'Papa,' Alice broke in, attempting to sooth his ruffled feelings, 'the Doctor and Miss Smith are our guests. They're going to help Sir Alexander in the morning. Try to be a little kinder.'

'Sir Alexander?' her father asked. 'Whatever does he want their help with?'

'There's been a death in the village,' the Doctor explained.

'Really?' asked Ross, his curiosity clearly piqued. 'An unnatural one, I take it?'

'Very,' agreed the Doctor. He grinned. 'An eventful night, wouldn't you say?'

'Definitely,' Ross agreed. He gave a thin smile. 'And in such a pleasant, isolated community, too.'

'Odd, isn't it?' The Doctor returned the smile. 'And why are you here? Not a local, are you?'

'No more than you are, Doctor,' Ross replied. He made no effort to answer the other question, however.

Sarah frowned. There were obviously undercurrents at work here. She caught the black look that Sir Edward darted in Ross's direction. Obviously the host wasn't too much at ease with the guest. 'Look,' she broke in, 'it's late, and we're all tired. My feet are killing me. Can't we call it a night and start arguing again in the morning?'

'Miss Smith is right, Papa,' Alice said. 'We're all tired.' She smiled and rested her hand on his arm. 'And you

57

are getting a little grouchy.'

For a moment it seemed as if Sir Edward was about to throw another tantrum. Then he patted his daughter's hand fondly. 'You're quite right, Alice. It is time to retire. Tomorrow is likely to be a busy day for us all.' He glared at the Doctor. 'Do you and your friend have anywhere to stay the night?' he growled. 'Courtesy forces me to offer you a room.'

'And forces me to accept,' the Doctor answered lightly. 'Thank you.'

Alice took Sarah's arm. 'You shall have the room adjoining mine,' she said. 'I'll show you the way and loan you a few necessities.'

'Thanks,' Sarah gave her a warm smile. It was impossible not to like the young woman. Anyone less like her aggressive, cantankerous father was difficult to imagine. Sarah nodded to the group. 'Good night.'

Alice gave her father a peck on the cheek, and another to her fiancé. 'Good night.' Then she led Sarah up the marble stairs. 'You must forgive my father,' she said softly. 'He has a lot of responsibilities.'

'I understand,' Sarah told her. 'And you'll have to excuse my friend. He sometimes gets a little carried away with his ideas.'

Alice smiled. 'It sounds like we both have a lot of practice being tolerant,' she said. 'I'm glad to have met you, Miss Smith.'

'Sarah,' Sarah told her. 'You make me sound like a schoolteacher.'

'Sarah,' agreed Alice. She smiled. 'I hope we can be friends.'

'That would be nice.' Sarah couldn't help liking the young woman. She was very open and friendly. She only hoped that the Doctor and her father could resolve their differences. It would make things so much easier.

She knew from experience, however, how little chance there was of that occurring.

He lay in his lair, panting from exertion and licking his sore paws. His sides heaved and his head rang. It had been a hard chase, and he had been hunted as though he were some monster. But he wasn't! He couldn't help what he had become!

And he'd been forced to abandon his prey before he had done little more than taste it. His stomach cried out for food, but he didn't dare leave his lair again tonight. The men might still be waiting for him, with their guns. He didn't want to die, even if his fate was repugnant to him. He hated being the monster he had become, but he feared death more.

Why couldn't they just leave him alone? He didn't want to hurt anyone, even though he knew it would be easy to use his powerful jaws on a person. It would take less effort to kill a man than a pony. Men couldn't run as far or as fast.

But he couldn't kill! He had been human once. But not any more. Men treated him like he was a monster, hunting him, hounding him, never allowing him peace. Well, if that was what they wanted to make of him, maybe he should become what they expected. Maybe he should accept his fate, and be the monster that he had been transformed into against his will. He recalled the look of revulsion and terror on the face of that lady he'd jumped over. He'd been careful not to hurt her, and she'd still been terrified and repulsed by him.

Well, if that was all they saw in him, then maybe that was all he should be.

He had to eat tomorrow. And if any hunter tried to stop him, then he would have no choice.

He would have to kill.

Interlude 1

Lucy

She was growing used to her new world, and that scared her more than anything had so far in her life. She was used to fear. And uncertainty. And abuse. And hunger. She wasn't used to feeling useful, and that was what was scaring her. Of course, there was plenty to hate in this new world. The work, for one thing. The Guards forced everyone to work, even when the jobs didn't make sense, and sometimes even when they were obviously pointless. Lucy realized that it wasn't the work that mattered, just that they were all forced to do it. It showed Lucy and the others that their place in this new world was one of slaves.

That Lucy could understand. Her life before this had been bad enough. This was hardly much worse, if you didn't count the Change.

Of course, how could you not count the Change? That was what had brought them here, to this new world of theirs. It was different from the old world physically, but not much else had altered. She was still an orphan, still unprotected, still forced to live on the edge of death constantly. But now she had responsibilities too. The Guards had made that much clear. She'd been the first, and she was the oldest here. It was her duty to teach the newcomers, to help them to adjust to the Change. To stop them killing themselves in despair. And to see that they worked. If they didn't work, the Guards would rough them up. And if they caused too many problems, like Tim had done, then the Guards killed.

And they forced the others to watch.

Lucy still had nightmares, still hearing Tim's screams, seeing the blood fountaining from his body as the Guards tore him apart. That had been horrifying, but what was worse was that the Guards had enjoyed it. They had been longing for someone else to give them the excuse to kill again. So far, Lucy had made certain that it had never occurred.

The day's work was done, and the Guards prodded them all back into the dormitory for the night. They had all eaten – and there had been many days in her old life when Lucy had gone to bed feeling hunger eating at her insides. At least here they all ate, even if it was a monotonous diet. Her muscles ached from working, but she felt fairly good otherwise. It was nice to go to bed with a full stomach.

'Come along, everyone,' she called to the younger ones. 'It's time for bed now.'

'Tell us a story,' begged Vicki. She was one of the youngest here, only about eight. There were twenty of them now since Joshua had arrived two days ago. He still hurt from the Change, Lucy knew. And he was having troubles adjusting to this new life.

'Yes,' Joshua agreed. 'Tell us a story.'

Lucy hesitated. It would help him and the others if she could take their minds off their states. 'I don't know any,' she confessed miserably. 'I never learned to read, and my folks died when I was too young to be told any.'

'You know one story,' Vicki objected. 'You know your own.'

Lucy smiled. 'But you've heard that one dozens of times already,' she objected. 'You must know it by heart.'

'Joshua doesn't,' Lizzy pointed out. 'He's new. He'd like to hear it. You tell it so well.'

'Yes,' agreed Joshua eagerly. 'I want to hear it.'

Lucy shook her head and laughed, a clear, tinkling laugh of pure happiness. 'Oh, very well,' she agreed. As they gathered around her, she looked out at their expectant faces. 'Well, every good story starts with "Once upon a time . . ."'

Once upon a time, I lived in a nightmare. I don't remember my parents at all. When I grew up, I lived with an old man called Cherry. He was gruff and sometimes mean, but usually only when he got drunk. He didn't have much money, so he couldn't get drunk too often. When he did, I tried to hide away until he passed out. If I couldn't, he'd hit me, and knock me around the little hut we lived in. He told me once that my father had been a sailor drowned at sea, and that my mother had died of grief, leaving me an unwanted orphan. He'd taken me in because he'd been related to my mother, and it was only out of the kindness of his heart. I didn't know he had any kindness, because he never showed it to me.

As soon as I could walk, he took me out onto the beaches and rocks. There he showed me how to scavenge for things brought in by the tide. Pieces of wood, mostly. He had a big knife that he used to carve the wood into all sorts of shapes. Some of them I knew, like boats and things. Some of them I'd never seen: seals, for example. He used to be a whaler, he told me, and had often seen seals. He had gone off on a ship to a land of ice, where night had never come. I laughed once when he told me this, thinking he was making it up. That made him mad, and he hit me and swore it was all true.

It was funny, really. He didn't have much goodness inside of him, but he could really carve the wood into beautiful shapes. Then he'd take them into town once a week or so and sell them. With the money he'd get good and drunk, so I soon learned to hide away until he got over it. He felt sorry for himself because he couldn't go back on the ships and off to hunt the whales and seals, you see. On his last trip his foot had been hurt, and he'd lost it. Instead of a real foot, he had a long piece of wood that he'd stomp about on. It made him slow, so I could dodge out of his way if I was lucky.

It hurt him to move about on this wooden foot, so I soon found out that the real reason he'd taken me in had nothing to do with him taking pity on me, or me being a relative of his. I think he just lied about that part. I was there to do all the things he couldn't manage, like getting the wood from the rocks for his carvings. Or getting food from town, if he had any money left after his drinking. Usually I had to steal the food, or take it from the farmers' fields. That was scary, because some of the farmers would have killed me if they'd caught me. I got to be pretty good at hiding, what with the farmers and old man Cherry. But I wasn't good enough when it mattered.

Sometimes, if a ship was wrecked at sea, I'd find other things on the rocks when the tide washed them in. I found a whole box filled with eating things once. Not food, the stuff you eat food with: knives and forks and spoons. Cherry was very pleased with that find because the things were made out of silver, which he told me was worth a lot of money. He got really drunk three times after he sold those things. Once I found some books, but they were all soggy and you couldn't read them because they'd been ruined by the water. I didn't much care, since I can't read anyway, but it might have been nice just to look at the pictures. I found all sorts of stuff, and Cherry would sell them and then get drunk.

I was about ten when he died, and everything changed.

That was almost two years ago. He'd been getting worse and worse all the time, with his temper and everything. And I was growing up and getting stronger and different. He started to look at me all funny, and sometimes instead of yelling and throwing things at me, he'd make me come over to him and he'd touch me. It was horrible, and I'm not going to tell you those bits because it would scare you and disgust you. He was a horrible old man, and I hated him more and more every day that passed. Sometimes I'd go to bed at night and pray that God would kill him. I wanted the sky to open up and a thunderbolt to come down and burn Cherry up. In the end he did die, but it wasn't a thunderbolt that killed him. It was his own knife.

He'd had one of his good selling days in town again, and had gone to get drunk. I knew what that would mean when he got back. He'd either hit me or touch me, and I wasn't about to stand for either. I knew that when he went off drinking, it would be hours and hours he'd be gone, until either the pubs would close, or they'd throw him out, or he'd run out of money. Well, I knew he had lots of money because I'd found a box on the beach that had sailor stuff in it. Metal instruments that could see far away and things like that. He'd sold them for a lot of money, so he was bound to get good and drunk.

I made up my mind that when he came back, he wouldn't have me there for him any more. I didn't have any things of my own, except for a few tattered old clothes he'd bought me from time to time, so I didn't need to pack much. And I had a few coins I'd managed to find around, or steal when he'd been too drunk to notice. I'd planned all this for a long time, you see, till I got enough courage to try it.

Of course, despite all my planning, things went terribly wrong. I had expected Cherry to spend the whole evening at the pub, but he'd met two men there and they had started talking. The men had persuaded him to buy drinks to bring home with him so they could all get drunk together. So when I slipped out of the cabin door, instead of being able to escape in the night, I ran right into the three of them as they arrived.

Cherry was slightly drunk, but he wasn't stupid. He could see what I was up to, and he was furious, of course. If there had just been him I could have escaped, because he couldn't move as quickly as I could with his wooden leg. But there was nothing wrong with his companions. One of them, a rat-faced man they called Raintree, grabbed me before I could run. The other man was tall and almost all muscle, named Brogan. You've all met the two of them, since they brought us all here, but they had just begun their work at this point, and were celebrating with Cherry. They were all a little drunk, and that made them even nastier than normal.

Raintree held me too tightly for me to break free, with his thin arm around my throat. He and Brogan encouraged Cherry as the old man ranted and raged about how ungrateful I was, and how evil I was, and how terrible I was to leave him alone in his old age to die. Raintree kept slipping his sly little comments in, working Cherry up. He wanted to see me hurt. It wasn't that he disliked me any more than he disliked the rest of the world, but he enjoyed seeing people hurt. Finally Cherry drew that carving knife of his.

'I've carved many things with this,' he told me, waving it drunkenly under my face. 'You won't be the first person, either. And I'll be very artistic with it. I'll cut you so that you won't die. You'll just wish you would. When people look at you from now on, they'll shudder at what they see. And they'll know better than to ever cross Cherry again.'

I knew he meant it, too. He was going to use his knife

65

to give me dreadful pain, and then to leave scars all over me so I'd be hideous and repulsive. He knew I couldn't get away, and Raintree and Brogan were laughing and crying aloud to see me hurt. I was terribly afraid, because I knew he'd make me suffer.

But Raintree was so intent on what was promising to be his idea of sport that he wasn't as careful as he should have been. The terrible, choking grip he had on me loosened just enough. I could take several gasping breaths, and I knew I had only once chance. I bit his arm as hard as I could. He screamed and his grip faltered again. Spitting out his vile blood, I pulled myself free.

At that second, Cherry lunged at me with his knife. I didn't have any choice but to dive forward to try and escape him. Cherry collided with Raintree instead of cutting me, and his knife sliced Raintree's hurt arm even more. I rolled out of the way, and staggered to my feet. As I was about to flee, I looked back.

With a roar of pain and rage, Raintree lashed out at Cherry. Unsteady on his feet because of the drink and his wooden leg, the old man fell down. Raintree grabbed the carving knife from Cherry's hands and plunged it down into the fallen man's stomach. Cherry gave a horrible scream, and twisted. He died slowly. I couldn't move, I was so terrified and sickened.

Then I felt Brogan's huge hand grab my arm, and I was a captive again. I couldn't escape his strong grip, and he dragged me back to where Raintree was getting back to his feet and staring down at the screaming, dying old man. I was horrified, but I couldn't feel any pity for Cherry. I was glad he'd finally met the end he deserved. He couldn't beat me or touch me ever again. But I was still in a great deal of trouble.

'You've killed him,' Brogan told his ratty friend. 'Now what do we do?'

Raintree looked at me with his little, evil eyes. I knew that he wanted to kill me so there wouldn't be any witnesses. But I was lucky, because greed was stronger in him than his love for blood. 'We get away from here,' he said. 'And she comes with us.'

Brogan stared at me. He wasn't very bright, and he didn't understand. 'Why don't I just break her neck?' he asked. 'That way, nobody will know anything.'

'Idiot,' Raintree said. 'We're being paid to get children for the doctor, aren't we? And isn't she a child?'

'Oh, I get it,' Brogan said. 'Once she's been changed, she won't be able to tell anyone, will she?'

'Right,' agreed Raintree. 'And if she dies . . . Then *we* didn't kill her, did we?'

As you can imagine, I didn't have a clue about what they meant. All I knew was that Cherry was rattling his way to death, blood and stuff spilling out of his stomach, and that I was free of him. Raintree and Brogan had something in mind for me that was probably horrible and scary, but I didn't much care right then. I was free of Cherry at last.

Lucy stopped her story and smiled at the younger ones about her. 'That's enough for one time,' she told them.

There was a chorus of moans. 'You can't stop now,' complained Joshua. 'What happened next?'

'I'll tell you the rest after work tomorrow,' promised Lucy. She ignored the complaints. 'If we talk too long, the Guards get angry,' she explained. 'So we'd better get our rest. We'll have a lot of work to do tomorrow, you know. They always make sure of that.'

With the odd grumble, the children began settling down for the night. Lucy checked on them, making sure they were comfortable. She left Joshua for last. He smiled up at her.

'You're very brave,' he told her, admiringly.

'We all are,' she answered. 'We have to be. You're one of us, now. I'm sorry you were chosen, but you are welcome as part of our family. We have to look after each other, because nobody else will look out for us.'

Joshua nodded and gripped her hand tightly. 'You'll be here for us,' he said. 'I trust you.'

'Good night,' she replied. Then she gently pulled her hand free. As he settled down, she crossed to her own sleeping area. She knew that the other children were drawing on her strength to survive the Change with their minds intact. If only she was as certain that she could hold up under the stress as they seemed to be. But she had to go on, despite everything, for their sake. They needed her so much. She couldn't let them down.

3

Bodies

Though morning seemed to come too early, Sarah managed to rouse herself. The bed she'd slept in was so comfortable that it was a struggle to get up, but she'd eventually won the fight. She scrambled back into the clothes she'd worn the previous day, wishing she'd thought to bring along a change from the TARDIS. Of course, she'd not expected the events of the previous day. What she'd hoped for was a pleasant chat with Rudyard Kipling on a veranda in India somewhere, and then back to the TARDIS.

She should have known better by now.

There was a pitcher and basin on the dressing table, both made from china decorated with red flowers of some indeterminate species. She splashed water on her face, then used a brush that Alice had loaned her to comb out her hair. It wasn't a very good toilet, but it was the best she could do in this place. What she'd give to be back in the TARDIS's bathroom!

There was a gentle rap on the door. When Sarah opened it, Alice was waiting outside. 'I thought a little breakfast and a cup of tea might help you before your journey into town,' she said. 'The breakfast room is being prepared, and I'll take you down.'

'Bless you!' said Sarah happily. 'I could just murder a cup of tea.'

Alice laughed. 'You have a strange way of speaking, Sarah.'

'I've got a lot of strange ways,' Sarah answered, as they walked down the elegant corridor together. 'That's what happens when you travel as much as I do, I suppose.'

'It must be nice,' Alice remarked wistfully. 'I've not been about much. When Roger and I are married, though, he has promised me that we shall honeymoon in Paris.' Her eyes sparkled. 'That sounds quite exciting. Have you ever been to Paris?'

'Lots of times,' Sarah admitted. 'It's a great place. I'm sure you'll love it there.'

Alice sighed. 'Oh, how I envy you. You seem to have done so much, and I so little.'

Sarah laughed. 'You don't know the half of it.'

It took a great deal of effort, but Sir Edward Fulbright managed to hold his temper in check. It seemed as though his house was filled at the moment with guests that he either disliked or distrusted. In Ross's case, perhaps both. After dressing for breakfast, he emerged from his room to almost run into another barely welcome guest.

'Good morning,' said the Doctor, politely doffing his hat. 'I hope you slept well?'

'Tolerably,' growled Fulbright.

The Doctor gave him a warm smile. 'I suspect we got off on the wrong foot last night, Sir Edward,' he said. 'I'm certain that we both want the same thing – the removal of the creature that hunts on the moors at night. Our only difference is that you wish to slay it and I wish to remove it for study. I'm sure we're both reasonable men; can't we come to some sort of amicable arrangement here?'

Fulbright grudgingly had to admit that the man had a point. 'What do you suggest?'

'Let me make one attempt to capture it,' the Doctor offered. 'If that fails, then you can have a try at killing it.'

He grinned. 'I'd let you have the first go, but your solution is a trifle more permanent than mine.'

Fulbright grunted. 'I'll consider it, Doctor,' he finally said. 'If you can come up with a scheme that sounds like it'll work, I'll go along with it.'

'More than fair,' the Doctor answered happily.

Perhaps he'd misjudged this fellow, after all. Fulbright had to concede that he hadn't been in the best of tempers the previous evening, and the chappie seemed to be pretty reasonable. 'Do you think you can help Sir Alexander with this mysterious death in the village?' he asked.

'I can but try,' the Doctor answered. 'I've some small acquaintance with matters of mystery.'

'And,' broke in Ross's voice, 'some contributions of your own to the cause of mystery. Your last name, for instance.'

Fulbright's brightening mood instantly started to cloud over once again. He hadn't even heard the man approaching. 'The Doctor is trying to help,' Fulbright pointed out. 'Which is more than you appear to be doing.'

Ross raised an eyebrow. 'I see. So my leading the hunt for that monster last night was no help at all?'

'I'm still not convinced that you've told us all that you know about that apparition,' Fulbright snapped. 'You have a secretive air about you.'

'And this Doctor doesn't?' asked Ross, mockingly. He turned to the stranger. 'You still haven't told us your last name.'

'No,' agreed the Doctor amiably. 'I haven't. And why are you here?'

'Counter-attack, eh?' Ross appeared to be amused. 'As a guest of Sir Edward's daughter and future son-in-law.'

The Doctor shook his head slowly. 'Oh, no. That's not

it at all, Colonel. Sir Edward is perfectly correct — there's something you know that you're not telling us.'

Ross smiled. 'I see. And you, of course, have been perfectly candid with everyone?'

The Doctor matched his smile. 'As much as I can be. Do you intend to take part in this autopsy today also?'

'Goodness me, no!' Ross shook his head. 'It all sounds very messy and quite disgusting. I had thought that my man Abercrombie and I would take a stroll on the moors.'

'Bird-watching?' asked Sir Edward acidly. 'Your man said he's no ornithologist.'

Ross didn't look at all embarrassed. 'I doubt he could pronounce the word. Actually, I had thought about collecting a few wild flowers.' He bowed to them both. 'If you'll excuse me?'

Fulbright watched the man leave, scowling. 'I don't trust him at all,' he admitted candidly. There was something about the Doctor, though, that made him seem to be trustworthy. And something about the way he dressed. Fulbright shuddered at the garish scarf and silly clothing. 'Do you intend to go along dressed like that?' he asked.

The Doctor appeared bemused, as though he'd never considered anything else. 'Why? Too flashy, you think?'

Fulbright snorted. 'Sir Alexander is rather . . . traditionally minded,' he commented. 'If you wish to make a good impression, you'd dress more conservatively.'

The Doctor looked confused. 'I'm afraid all of my luggage is stuck out on the moors right now.'

'Not a problem,' Fulbright assured him. 'You're about my size. I'm sure I can loan you a few items to tide you over.'

'Most generous,' the Doctor replied. 'I'd be very grateful.'

'This way, then.'

* * *

Sarah had polished off a plate of kippers and three cups of tea when the footman announced that the coach was ready. She felt much more prepared to face whatever the day would bring, and the news that she wouldn't be walking into the village cheered her even more. Saying goodbye to Alice, she followed the servant out of the large main doors. In front of the steps stood a landau, with a coachman already at the reins. Beside the carriage, chattering animatedly, stood the Doctor, Sir Edward and Sir Alexander. Sarah couldn't help smiling at the Doctor's appearance.

He'd put aside his normal attire for once, and actually looked rather dashing. He wore a chequered cape coat and a deerstalker hat. Sarah slipped up beside him. 'Didn't you get a pipe with that outfit?' she joked.

'It's in my pocket,' the Doctor replied gravely. 'Thankfully it isn't lit.'

'Ah, Miss Smith,' said the magistrate, bowing over her hand. He turned to Fulbright. 'Well, old man, it looks as though we're ready to go now.'

'You will all return for dinner, I trust?' asked Fulbright.

Sarah grinned. 'If it's half as good as breakfast, Sir Edward,' she assured him, 'wild horses couldn't keep me away.'

'Or wild hounds, either,' added the Doctor.

'Splendid.' Fulbright beamed at them both. 'Well, I mustn't keep you from your work. Good luck, all of you.'

Alice watched the carriage leave the driveway, smiling to herself. She was certain that she'd discovered a new friend in Sarah. She might be a trifle unusual, due to her nomadic lifestyle, but she was pleasant and personable, and Alice was glad of another woman her age about the

73

house. It was nice to have men about, but she liked another woman to talk with.

She was about to move on from the window alcove she'd been observing the grounds from when she heard Edmund Ross's voice. She rather liked the young officer, whom Roger had known for several years, even though she knew her father was not so fond of the man. Before she could emerge to introduce herself into the conversation, however, she realized Ross was speaking to that strange little servant of his, Abercrombie.

'It's a shame that Sir Edward didn't go with the others, Abercrombie,' Ross commented. 'It would have made searching the house so much easier.'

Alice stopped still, shocked at what she had just heard. It would not be a wise move to show herself now, she decided. Instead she waited, hoping to hear more.

'You want me to have a nose about?' asked Abercrombie.

'Yes,' replied Ross. 'And do try to be a little more circumspect. The maids have been noticing you, and not because of your debonair charms. I thought you were supposed to be the best burglar in the West End?'

'Yeah, but this ain't the West End,' Abercrombie complained. 'I'm doing my best.'

'I'm sure you are, but do better.' Ross paused a moment, then added, 'I'm going to search inside the house. If you see anything of value, you know how to contact me.'

Alice hardly dared breathe in case she was discovered. With relief, she heard the men move away from the alcove. She waited another couple of minutes, and then timidly peered around the corner. The corridor was empty; the men had gone.

What should she do now? It was quite clear that Ross was not here as Roger's friend, whatever he had claimed.

74

And he had called that creature of his a burglar! It was obvious to her that Ross was here to steal something from the house. She felt angry and betrayed, but she didn't know how to handle this. If she told her father what she'd heard, Papa would probably have Ross horsewhipped. The only thing Alice could think of was to tell Roger and let him handle his so-called friend. She hurried off to find her fiancé.

Doyle had breakfasted and shaved by the time that the one-armed ex-sailor, Brackley, turned up on the *Hope* to say that Constable Faversham would like him to come along. Doyle had already cleared this with Captain Gray, so he scooped up his medical bag and followed Brackley with anticipation of an interesting day.

He'd had a good night's sleep, and had risen early to check through the few medical volumes he'd brought with him on the voyage. There had been references to shark attacks in one of these but, as Doyle had already felt certain, the patterns didn't match the case of the previous evening. Nothing more had really occurred to him, but the conviction had grown that this was no shark attack, and that there was a definite mystery behind the corpse.

'Whatever happened to the poor man's boat?' he asked Brackley, as they hurried along the quay toward the Pig and Thistle.

'The men brought it in, sir,' the retired sailor answered. 'It's berthed behind the tavern. Will you be wanting to see it later?'

'I believe so,' Doyle replied. 'There may be evidence or clues aboard it that will aid in the investigation of this matter.' Taking one of his few remaining half-crowns from his pocket, he slipped it to the one-armed man. This would be a good investment if a story came out of this mystery. 'See that it remains undisturbed, will you?'

Brackley gave him a broken-toothed grin. 'You can count on me, sir.'

'I'm sure I can.' Doyle felt that he'd done all that he could for the moment. There was a real sense of excitement growing within him. It was a shame that the old man had died – and perished so brutally – but it might be the opportunity he'd been praying for.

The Pig and Thistle was a smallish building, a typical country pub. There was a tap bar and a smoking lounge, plus a couple of rooms upstairs for the landlord and his wife, and one for the barmaid. There were two other rooms that were rented out if they were needed, but Doyle knew they were currently empty. There weren't a lot of travellers that passed through Bodham. If the *Hope* sailed on before he was done, Doyle was certain he could take one of the rooms for a modest price to enable him to see this through to the end.

The body of old Ben Tolliver was laid out in the stables behind the tavern. Constable Faversham was seated outside the small building, dozing slightly in the morning sunshine. Doyle wondered if the man had stood – or sat – on guard all night. He had mentioned something about being the only law officer in the area. He was probably glad to have Brackley around to carry messages for him.

Faversham snapped awake with a jerk as Doyle hurried over. 'Good morning, Sir,' the constable said, rising uncomfortably to his feet and straightening his tie. 'I was just catching a few nods, waiting for you all to arrive.'

Doyle pulled out his watch. 'Almost eight thirty,' he observed. 'Do you think that Sir Edward will be here soon?'

'I'm expecting him any time, sir,' Faversham answered. 'Ah, this is Doctor Martinson now.'

Doyle glanced around to see an elderly man walking carefully across the tavern's cobbled yard. Some of the stones were rather slippery from ale spilled the previous night. Martinson was clearly into his sixties, but a spry old bird for all that. He had an aquiline nose and a shock of white hair that gave him more than a passing resemblance to an eagle. Doyle stuck out his hand as the older man approached.

'Ship's Surgeon Doyle,' he introduced himself.

'Martinson,' the other replied, shaking his hand firmly. 'I gather from Faversham here that you made a preliminary examination of the body last night?'

'Purely a cursory one, I'm afraid,' Doyle answered. 'The light was very poor, but I feel certain that Tolliver was not attacked by a shark. What did kill him is a mystery thus far.'

'Ah.' Martinson chuckled. 'I, too, am sure he wasn't killed by a shark,' he commented. 'I didn't need to examine the body to tell you that. There have been no such attacks around here for decades, to my knowledge, and certainly not in Bodham Bay.' He winked. 'So we'll have our work cut out for us today, I imagine.'

'Rather,' agreed Doyle. He was quite warming up to the old man. 'I trust you have no objection to my assisting you?'

'My dear chap, of course not! Many hands make light work, as they say, and at my age you appreciate the lightest possible work.' He spun around to face the street. 'Ah, this must be Sir Alexander! Capital, we can soon commence!'

A landau drew to a halt outside the tavern entrance and the footman jumped down to offer his hand to the first passenger that descended. To Doyle's surprise and pleasure, it was a young woman. And a pretty one, too! She was followed by an older man, richly dressed, and clearly the Justice himself. The final figure who emerged from the carriage caught Doyle's eye. He was almost as interesting as the young woman. In his cape coat and deerstalker hat, with a prominent nose and a steely eye, he was clearly a man to be reckoned with.

The trio came through the gateway and into the courtyard. Doctor Martinson waved as they approached. 'Glad you could make it, Sir Alexander,' he called. 'Who are your friends?'

Sir Alexander shook the medical man's hand. 'Glad you're here, Walter. Allow me to introduce Miss Sarah Jane Smith and the Doctor.'

'Doctor, eh?' asked Martinson. 'Of what?'

'Everything but medicine,' the Doctor replied, his gaze resting on Doyle. 'Haven't we met somewhere before?'

'I don't believe so,' Doyle replied. 'You don't look like the sort of man I'd forget in a hurry.' He held out his hand. 'Ship's Surgeon Doyle.'

Sarah's eyes lit up at this. 'Off the *Hope*?' she asked eagerly.

Doyle was taken somewhat aback at her knowledge. 'Why, yes. But how the blazes did you know that?'

Sarah laughed in delight. 'I've read your stories,' she told him. To his surprise, she shook his hand as a man would have done. 'You're one of my favourite authors, you know. Arthur Conan Doyle.'

Doyle felt himself blushing. 'Actually you flatter me too much, Miss Smith,' he replied. 'I've had only one story published so far, but it's most gratifying to know that you enjoyed it so much.'

'I'm sure we'll be reading much more by you in the future,' Sarah told him. 'You're a natural.'

'Well,' broke in Sir Alexander, 'I hate to stop all this cheeriness, but we do have work to do, gentlemen – and lady.'

Faversham stepped forward. 'Ah, begging your pardon, sir, but . . .' He shuffled somewhat uncomfortably. 'I don't think that the body is a fit sight for a lady.'

'Oh. Quite.' The Justice turned to Sarah. 'Perhaps you had better wait for us here, young lady.'

'What?' Sarah's face fell. 'Come off it! I'm not squeamish, I'll have you know.'

The Doctor patted her shoulder. 'I think it would be better if you waited, Sarah,' he said. 'I'll fill you in later.'

'Well, thanks a lot!' said Sarah huffily. She threw her hands in the air and stalked off. Typical! Going off to have all the fun and leaving her to her own devices. As if she hadn't seen plenty of dead bodies in her travels with the Doctor. 'What a start to the day,' she grumbled. 'I'll bet it just gets worse.'

There was a low whistle from outside the gateway. Sarah hurried over and peered around the corner – straight into three familiar faces.

'Morning!' said Rudyard Kipling breezily.

'It just got worse,' sighed Sarah.

The stable had clearly been neglected for a number of years. There were small holes in the walls that allowed light in, and windows that were so encrusted with dirt that they didn't. Cobwebs laced the whole structure – possibly helping to hold it together, Doyle mused – and the only evidence of any recent use was the empty ale barrels stacked for collection. There was a musty smell, mixed with the sickly stench of decay permeating from the direction of the body. Faversham had been thoughtful enough to provide nosegays for them, which offset this a trifle.

Half a dozen barrels had been pressed into service to act as a table to bear Tolliver's corpse. It was still covered over with the tarpaulin, presumably to keep off the rats that Doyle had heard scurrying for cover when they had entered the stable.

Faversham started to unlace the covering, and glanced up at the Doctor. 'Would you happen to be the gentleman that Scotland Yard promised to send out, sir?'

The Doctor frowned. 'You couldn't possibly have contacted the Yard yet about this matter,' he observed.

'No, sir, not about this. About the children.'

'Ah!' The Doctor shook his head slightly. 'I have on occasion worked with Scotland Yard, constable, but I remain for the most part an independent observer. I am here only to offer my expertise if Sir Alexander or either of these medical gentlemen wish to avail themselves of it.'

'I see, sir.' Faversham sounded disappointed. Doyle asked, 'Children?'

Sir Alexander sighed. 'Some of the local urchins have gone missing, it appears. It didn't seem to me to be anything for concern, as Constable Faversham is quite capable. But one of the boys from Westward Ho!, the local school, went missing several days ago. His parents are apparently well connected, and they demanded a plea for aid from the Yard. So far, other than promises, nothing much has materialized.'

'Would that be a boy named Anders?' asked the Doctor.

'That's right, sir,' Faversham said, pausing in his work of uncovering the corpse. 'Joshua Anders. I thought you weren't involved with that?'

'I didn't think I was,' the Doctor said thoughtfully. 'But Miss Smith and I met three of his friends last night. They mentioned his name. How many are missing in all?'

'Hard to say, sir,' Faversham informed him. 'Seeing as how most of them have neither kin nor friends, it's hard to be exact.'

'Be inexact then.'

'About fifteen, perhaps more,' Faversham admitted.

'Fifteen children missing!' the Doctor exclaimed. He

rounded on Sir Alexander. 'And you didn't think that significant?'

'They are merely wharf rats and street urchins, Doctor,' the Justice protested. 'We don't know that anything has happened to them at all.'

'Of course not,' the Doctor agreed sarcastically. 'Probably just popped off down to Brighton for a paddle in the sea. Hello!'

The constable had finished unwrapping the body now, and pulled off the tarpaulin. The Doctor peered at it in fascination. Both Sir Alexander and Doctor Martinson paled and turned away. 'What do you make of it, Doyle?' asked the Doctor.

Doyle stepped forward eagerly. 'As you can see, Doctor,' he explained, 'Tolliver was killed by the bite to the face. The teeth have left striations on what remains of the frontal and sphenoidal bones. The arm was taken off in a subsequent attack after he was already dead. There is too little blood marking the side of his jacket, so the heart must have stopped pumping by that point in time.'

The Doctor nodded approvingly. 'Excellent deduction, Doctor.' He whipped a small magnifying glass from a pocket and bent over the grisly remains of the head, apparently oblivious to the nauseating stench. 'And what do you make of the angle of incisions?'

Doyle frowned. 'I'm not sure I follow you, Doctor.'

'Well, look at the way the bones have been shattered in the face and how the flesh is torn from the arm.' He glanced back at the two older men. 'I'm sorry; would either of you care to take a closer look? I didn't mean to hog the best position.'

'No, Doctor,' Sir Alexander replied, blanching at the suggestion. 'Please, carry on. I'm more than happy to listen.'

'As you wish.' The Doctor seemed puzzled at this

reaction. Ignoring it, he turned back to Doyle. 'Do you think a shark could have done this?'

Grinning, Doyle shook his head. 'No. Sharks always attack the limbs, and invariably the limbs of a person in the water. But the limb was severed after the bite to the face. And Tolliver was never in the water.' He gestured at the corpse's waistcoat pocket. 'As you see, his baccy pouch is dry.'

'Capital!' approved the Doctor, slapping Doyle heartily on the back. 'Absolutely sound reasoning. You noticed, also, no doubt, that the angle of the bite is all wrong. I think we can safely assume that poor Tolliver here was staring down at whatever killed him. The attacker ripped off the front of his face. Sharks have their mouths on the underside of their heads, so to be able to rip off the face, a shark would have had to have been swimming on its back at the time. So we can discount that. Whatever creature did this has to have its mouth forward on its head – and offhand I can think of no species of aquatic animal that is native to the Earth that might be held accountable.'

Doctor Martinson took a nervous step forward. 'Does it have to be a marine creature that killed him, Doctor?' he asked. 'After all, Tolliver was found on his boat, which was drifting. Is it not possible that there was on board with him some terrestrial animal, such as a savage dog, that killed him?'

'And then vanished?' asked the Doctor sceptically. He shrugged. 'It is a possibility,' he agreed. 'After all, Sir Edward and his friends were hunting some such creature on the moors last night.'

'Well, there you are then,' Martinson exclaimed. 'Surely that is the creature we're after?'

'I don't believe so.' The Doctor looked very thoughtful. 'For one thing, it was quite a distance inland and not much later than the time when Tolliver died. I myself saw the beast, and it showed no signs of having been for a swim.' He gave a sudden smile. 'Still, there's one way to be certain, isn't there?' He turned to Faversham. 'I take it that Tolliver's boat is somewhere around and hasn't been touched?'

'Aye, sir. It's moored up just behind the tavern.'

'And,' added Doyle, 'I paid Brackley to keep an eye on it and see that it wasn't disturbed.'

'Excellent,' approved the Doctor. 'I'm beginning to think that I'm really not needed here at all. You seem to be proceeding perfectly well without my aid.'

Sir Alexander frowned. 'But what will the boat tell us about Tolliver's death?' he asked.

'Where it occurred,' the Doctor answered.

'But we know where it occurred,' the Justice retorted. 'At sea.'

'Yes, but from the sea or from the boat?' asked the Doctor. 'If the creature that killed him was on the vessel with him, then there will be buckets of blood all over the deck. If it was from the sea, then the majority of the blood would have gone into the water and the decks will be relatively clean.'

'Wonderful!' exclaimed Doyle. 'You are most certainly proving your worth, Doctor. Well, are we done here?'

'Almost,' the Doctor answered. 'Let's see if we can't make poor Tolliver bear a little further witness against his slayer first.'

'Surely,' objected Doctor Martinson, 'we've got all we can already from this noisome relic?'

The Doctor gave him a wide smile. 'Bear with me, Doctor. Let's make a few small assumptions. First of all, whatever killed Tolliver didn't do it for food. An animal that hunts aims the blow at a vulnerable area – a limb or the throat, depending on whether it kills by biting or strangulation. This creature instead attacked the face. A small target, if you think about it.'

'But the only one offered if Tolliver was leaning across the bows of his boat,' Sir Alexander put in.

'Correct!' The Doctor's eyes sparkled. 'Another blow against the idea that his killer was on the boat with him. Now, the body was on the boat when it was found, so Tolliver must have fallen backwards. The missing limb led Doyle to suggest that the killer attacked the corpse again as it fell. There wasn't a great deal of time for that, so the odds are that there were in fact two creatures that attacked him, almost simultaneously: one killing first with the bite to the head, the second severing the limb.'

'I say!' exclaimed Sir Alexander. 'So now instead of one mysterious killer creature, we now have two?'

'More than that,' the Doctor commented. 'Two hunting together. Intriguing, isn't it?'

'Intriguing?' The Justice shivered. 'It's downright scary.'

'That too,' agreed the Doctor. He turned to Faversham. 'Well, that's about it for here. Perhaps we could examine the boat now?'

'Very good, sir. If you care to go on ahead, I'll cover the body again.' The constable turned to Sir Alexander. 'Can I inform the rector that the body is ready for burial now, sir?'

'You can indeed,' Sir Alexander answered. 'The sooner the better, if you ask me.'

Sarah grimaced and stared at her three admirers. 'Don't you have something better to do?' she asked them. 'Like lessons, for instance?'

'No,' Kipling replied. 'Term starts next week, so we're free.'

'And at a loose end,' added Dunsterville. 'So here we are.'

'And you're awfully pretty,' Beresford finished, 'so we don't mind being seen with you. It'll do our reps scads of good.'

'Wonderful,' Sarah muttered. 'And my nerves irreparable harm, probably.' She was starting to wish she hadn't wanted to meet Kipling. As an adult he would have been fascinating, but as a fifteen-year-old boy . . . well, he was a fifteen-year-old boy, and that said it all. Now what? Well, since the men had effectively shut her out from their autopsy, she might as well get to work on something else. 'This friend of yours who vanished,' she said, hoping that this would distract their attention from her body for a while. 'Tell me about him.'

'Well, he wasn't really our friend,' Dunsterville confessed. 'He's only ten, after all.'

'And not at all sophisticated, like us,' Kipling added.

'Give me a break,' muttered Sarah.

'And he's more like a responsibility,' Dunsterville said, staring at Beresford.

Beresford nodded. 'His pater and mine are chums, you see, and we were asked to sort of keep an eye on him.' He pouted. 'And you know how infernally dull that can be.'

Sarah was starting to catch on. 'And what did you do with him?' she asked.

'Nothing!' Beresford protested.

'Well, almost nothing,' Kipling amended.

Raising an eyebrow, Sarah surveyed them sceptically. 'Let's have it.'

Both the other boys looked at Beresford, who shuffled his feet uncomfortably. 'Well, the truth of the matter is that we ragged him a bit. Told him a few fibs about ourselves, and said he'd got a lot to learn.'

'Such as?' Sarah prompted.

'Well, about women, for example,' Beresford admitted. 'We spun a few yarns – '

85

'You did,' said Kipling smugly. 'Mine were all true.'

' – a few yarns,' Beresford continued, 'about the fish-girls here in the village. So he skipped out one night last week and never came back.'

'I see.' Sarah sighed. It was typical of teenaged boys, but Anders had been a young and impressionable target. 'So how much of this did you actually tell the police?'

'Faversham?' Dunsterville looked appalled. 'Just that Anders left early in the evening, nothing more. He wouldn't understand what it is to be a man of the world, like you do.'

'Thanks, I think,' said Sarah dryly. 'Okay, let's start from there. Do you happen to recall if you mentioned any names to Anders, or were you too polite for that?'

Kipling sniggered. 'We did casually let Jen Walker's name crop up.'

Now she was getting somewhere. 'And did this lady ever see Anders?'

Dunsterville shrugged. 'We don't know. She isn't speaking to us just at this moment.'

'I can't imagine why,' Sarah said. 'So where can I find her?'

Kipling hooked a finger over his shoulder. 'She works here, as the barmaid,' he told her. 'Dark-haired and almost as pretty as you are.' He glanced at Sarah's ankles. 'I'll bet you have nicer legs though,' he added hopefully.

'Dream about them,' Sarah suggested. 'Right – you lot stay here. I'll go and have a chat with this Jen Walker.' As she started to move off, she added, 'And try not to harass anyone while I'm gone, okay?'

'Us?' asked Kipling, the picture of innocence. 'Would we do that?'

'You'd better not,' Sarah advised him. 'Or there's likely to be three more missing kids by this evening.'

* * *

Tolliver's boat was a typical small fishing vessel. The nets were still on the deck and the sail had been furled, obviously after it had been moored. Otherwise, Brackley assured them, the boat was exactly how it had been when the men had found it adrift.

The Doctor scurried aboard and began peering at the gunwales. Doyle, Martinson and Sir Alexander followed him. Brackley hovered at the top of the plank.

'Where was the body discovered?' Doyle asked.

'Fore of the cabin, sir,' Brackley replied.

Doyle nodded, and skirted about the tiny structure. On the deck was a splash of dried blood. 'Ah!' he exclaimed. 'Not sufficient for Tolliver to have been attacked on board.' He glanced at the cabin. 'And nowhere for any terrestrial animal to hide, either. So he was definitely attacked from the sea.'

'I agree,' the Doctor commented, kneeling beside the gunwale close by Doyle. 'What do you make of this?'

Doyle bent to examine the marks the Doctor had found. The Doctor offered the use of his magnifying glass, which Doyle accepted. 'Scratches in the wood,' he observed, puzzled. 'I'm afraid that the significance of it escapes me.'

'Recent,' the Doctor commented. 'The wood exposed is unweathered. And it's close to where the body fell. I'd say that whatever killed Tolliver made these marks. There are just the two of them, here and here.' He pointed to the two gashes, about two and a half feet apart. 'That suggests a width for the creature. The marks are probably the result of its flippers or fins striking the wood.'

'There's no sign of blood in the marks,' objected Doyle. 'Surely any blows sufficient to make these gashes would have scored the skin of the attacker and drawn blood.'

'Unless the hide was too tough,' the Doctor said. 'In

many aquatic creatures the skin, especially on the flippers, is extremely tough.'

Sir Alexander frowned. 'Are you suggesting that he was killed by something like a seal? Your mention of flippers suggests that conclusion.'

The Doctor gave a large smile. 'And some seals have very sharp teeth,' he pointed out. 'They are carnivores, after all, and their mouths are positioned well for the attack.'

'But they have never been known to attack a man!' protested Martinson.

'No,' agreed the Doctor thoughtfully. 'But this has all the indications that they have started now.' He pondered ideas for a moment. 'And they are trainable,' he mused. 'I wonder . . .'

Sir Alexander was almost spluttering. 'But there are only a few grey seals about this coast,' he protested. 'And they are perfectly harmless.'

'I agree,' the Doctor said. He looked up at Doyle suddenly. 'Is the *Hope* a whaler alone?'

'Why, no,' Doyle replied. 'We've also got a fair supply of seal skins.'

'No live ones, though?'

'Of course not,' Doyle answered. 'There's no market for them.'

The Doctor removed his cap and ran his hand through his mane of curly hair. 'Isn't your vessel out of some Scottish port?' he asked.

'Peterhead.'

'Ah!' The Doctor gave another of his smiles. 'And what brings it to Devon, then?'

Doyle shrugged. 'Captain Gray had business here; that's all I know.'

'Look here,' broke in Sir Alexander, 'surely that is irrelevant to the matter of Tolliver's death?'

88

'Irrelevant?' The Doctor stared at the Justice as if he were a silly child. 'A whaling ship stops off here instead of Scotland, barely hours before a man is killed and it's *irrelevant*? It has a cargo of seal skins, and the man is apparently killed by a pair of attack seals, and it's *irrelevant*?' He whirled around to face Doyle. 'I'd like to have a word with this captain of yours.'

Doyle shrugged. 'I can introduce you to him when he returns to the ship this evening, but he's not aboard right now.'

The Doctor nodded. 'And who is it that he has business with?'

'A man called Breckinridge, that's all I know,' Doyle answered.

Sir Alexander smiled. 'Well then, that's no problem, is it?'

The Doctor glared at him. 'It might not be,' he snapped. 'It might help if I knew who this Breckinridge was.'

The Justice stared at him in amazement. 'Surely you must have heard of him.'

'If I had,' the Doctor retorted, 'I wouldn't need to ask questions, would I?'

'Well,' Sir Alexander said, taken aback, 'he's an industrialist who built a factory on the edge of the village last year. He's very well known, and quite a pleasant chappie.'

'You know him?'

'Well,' Sir Alexander admitted, 'I think he's done splendid work since he arrived here, and he's given many of the locals jobs when they would otherwise be starving. He's a very generous and kind man. I'm sure you'd like him.'

'I'd appreciate the chance to meet him,' the Doctor agreed. He looked around as Faversham hurried up the jetty toward the boat. 'Ah, there you are. What kept you?'

The policeman was almost out of breath. 'Another crime has just been reported,' he announced, huffing and panting.

'And I thought this was such a quiet little town,' the Doctor observed dryly. 'Well, what's the latest event in this crime spree?'

'Somebody broke into the cemetery last night,' Faversham said. 'They dug up the grave of Missus Bellaver and stole her corpse.'

4

Wild Hunt

'Curiouser and curiouser,' said the Doctor, intrigued. Sir Alexander stared at him. 'Surely you don't believe that there's any connection between Tolliver's death and the stolen body?'

The Doctor rolled his eyes. 'Unless this sleepy little town has suddenly developed a crime wave of epidemic proportions, we have to assume a connection.'

Doyle looked puzzled. 'I can't see one.'

'Nor can I – yet,' admitted the Doctor. 'What did this Missus Bellaver die from?'

'Purely natural causes,' Doctor Martinson broke in hastily. 'I myself was there when she expired. She was eighty-seven years old and very frail. She died three nights ago, before the *Hope* arrived.'

'So,' Sir Alexander said gruffly, 'there is no connection.'

'No,' the Doctor argued. 'We simply haven't found one yet.' He stared thoughtfully at the constable. 'Is this the first time somebody dead has turned up missing?' When Faversham didn't answer immediately, the Doctor turned to Sir Alexander. 'Well, is it?'

'There have been two other cases recently,' the Justice admitted carefully.

'Then why didn't you say so?' the Doctor snapped. 'I know, I know, they didn't seem relevant. Well, how recently?'

'Just over six months ago and about twelve weeks ago.' Sir Alexander looked a little crestfallen.

'And when does the first missing child date back to?' asked the Doctor, with all the patience he could muster.

'Approximately the same length of time, sir,' Faversham admitted.

'I see.' The Doctor glared from the constable to his superior. 'And you didn't see any connection?'

'How could there be one?' argued Sir Alexander, reddening slightly.

'How could there not be?' the Doctor countered. 'And all this began happening since your philanthropic Mister Breckinridge arrived in town?'

'My dear Doctor!' exclaimed Doctor Martinson. 'Surely you are making too many inferences from too few facts.'

The Doctor considered the point. 'Perhaps I am,' he agreed. 'But that points to the need to gather more facts, doesn't it?'

'We were working on the assumption,' Sir Alexander said, 'that Resurrectionists were responsible for the missing bodies, and that it is entirely unrelated to the missing children.'

'Were you indeed?' asked the Doctor. 'This information changes everything, though. I had hoped that the children were alive, but if there are Resurrectionists involved, isn't it possible that the missing children were murdered and used as a substitute form of bodies?'

'Just a moment,' argued Doyle. 'I don't believe that Resurrectionists could be involved here. For one thing, their foul trade hinges on their procuring fresh corpses for the teaching hospitals. There are no such hospitals within a hundred miles of this place. The bodies would begin to decay long before they reached a hospital. Added to that, Missus Bellaver died three days ago, so her body was hardly fresh in any event.'

'Capital reasoning, Doctor,' said the Doctor. 'I couldn't

have put it better myself.' He turned to the constable. 'I think you had better let us have a look at the scene of this fresh crime, don't you? Then we'll be able to deduce whether all these events are linked or separate.'

Sir Alexander glared at him. 'I doubt that you'll find your hypothetical killer seals are responsible for digging up Missus Bellaver.'

'Why don't we wait until we've had a chance to examine the site before making decisions?' snapped the Doctor. He thrust his deerstalker back on his head. 'Come along, Doctors. Faversham – lead the way!'

The three schoolboys had been right in saying that Jen Walker was pretty. It was an unrefined prettiness, of course, since this was well out in the provinces, but she clearly had no lack of admirers as well as the boys. When Sarah found the barmaid she was flirting gently with one of the local fisherlads.

'Could we talk?' Sarah asked, giving the youth a pointed stare.

'Off you go, Tom,' Jen said, tossing her dark curls. 'No doubt I'll be seeing you later this night?'

'For as much of it as you like,' agreed Tom cheekily.

'Be off with you!' Jen laughed. Then she turned to Sarah. 'And what would you like to talk about, miss?' she asked.

'Schoolboys,' Sarah replied.

'Oh.' Jen scowled. 'I thought I seen Gigger and his mates around earlier. Cheeky little buggers, aren't they? They been giving you trouble, too?'

'None I can't handle,' Sarah informed her. 'But they told me that you might have seen one of their friends.'

Jen scowled in sudden suspicion. 'You the sister of one of them, come to complain?' she asked sharply. 'I don't need no lip from the likes of you. Boys will be boys, and they have to learn their experiences somewhere.'

Sarah stared at the barmaid in disgust. 'Look, I'm not here to get you into trouble,' she snapped. 'I'm looking for a missing boy, not for someone who seems to enjoy under-aged suitors. And I hope even you would draw the line at ten-year-olds.'

'Oh.' Jen twitched her nose. 'That missing kid, Anders, you mean? Well, honest to God, I never seen him in me life.'

'He was on his way to see you when he vanished,' Sarah replied. 'Apparently Gigger and his chums talked up your charms and availability, and he wanted to become a man.'

'Well, he never did with me!' Jen replied. 'Strike me dead if I'm lying. I never saw the kid. And I wouldn't have done nothing if I had. I have me morals, you know.'

'Really?' asked Sarah sceptically. 'I'll take your word for that. So you have no idea what might have happened to the boy, then?'

Jen's eyes narrowed. 'Now I didn't say that. I just said I didn't have anything to do with it. I might be able to help a little, if you can make it worth me while. Get my drift?' She scratched at her palm.

Sarah's blood was starting to boil. 'I get your drift,' she said, striving to keep her temper. 'And if you aim to keep those good looks that bring in the customers, you'd better tell me what you know.' She examined her nails thoughtfully. 'I doubt you'd earn so much from even curious boys if you had scars down both cheeks.'

Realizing she'd gone too far, Jen backed away slightly. 'I didn't mean nothing,' she whined. 'Just trying to make an honest living. You can't fault me for that, can you?'

'Guess again,' Sarah answered coldly. 'You've got ten seconds to say something I want to hear.'

94

'Like I said,' Jen answered hastily, 'I don't know nothing myself. But you should talk to Billy. He knows everything that happens in the village.'

'Billy?'

'Yeah. He's one of the wharf rats, you know.' Jen pointed down to the shore. 'He's got a little lean-to by the docks. There's a house down there with a red roof and door. Past that, down the shore a bit is where Billy lives. Tell him I sent you, and he'll talk to you. I'll bet he knows something.'

'Something he wouldn't tell the police, you mean?' asked Sarah.

'Police!' snorted Jen. 'Billy wouldn't have nothing to do with the police. Better sense than that, Billy's got. But you speak to him.'

Sarah nodded, and left the tavern. As she'd dreaded, Kipling and his two pals were eagerly waiting for her.

'Learn anything?' Beresford asked.

'More than you have in years of schooling,' Sarah told him. 'If I find out what happened to Anders, I'll let you know. Now buzz off.'

'Never!' said Kipling defiantly. 'We're here to offer you our protection and assistance.'

'And crude comments too,' Sarah retorted. 'I don't need any of them. Clear off.'

Kipling's face fell. 'Oh, come on,' he begged. 'He's our responsibility, you know. Well, McBee's at least. And we could be useful, couldn't we?' He gave her a pathetic look of hope.

Against her better judgement, Sarah took pity on them. 'Oh, all right,' she agreed crossly. 'But one untoward comment from any of you, and I'm sending you back to school with a flea in your ears. And don't think I wouldn't.'

'Honestly,' Dunsterville assured her, 'we believe every

last word you say, Miss Smith.'

'Now you're starting to learn,' Sarah approved.

'I can quite understand your concern, Alice,' Bridewell told her, holding her hand comfortingly. 'I will confess, what you overheard does sound rather bad for Edmund.'

'Bad?' Alice stared at her fiancé. 'He is planning to rob this house, Roger! That manservant of his is a common thief!'

'Alice,' Roger said, his face twisted by indecision, 'please trust me. I know it looks bad, but please believe me. I know that Edmund is planning nothing that would hurt you in any way. Despite what you heard – '

'Then tell me what he is planning, if you know,' begged Alice.

'I can't,' Roger replied, not looking at her. 'But if you love me, Alice, trust me on this matter.'

Alice was torn: she did love him, but he was asking a great deal of her. His explanations – if they were in fact explanations and not evasions – were not making her feel any better. 'Roger, I want to trust you. But I can't trust him without some reason.'

Roger nodded miserably. 'I shall have a word with Edmund,' he promised. 'Perhaps that will help.'

'Perhaps,' agreed Alice, unconvinced. Roger kissed her hand rather perfunctorily and then fled down the corridor. She stared after him, wondering how well she really knew her fiancé. He was certainly keeping some secret about Edmund from her, but what? What kind of a hold did the suave Colonel Ross have over Roger? Friendship? Money? Blackmail? She didn't know, and if Roger wouldn't confide in her then perhaps she had better do a little prying of her own. She was not about to trust Ross without some convincing proof of the innocence of his intentions. And Roger was about to warn the man of her suspicions.

Making up her mind, she headed for Ross's rooms. She felt dreadful about searching them, but what else could she do? Perhaps something would be revealed to resolve her quandary.

The graveyard was small, and set on one of the hills overlooking Bodham Bay. An ancient, weather-beaten stone church guarded the high spot on the rise. The tower was definitely Saxon in styling and in need of a little work, and the windows in the grey stonework were small. The graves were gathered about the church, as if seeking the protection of those old stones.

Most were marked with simple headstones, many of which had been worn into virtual unreadability. There had been some efforts to tend the graves, but several were overgrown with patchy clumps of unkempt grass. Against the grey sky, the whole site looked dreadfully depressing to Doyle.

Faversham led the way across the graveyard as the harsh wind tugged at their coats. The Doctor, hands thrust in his pockets, his face inscrutable, followed. Behind Doyle, limping slightly, came Sir Alexander and Doctor Martinson. The policeman halted beside a dark gash in the ground. The gravestone had been knocked over, and a hole dug straight through the fresh earth. The Doctor peered in the gap, and Doyle stared down over his shoulder.

The coffin was still down there, a simple wooden affair of local timber. The top had been staved in by a spade, and the body had been dragged out through the gap. A piece of the shroud had caught on a long splinter of wood in the coffin lid, and flapped like a trapped butterfly vainly striving to escape.

The Doctor looked up, his face grim. 'Stay back,' he

called over his shoulder to Martinson and Sir Alexander. He glanced at Faversham and Doyle. 'Both of you stay where you are,' he said. Without explanation he went down on one knee and began to stare at the ground around the grave.

Doyle stared at him in fascination. 'What are you doing, Doctor?' he asked.

'Looking for clues,' he snapped. 'Be quiet.' He sprang to his feet and wandered across the grounds, staring intently at the ground. Making his way back to the small stone wall surrounding the church, he examined the top stones, and then walked slowly back to the grave. 'There were two men,' he announced. 'One was tall and heavy-set, the other shorter and thin. They came from the village and went back that way with the corpse.'

Doyle was astonished. 'How on earth could you possibly know that?'

The Doctor cracked one of his wide, toothy smiles. 'Elementary, my dear Doyle.' He pointed to the ground. 'Aside from a set of woman's shoe-prints that I assume to be the cleaner who discovered the robbery, there are two recent sets of shoe-prints. One is a large size, and sinks deeply into the disturbed fresh earth. Hence a large man, and rather heavy. The other set is small, and not as deep: a smaller, lighter man. The same prints show on the pathway from the village at the gate, and they return that way also. On the return trip, the large man's prints sink even deeper, so he was carrying the woman's corpse with him.'

'That's remarkable!' exclaimed Sir Alexander. 'And can you tell us where the men went in the village?'

The Doctor shook his head. 'The ground is too rocky, and by the time we get down to the village, the cobble-stoned streets will not carry prints. This is all I can tell you for the moment, gentlemen. But the culprits must still be somewhere in the vicinity.'

'That's quite astounding,' Doyle enthused.

'Scientific method,' the Doctor answered. 'Now, we have several separate mysteries that I feel certain must be intertwined. You know what we need now?'

'What?' asked Doyle.

'Lunch. I'm starving. Come on!' The Doctor rubbed his hands together and started back towards the village.

'You've left me in the deuce of an uncomfortable position, old man,' Roger complained. 'I know I promised to help all I could, but with Alice getting suspicious – '

Ross nodded thoughtfully. 'I know, Roger, and I'm sorry. I suppose the best thing to do would be for me either to leave or come clean. But I'm so close now. I know it! I'm fairly certain that what I'm after isn't here at all.'

'Which I told you from the start,' Roger pointed out.

'I know you did,' agreed Ross. 'But you know I couldn't simply take your word for it. Now I have Abercrombie checking out other possibilities. The problem is that matters have become rather more complex than I had anticipated. This Doctor fellow, for example. He's a factor I hadn't foreseen, and I'm not at all certain whose side he's on – or what his reasons are for getting involved with this in the first place. Then there's that whaling ship, the *Hope*. It can't be a coincidence that it was diverted here at this time. But how does it figure in? Will it interfere with my plans?' Ross sighed. 'I had anticipated a fairly straightforward time here, but it's definitely far too complex now. Still, that's my problem, and I shall have to make the best of it.'

'Then what do you aim to do?' asked Roger.

His friend patted his arm in a kindly fashion. 'What I don't aim to do is to come between you and your fiancée, old man. I promise you, I'll square things with her somehow. I just have to work out what would be best.'

Roger smiled with relief. 'Thanks. I'd certainly appreciate your getting me off the hook with Alice.'

The room that Ross had been given was in the west wing. Alice slipped inside it and gazed around. It was a simple bedroom, with little adornment other than a few paintings on the wall. There were two large trunks positioned beside the chest of drawers, one of which was unstrapped. Both trunks were covered with small stickers. Alice took a closer look and saw that they were paste-on labels from hotels all around the world: Cairo, Cadiz, San Francisco, Panama, Rio de Janeiro. Obviously Edmund Ross – or at least his luggage – was well travelled.

Feeling a twinge of guilt, Alice used the straps to open the unlocked trunk. As she did so, she felt a slight prick in the end of her finger. She winced and then saw a drop of blood forming. Some kind of needle in the strap must have . . .

She felt herself growing rather heady. She gasped, and tried to straighten up. But her legs refused to obey her, and she couldn't stand. Her knees gave way and with a sigh she collapsed to the floor, unconscious.

A few moments later, Ross strode into the room. He stopped in his tracks and stared in despair at the girl on the floor. 'Oh dear,' he sighed. 'This does complicate matters rather more.' It was certainly not turning out to be one of his better days.

Sarah led Kipling, Dunsterville and Beresford to the small lean-to shack that the barmaid had described. It was even flimsier and filthier than Sarah had been expecting, and it was hard to imagine that anyone actually lived here. The wind was rising now, whipping at any exposed portions of Sarah's skin. She could imagine what it would be like here in the winter, and was astounded that the rickety little hut managed to survive those months.

As the four of them approached the dwelling, there was a sudden movement. A small girl, dressed in dark clothing that flapped raggedly, seemed to flash from behind a rock on the sea walk and into the hut. A look-out, obviously, probably gone to warn whoever else lived in the hut that visitors were coming.

'Right,' she said firmly to her companions. 'You three stay here.'

'We want to help,' Kipling objected.

'As far as these kids are concerned,' Sarah pointed out, 'you're rich brats. They won't trust you.'

'And they will trust you?' asked Beresford scornfully.

'They might,' Sarah answered. She had been wondering the same thing herself. These wharf rats had never been treated as anything other than vermin in their lives. Would they even want to talk to her? 'I'm going to try. So stay put, and stay out of trouble.' She ignored Kipling and his friends and marched on down the quay towards the hut.

The door opened as she drew close, and a tall, thin boy stepped out. He was obviously underfed, and his clothing was tattered and didn't fit at all well. His dark eyes were haunted and angry, and he ran thin fingers through dusty blond hair that had probably only been washed if he had fallen into the ocean.

'What you want?' he asked. His voice was cold, angry and impatient. 'You ain't welcome, you know.'

'I only want to talk, Billy,' Sarah said, pitching her voice low and warm. 'I think we may have a problem in common.'

Billy laughed sharply. 'You and me?' he snorted. 'Get on! We got nowt in common.'

'Missing children,' Sarah said.

101

That made his eyes narrow. His right hand came up, and Sarah saw that he held a fish-gutting knife at the ready. Unlike Billy, the knife was clean and obviously well used. She suspected that Billy had used it to defend himself many times in the past. 'What do you mean?' he growled suspiciously.

'Those three boys,' Sarah waved vaguely in Kipling's direction. Billy's eyes flickered off her face for only a second, and then returned. 'One of their friends has gone missing. I talked to Jen Walker and she said that some of your friends have gone missing too. And she said that you might be able to help me find them.'

'She says too much,' Billy complained. 'She shouldn't talk so much.'

Sarah smiled. 'Maybe, Billy. But have some of your friends disappeared too?'

'What do you care?' asked Billy. 'They're just street rats. Nobody cares about they except I.'

'I care,' Sarah told him. 'Whatever they are, they're human beings. I know the police don't care much, but I promise you that they matter to me.'

'You're just saying that,' the boy retorted angrily. 'You're like the rest, want us gone. Why should I trust you?'

Sarah shrugged. 'No reason at all, Billy. I can't prove that I care, or that I'm telling the truth. But unless you give me a chance you'll never know, will you?' Was she getting through to him at all? He had obviously lived on the streets and off his wits almost all his young life. Suspicion and fear were his constant companions. Could she possibly break through those barriers and reach him? 'All I'm asking for is a little help from you so that I can help you in return.'

'We don't need your help,' he answered, brandishing the knife. 'We look after ourselves.'

'You do need help,' Sarah countered. 'Because some of your friends have disappeared, haven't they? And you haven't been able to stop it. Well, maybe I can – if I have some idea where to start looking.'

Billy thought hard for a moment. Sarah stayed silent, knowing this was a battle he'd be waging with himself, and that anything else she said now might swing him the wrong way. It would not be an easy matter for him to trust her, but had she made him realize that he had no other genuine option?

'No skin off my nose,' he finally announced ambiguously. 'If you get yourself killed,' he added.

'Then you do have some idea what may have happened to the missing children?' asked Sarah.

He shrugged. 'No,' he answered, dashing her hopes. 'But I know who might. Factory man.'

Sarah started to feel hopeful once again. 'Factory man?' she asked.

Billy gestured with the knife. 'Go see him,' he suggested. 'Look hard. Now just *go*.'

Knowing she'd get no more this time, Sarah nodded. 'All right, Billy. Thank you for your help. I promise I will do my best to find your friends, too. I'll let you know if I find anything out.'

'Don't do me favours,' Billy snapped. But he looked at least part-way pleased at her response.

Returning to Kipling and his companions, Sarah asked, 'What do you know about a factory man?'

Kipling scowled. 'You must mean old Breckinridge. He owns a factory on the outskirts of Bodham. You must have seen it as you came into town. Big, modern and very impressive. He's really into progress and what-have-you. Shame he's such an unpleasant fellow, though.'

'Does the fish-boy think that Breckers has something to do with Anders' disappearance?' asked Beresford.

'*Billy* does,' Sarah said, stressing the youngster's name. 'And with a few others, too.'

'Can't think why he'd want to,' Dunsterville said. 'He's a mean sort, but not such a bad egg.'

'Maybe he's a worse egg than you think,' Sarah told him. 'Why don't we go and see if we can have a chat with him?'

'I'm game,' agreed Kipling. 'I'll be scout.' He set off down the road.

Sarah followed behind, ignoring Beresford's comments as he droned away. She couldn't help wondering whether Dunsterville had a point: why would a successful factory owner be connected to missing children? Was it possible that Billy was sending her on a wild goose chase just to get rid of her?

As the Doctor reached the Pig and Thistle, he halted and turned to Sir Alexander. 'Why don't you and Doctor Martinson order up some lunch?' he suggested. 'I'd like to see if Captain Gray is back on the *Hope* yet. I've an idea that he may be able to clear up a few items that are nagging at the back of my mind. If he's not back yet, Doyle can leave him a note to get in contact with us when he does return.'

'Oh, very well,' the magistrate agreed. 'Though I still think you're off hunting red herrings, Doctor.'

The Doctor grinned. 'I've a particular fondness for herrings,' he replied. 'Come on, Doyle.' He started down the wharf toward where the *Hope* lay at anchor. 'Do you think I'm off on a tangent here also?'

Doyle shrugged. 'I have to admit, Doctor, that it does look like you're connecting matters that are unrelated. On the other hand, your scientific methods are impeccable, and you are certainly skilled at deduction. I'm willing to indulge in a few wild ideas if they help to settle this case.'

He rubbed his hands together eagerly. 'And it certainly is proving to be a most fascinating affair, isn't it?'

'It would be more fascinating,' the Doctor replied, 'if people weren't dying. But it is unique.' They had reached the plank leading up to the whaler now. 'After you, my dear chap.'

'Thank you.' Doyle led the way aboard. There was no one in sight on deck, and Doyle gestured. 'The captain's quarters are over here,' he said.

'Where is everyone?' the Doctor asked.

'Shore leave,' Doyle informed him. 'The captain gave us a day or so off while he concluded his deal, then the ship will head back home. I imagine most of the crew are off getting blind drunk while they can.'

The Doctor nodded. It sounded more than reasonable. They reached the door to the captain's cabin, and Doyle rapped on it.

The door swung slowly open.

'Odd,' Doyle muttered. 'This is usually kept locked if –'

There was a sudden flurry of movement and a hunched form shot out of the cabin, slamming into Doyle and knocking the medical man backward with a whoosh of breath. Doyle slammed into the Doctor, and they collapsed in a tangle of arms and legs. It took Doyle a moment to catch his breath and stagger back to his feet.

'The scoundrel's getting away,' he wheezed, clutching his stomach with one hand and the wall of the cabin with the other.

'Got away,' corrected the Doctor, regaining his own feet. 'I doubt either of us could catch up with him now. Besides, I know where I can find him anyway.'

'You do?' asked Doyle, his face returning to its normal colour and his breathing regular once more. 'You recognized the man, then?'

'Yes,' the Doctor said. 'I only saw him briefly last night, but there's no mistaking that nose and build. His name is Abercrombie, and he works for a Colonel Ross.'

Frowning, Doyle followed the Doctor into Gray's cabin. 'He must have been here to rob the captain,' he said. 'We'd better let Faversham know, so he can arrest the villain.'

'Not yet,' the Doctor cautioned. 'I'd like to know what he expected to find in here that's worth his while. Men who spend several months in the Arctic don't usually take many valuables with them, do they? If Gray is off-ship, he's not likely to leave much cash around either.'

'True,' agreed Doyle, puzzled. 'We won't really get any money till we dock again in Peterhead and sell the bulk of the cargo.' He glanced around the cabin. 'Not much has been disturbed,' he observed.

'Except this,' the Doctor answered. He gestured to the ship's log, which was open on the captain's desk. 'To today's entries in fact.' He scanned the page. 'Hello! Now that is interesting.'

'What?' Doyle peered over the Doctor's shoulder.

' "Met with Breckinridge and Ross",' the Doctor read. He grinned. 'That was yesterday,' he said thoughtfully. 'Breckinridge again. He seems to be turning up at every twist in the road, doesn't he? And I wonder why your captain met with this mysterious Colonel Ross?'

'And why was Ross's man here reading that?' Doyle asked, perplexed. 'Unless maybe he aimed to destroy the reference so we couldn't read it?'

The Doctor snorted. 'Come on, Doyle. We wouldn't have even looked at it if Abercrombie hadn't left the page open.' He shook his head. 'Another mystery.'

Doyle sighed. 'It seems as if at every turn, matters get more complex and confusing,' he complained.

'I know,' agreed the Doctor happily. 'Isn't it fun?

Right, leave Gray a note asking him to contact us as soon as he can, and let's be going. I'm famished.'

'There it is,' said Kipling. Sarah couldn't help noticing a distinct trace of pride in his voice. She remembered that he was very keen on progress, and had even written a couple of science-fiction stories as a young writer. 'Breckinridge's factory.'

It looked like one of Blake's 'dark, satanic mills' to Sarah. It was large, block-shaped and grim. Three tall chimneys were pouring thick, gritty fumes into the atmosphere. There were few windows visible in the walls, and the entire bottom half of the building was invisible behind a tall stone wall. A single road led to the structure, and the sound of machinery came from within, audible even at this distance of about a mile.

'So what does he make?' she asked as they strode along briskly. She was glad that she had had a good breakfast and a rest before all this marching around. Bodham was only a small town, but it seemed as if everything she wanted to see was at opposite ends of it. The factory was on a small hill to the west of town, facing out into the bay. She could make out a pipe that led from the base of the hill and which was discharging into the sea. Pollutants, no doubt.

'A jolly good living,' Kipling answered, grinning. 'Aside from that, wire and cables, I believe.'

'Wire and cables?' Sarah was puzzled. 'Isn't this a trifle out of the way for such things? I would expect the market for them to be closer to London.'

Kipling shook his head. 'Ah, but Breckinridge is a great believer in progress. He's talking about laying a telegraph line between England and the United States that would carry ten times the load of the ones Lord Kelvin laid fifteen years ago.'

107

'And if that was done,' Sarah said, catching on, 'he'd be able to supply the necessary materials from here instead of having to ship them out from London. Clever!'

'Rather,' agreed Kipling. 'This man has an eye on the future, no doubt about that. And he's very interested in the telephone. He came to our school last term and gave a talk about it being the future of communications, and even envisions a time when telephonic lines will cross the Atlantic and replace telegraphs. It's jolly interesting stuff.'

Of course! This was 1880, and it was only a year since Bell had demonstrated the telephone to Queen Victoria. The great explosive growth of this new industry was poised to start. Breckinridge was definitely being visionary if he was already planning to take advantage of that new technology to lay submarine cables for it.

Then why had she never heard of his name in that connection? He was certainly in the right place at the right time with the right product. Why hadn't he been one of the first media barons, then? Did his failure have something to do with the events that were unfolding? It was lucky that the TARDIS had brought them here, then, instead of meeting up with Kipling in ten years' time in India.

Or was it luck? Too often, Sarah reflected, the ship had landed her and the Doctor right in the thick of things. Could it be nothing more than coincidence? Or was it possible that the TARDIS – or some other force, unknown as yet – was deliberately bringing the Doctor to points in space and time where help was needed?

As she mused on this thought, they drew closer to the factory. There was a definite odour in the air now. All factories seemed to be intent on producing stench as a primary product, she reflected. There was a small guard box beside the door, and a bored-looking rat-faced man inside it. He glared at the four of them as they approached, as if irritated that they should deign to disturb his rest.

'I'd like to see Mister Breckinridge, please,' Sarah said firmly.

'Sorry,' the guard replied. 'He's not available for visitors.'

That wasn't a very encouraging start. 'When will he be back, then?'

Rat-face sniggered. 'Did I say he was out? I just told you, he's not seeing visitors.' He was clearly enjoying his role as guardian of the gates.

Sarah examined the gates carefully. There was no way through them without the man's permission, that was clear, and it didn't look as if he was interested in letting anyone pass. 'I'd prefer to hear Mister Breckinridge say that himself,' she snapped. 'Can you take a message to him?'

'I'm a guard, not a messenger,' the man replied haughtily. 'I guard. I don't carry messages. And I was told point-blank not to let in visitors.'

'Really?' Sarah glowered at him. 'Have you turned many others away today?'

'No. You're the first. Goodbye.'

'It's a waste of time,' Beresford said. 'Why don't we just go somewhere more interesting?'

Sarah shrugged. For once she was inclined to agree with Beresford, but she wasn't going without firing off one last salvo. 'Well, tell Mister Breckinridge that I was here, please. The name is Sarah Jane Smith, and I'm staying with Sir Edward Fulbright. You could mention that I was asking about missing children.'

Rat-face scowled at her. 'What's that supposed to mean?' he demanded.

Sarah smiled sweetly. 'If you were a messenger and not a guard, I might explain. Bye.' She waved, and started back towards the village. *Let's see what effect that produces*, she mused. If any, of course. Her three musketeers promptly fell in beside her. She'd have felt better about them if they weren't continually staring at her ankles or her chest. She knew she had their attention only because they were hoping to take advantage of her later. *Fat chance*, she thought.

She gave a start as Billy suddenly stepped out into the road ahead of them. He'd been behind a tree, and Kipling and his friends yelped and almost jumped out of their skins. Billy sneered at them.

'I can see why you needed my help,' he told Sarah. 'Brave as rabbits, they is.'

Beresford stepped forward. 'You want a serious duffing-up?' he growled.

Billy produced his knife, and Beresford retreated again. Giving a crooked grin, Billy winked at Sarah. 'I followed along to make sure ye were on the level,' he explained. 'You really are looking for the missing 'uns, aren't ye?'

'Yes,' Sarah agreed. She was starting to quite like this little hoodlum. For one thing, she liked the subduing effect he had on Kipling and company. 'But I didn't get very far, did I?'

'Didn't think the factory man would hand them over, did ye?'

'No,' admitted Sarah. 'But I would have liked the chance to meet this Breckinridge. I've got good instincts, and the nose of a reporter. If he tried to cover up anything, I'd know.'

'I like ye,' Billy said. He stuck out a filthy hand. 'I'll help ye.'

Wondering how many diseases she was risking, Sarah shook his hand gingerly. 'Thanks, Billy. But help me how?'

'Me mates'll look and listen,' he promised. 'Anything turns up, I'll fetch ye. You've me word on it.'

'You wouldn't trust a tramp like that, would you?' asked Dunsterville in disgust. 'I wouldn't trust him as far as I could throw him.'

'You wanna throw me,' Billy said slyly, 'you can try.'

'There's no need to fight,' Sarah told them all firmly. 'Yes, I do trust Billy. On his own, there's not much he can do. Joining forces with us makes us all stronger.' She turned to the beggar boy. 'You can find me – '

'I can find ye when I want,' Billy said, sniffing loudly in disdain. 'Don't need no map.' He tossed her a ragged salute and dived off the road into the trees again. Within seconds there was neither sight nor sound of him.

'Interesting character,' said Sarah. She was most amused by the look of disgust and irritation on the faces of the three boys left with her. They all knew they had been outdone, and by a boy they felt utter contempt for. 'Cheer up,' she told them. 'Maybe you'll actually be of some use later.' The looks on their faces almost made up for the troubles she'd endured at their hands so far. It was starting to shape up into a fine day after all.

Still, where was she actually getting? She'd really discovered nothing of much use, and her only gains thus far were to have three schoolboys and one drop-out join her side. She could only hope that the Doctor was having more luck.

Ross could only hope that Abercrombie was having more luck than he was. He had managed to carry Alice back to her own room unobserved, and quickly checked that his booby-trap hadn't caused any serious medical condition. She would wake up when his little drug wore off in a couple of hours, but he wasn't expecting her to have no clue as to what had happened to her. When she awoke, there was going to be trouble.

He couldn't afford to wait around for that. It was bad

111

enough that she suspected his motives and that her father was so implacable in his own suspicions. Now she finally had some proof for her theory that Ross was up to no good. After all, why would a man with nothing to hide set traps on his luggage for the unwary?

There was no option but for him to leave before she awoke. He couldn't possibly get out of here with all his luggage for the moment, which meant leaving it until later. On the other hand, he doubted that anyone else would be foolish enough to try and open it, given Alice's experience, so it should be safe enough for now.

If only there had been some sign of what she was after!

Carefully removing several items from his locked trunk, Ross reset the traps and then locked the case again. He slipped the items into his pockets, save for the rifle case. That he would have to carry. He glanced at his watch and frowned. Abercrombie should have been back by now if everything had gone well. That suggested another problem. Just what he needed. Why couldn't this whole thing have worked as smoothly as most of his jobs?

He eased open the door to his room and carefully scanned the corridor outside. There was no sign of any of the servants, so he slipped out. Staying close to the wall and poised to hide if necessary, he made his way to the stairs leading to the rear exit of the Hall. There he paused, hearing the soft sound of movement on the stairs. He glanced around and then moved to the closest door. It was locked, but to his skeleton keys that was no bar. He moved into the room and closed the door almost entirely, leaving the barest crack to peer through. The room was an unmade guest room, and smelled vaguely fusty.

He stiffened as there came the sound of someone entering the corridor, and then breathed a sigh of relief. It

112

was Abercrombie, trying to sneak into the Hall unobserved as he'd been instructed. As Abercrombie passed the room, Ross opened the door and tapped his companion on the shoulder.

Abercrombie squealed and jumped, then spun about so fast he almost fell over. 'Stone the crows,' he complained, seeing who it was. 'You enjoyed that, didn't you?'

'Yes,' admitted Ross. 'About face; we have to leave immediately.'

'How come?'

'Miss Fulbright attempted to open my luggage,' Ross answered, waving the little man back towards the stairwell.

'Blooming Ada,' Abercrombie muttered, scuttling back down the stairs. 'That's torn it.'

'It has indeed,' agreed Ross. 'We'd better lay low until this evening.' He hefted the wooden case he was carrying. 'I've brought the Townsend.'

Abercrombie made a face. 'You going to have to use it?'

Ross sighed. 'I doubt I'll have any option but to kill,' he replied. They had reached the base of the stairs. Beyond was a door to the servants' quarters, and he could hear sounds of activity and voices through there, but this side was clear. He led the way out to the rear of the Hall, and then sprinted for the closest trees. A moment later, Abercrombie joined him. 'Until this evening, we'd better lay low,' he said. 'Meanwhile, how did your research fare?'

'Good and bad,' his companion answered sourly. 'Did you bring any food? I'm famished.'

'No, there was no time. About your findings?'

Abercrombie scowled at the news, and then smiled as he delivered his own. 'He's here,' he reported. 'At the factory.'

'Excellent,' Ross replied. 'Typical, isn't it? Only two possible locations, and I selected the wrong one.'

Abercrombie shrugged. 'Can't win them all,' he opined. 'So, do we go down to break in now?'

'Not just yet,' Ross replied. 'First things first. The factory can wait until the morning, I think.'

'What about me stomach?' asked Abercrombie, rubbing it as he spoke. 'I need food to keep going.'

'We could try getting a bite to eat at the local tavern,' Ross suggested.

'That might not be such a great idea,' his companion replied. 'That Doctor bloke and another geezer spotted me on the ship.'

Ross gave him a severe look. 'You're slipping up. But you're right. We'd best not go back to the village, in case they arrest you.'

Abercrombie looked wistful. 'Yeah. But they'd feed me.' With a deep, mournful sigh, he followed Ross into the woods.

'Maybe we can find you some nuts,' Ross suggested with a smile.

'Do I look like a ruddy squirrel?'

Sarah was just getting her appetite when they arrived back at the tavern. There had been no sign of the Doctor or his companions at the barn, and even the body of old Ben Tolliver had vanished. Since the carriage was still waiting, Sarah realized that the Doctor was probably still investigating. As it was past noon, the tavern was open and several of the locals were already inside, pints and pipes in hand and mouth.

Jen Walker was there, collecting and refilling glasses. She nodded at the back room. 'Your mate's in there,' she said. 'Tucking into a pie.'

'What a marvellous idea,' said Kipling loudly.

'Come on,' Sarah said, realizing she was unlikely to be rid of her three shadows for a while. She crossed the smoke-filled lounge and moved into the slightly less smoky air of what passed for a dining room. As the barmaid had said, the Doctor was there, cheerfully eating a large wedge of some kind of local pie. Sir Alexander and Doctors Doyle and Martinson were also enjoying a meal and a glass of wine.

'Ah, there you are,' the Doctor called out. 'And your cheering section, too.' He gestured at the empty seats about the large table. 'Make yourselves comfortable.'

'Absolutely,' said Kipling, snatching up a spare plate and cutting himself a large chunk of the steaming pie. His two friends followed suit, and settled down to stuff their faces.

It was a good thing Sarah hadn't really been expecting better manners of them. She helped herself to a smaller piece of pie and sat beside the Doctor. 'So,' she asked conversationally, 'how was your morning?' Doyle passed her a glass of the white wine, which she accepted gratefully. The pie was delicious, and as she ate she listened to the Doctor and Doyle recounting their findings. Then she told them of her own escapades.

'You've done well, as always,' the Doctor said approvingly, as he cleaned his own plate. 'Smart move to win over young Billy like that.'

Doyle frowned. 'I think it's dashed irregular to use young urchins as agents,' he complained.

'But very wise,' the Doctor countered. 'People are used to seeing them about, and they can go places and listen in where an adult would be immediately suspected as a spy. And from the sound of things, young Billy is likely to turn up any amount of helpful information.'

'What concerns me, though,' Sir Alexander interjected, 'is all this stress you're laying on poor old Breckinridge.

The man's merely a businessman who's helped out the village when he didn't have to. I feel certain that he's innocent of involvement.'

'He may be,' agreed Sarah. 'But unless we can check him out, we won't know for certain.' She gave the magistrate a winning smile. 'You know him; can't you arrange for him to allow us to visit the factory?'

Sir Alexander flushed slightly, obviously appreciating her attention. 'I can but try, young lady. When I get home later, I'll send a man around to ask.'

The Doctor nodded. 'We'll assume that Breckinridge agrees,' he commented. 'That means tomorrow at the soonest will be a visit to the factory.'

'Is that a problem?'

'No.' The Doctor gave another of his wide smiles. 'After all, tonight we go out hunting the beast of the moors.' He smiled at Doyle. 'Are you up to that, do you think?'

Doyle nodded eagerly. 'Wouldn't miss it for the world,' he announced. 'The game's afoot!'

5

Hounded

Sir Alexander remained behind in the village when their late lunch was finished. Kipling, Beresford and Dunsterville reluctantly took their leave. Doctor Martinson shook the hands of the Doctor and Doyle before heading back to his own home to finish the death certificate on Tolliver. That left only Doyle to accompany the Doctor and Sarah back to Fulbright Hall.

As the coach ambled through the countryside, Sarah turned to the Doctor. 'Is any of this becoming clearer to you?' she asked.

'Not really,' he answered cheerfully. He had slouched down in the seat, the brim of his deerstalker pulled down over his eyes in an attempt to make it look as though he were sleeping. Sarah knew him too well to believe this ruse, and knew that he was merely attempting to avoid answering any questions she or Doyle might have.

'Do you have any idea what is going on here?' she persisted.

'I always have ideas,' he answered sombrely. 'But until I have more information, I'm not going to share them. If we can capture this beast tonight, then I'll be able to be more specific. Until then, all I have is theories.'

Doyle shifted eagerly in his own seat, opposite Sarah. 'What is this monstrous hound like?' he asked.

'Like a monstrous hound,' she answered. 'It's huge, and its mouth is filled with razor-sharp fangs. It's like nothing I've ever seen on Earth before.'

117

'Intriguing,' Doyle mused. 'An unearthly hound, eh? Sounds like the perfect idea for a story.'

Sarah couldn't hide a smile. 'Believe me, it is.' She gave one of the Doctor's knees a poke. 'Oi, you going to be like this all the way back?'

'Yes, and probably much later,' the Doctor muttered through his hat. 'I'm sure you can amuse yourself until the hunt.'

'I'm sure I'll have to,' Sarah answered. He was in his usual taciturn mood again, and she knew he was feverishly thinking through what they had discovered so far, as well as planning their evening's escapades. She chatted pleasantly with Doyle about his adventures on the whaler, and his plans to enter private practice when he returned to Edinburgh.

As the coach rolled to a halt outside Fulbright Hall, Sarah was startled to see Sir Edward come running down the steps, his face ashen. Ignoring the footman's offered hand, she jumped down to the gravel. 'What's wrong?' she asked.

'It's Alice,' he said. 'One of the servants found her in her room, unconscious. I hoped that the Doctor might be able to explain – '

Doyle and the Doctor virtually leaped from the landau, Doyle clutching his medical bag. 'I'm a doctor, sir,' he said briskly. 'I'd be happy to offer my opinion.'

'Thank you,' said Sir Edward gratefully. 'This way.' He led the three of them up to Alice's room. Roger was there, wringing his hands helplessly, as was one of the serving maids, presumably the girl who had discovered Alice.

It took Doyle and the Doctor a very brief time to come to the same conclusion. 'She's been drugged,' Doyle explained. 'The effects should wear off in a short while and leave her with no ill effects.'

'Drugged?' her father exclaimed, aghast. 'But who would do such a thing?'

The Doctor glanced around the room. 'Offhand,' he suggested, 'I'd suspect the one person missing from this picture. Which is Colonel Ross's room?'

Roger gave a strangled cry. 'You can't think that Edmund would possibly – '

'I can and I do,' the Doctor snapped. 'He's a very secretive person, and he's conspicuous by his absence.'

'But he's my friend,' protested Roger. 'I'm sure – '

'I'm sure you're a blithering idiot,' Sir Edmund grunted. 'Come along, Doctor. I've long said that the man is a scoundrel. Let's take a look in his room.'

Sarah was torn for a moment between staying to look after Alice, who she rather liked, and keeping up with the action. Action won, and she gave Doyle a quick wave before diving after the Doctor and Sir Edward.

Ross's room was further down the corridor, past the one Sarah had been given. Sir Edward rapped hard on the door and then threw it open. 'Nobody here,' he reported, disappointed.

'But his bags are,' the Doctor said, going to his knees in front of the first. He didn't touch it until he had conducted a thorough examination of the straps. 'Aha!' he exclaimed happily. 'Just as I expected.' Taking his magnifying glass from his pocket, he held up the strap using the handle. Sarah saw the glint of something in the leather. 'Ingenious. He's booby-trapped it so that anyone who opens his bags unaware gets drugged.'

Sarah frowned. 'So you're saying that Alice was trying to rummage through his things?'

'It looks that way,' the Doctor agreed. 'She was obviously suspicious of his motives and wanted some information.' His eyes sparkled. 'I wonder why Ross felt it necessary to rig this kind of trap for his bags? It's hardly the action of an honest man, is it?'

'The man's a scoundrel,' repeated Sir Edward. 'I should have Faversham arrest him.'

'On what charge?' asked the Doctor. 'He hasn't actually done anything criminal that we know of, and the only way your daughter could have been injected is if she were burgling his trunk. I think we'd be better off leaving the constable out of this.'

'But we have to do something,' protested Fulbright.

Sarah jerked her head at the two trunks. 'He won't go too far without his luggage, will he?' she said. 'That they're rigged suggests there's stuff in there he needs.' She looked down at the Doctor. 'You going to open them up?'

He shook his head. 'I don't think so. There may be other traps, and I doubt Ross would have left anything terribly incriminating behind. Let's just wait for him to turn up again, shall we?'

'So now what?' asked Sarah.

Getting to his feet, the Doctor slipped his glass back into his pocket. 'Rest,' he suggested. 'We'll need all our energies and wits tonight when the sun goes down.'

The hunger in his stomach almost overcame the fear in his soul. Waiting in the ancient mine for the sun to go down taxed him almost beyond endurance. He tried to sleep, but hunger continually wakened him. It was only the certainty that if he ventured out in the daylight then he might as well just kill himself that kept him from throwing aside caution and padding out onto the moors.

The wind had risen, whipping at the grasses and sparse shrubs, bringing to his sensitive nostrils the scents of life. He could almost taste the prey in his mouth, feel the blood pulsing in their furry bodies, hear their bones snap as he bit down . . . He whimpered in agonized indecision, desperately wanting to feed, but terrified of the consequences.

He had not asked for this fate, didn't deserve it. Why was he so tortured and so afflicted? He stared down at the paws he now possessed instead of hands. They were much more powerful in some ways than his old hands had been. He could kill with a single blow, and the claws he possessed could rip through branches, bone or flesh. But he couldn't hold a pencil. And his mouth! The fangs he had grown were capable of ripping the throat out of a horse, but he had lost the ability to speak. All he could manage were the whimperings he was now producing, or the growls, barks and howls that he gave vent to in the night.

Despite all of that, he knew that he had been human once. A long, long time ago. Now – what was he? Neither man nor beast but some terrible, cruel mixture of the two, twin natures that could never intermix as his physical forms had done.

He wanted to howl out his pain, his fear and his rage, but he knew that would bring the hunters to him faster. One day, he was sure, they would kill him. One day, perhaps, he would get some peace in the arms of death. He wasn't afraid of that so much. Death would be welcome, though he would never actively seek it. What terrified him the most was that he might not be killed. He'd been human once. He knew what people would do with him if they ever captured him.

Worse, he knew what Ross would do if he found him. This was all because of Ross in the first place! Had it not been for the man, he wouldn't be in this state. He would still be human. If he was doomed to die, he'd die happily if he could only kill the man who had done this to him. He envisioned fastening his fangs into Ross's throat and shaking the man like a rat until his spine cracked, his skull split and he could eat the fiend's brains for a final meal! Ah, then they could kill him!

But he knew that he was fooling himself. There was no chance that Ross would give him the opportunity for vengeance. Ross was too smart for that. He'd have others out to do his work. The hunters would be others, either bought by Ross or else fooled into doing his black deeds.

Hunger gnawed at his insides again, and he whimpered once more. He stopped pacing up and down in the confines of the tunnel and stared at the darkening sky. It would be twilight in an hour, and then he could venture out. In the darkness, he knew, he could give any human the slip. All he needed to do was to kill, quickly and silently, the first prey he came across.

And if it was a hunter, a human? Well, so much the worse for that man, then. He had only wished to be left alone, and the men with their guns wouldn't allow him to live. So be it. If there was to be a confrontation, he would not shy from killing.

And, though the thought was repugnant, his stomach insisted that good food could not be wasted. *Has it come to this?* he agonized. *Am I really considering cannibalism?*

But was it cannibalism? He had been human once — but he was not human now, and could never be again. He'd take animal flesh if he could, and he was more animal than human now. If that was right, how could it be wrong to feast on the flesh of those who would kill him? He resolved that he would kill whatever prey came to him first, man or beast. And he knew that he would eat anything that was presented to him.

He settled down to await the setting of the sun. Then the hunt would begin.

Alice joined the rest of them in the dining room for an early supper, though she didn't eat much. She insisted that she was feeling much better, but appeared pale and still tired despite her long, enforced rest. Roger fussed over her, and her father appeared much relieved. Sarah could see that Sir Edward was genuinely fond of his daughter. Despite his somewhat gruff manner, she realized that Fulbright was actually quite a pleasant person. He became much more animated with the reappearance of Alice.

After they had eaten, he led them all onto the patio overlooking the back lawns and the beautiful fountain. Sipping at her wine, Sarah found it very relaxing to be here. It was difficult to turn her mind to the evening's activities. She simply wanted to sit out here and enjoy the cool of the dying afternoon. Despite the rising breeze, it wasn't uncomfortable at all.

'I've arranged for the grooms to prepare four horses for us,' Sir Edward told the Doctor. 'I take it you can ride?'

'Naturally,' the Doctor answered. He looked satiated. Considering how much of the supper he'd packed away, Sarah reflected, he should. 'And so can Sarah.'

'Miss Smith?' Sir Edward stared from her to the Doctor. 'I assure you sir, this is no expedition for a woman.'

'And I assure you,' the Doctor retorted before Sarah could start her own protest, 'that I would sooner have Sarah beside me than any three men. I know I can rely on her implicitly.'

'Thank you,' Sarah said, touched by his compliment. He wasn't often that generous with his praise.

'But it's not right!' spluttered Sir Edward.

'You'd better accept that I'm coming,' Sarah told him. She turned to Alice. 'I hope I can borrow a pair of riding trousers, though.'

Sir Edward almost had apoplexy. 'Men's clothing? What is this world coming to?'

Alice patted his hand. 'Don't be so old-fashioned, Papa,' she said. 'I'm quite sure that Sarah and the Doctor know what they are doing. And a dress is so impractical for a hunt, isn't it?' She smiled wistfully. 'If I were not so weak, I'd want to come along as well.'

'Never!' her father vowed. Then he sighed. 'Oh, very well. I suppose I have no choice but to agree.' He took a swig of his own brandy. 'I'd better have them ready five horses, I suppose.'

'Four should be sufficient,' the Doctor replied. 'I think it would be better for Roger to stay here and look after Alice.'

'Here, I say!' Bridewell exclaimed. 'I'm jolly well coming if she is. I can handle a gun.'

'Probably not as well as Sarah,' the Doctor informed him. 'Anyway, I aim to capture the creature, not blow its brains out.' He gave Bridewell a wide grin. 'Besides, if your friend Ross reappears, I think it would be better for you to be here to question him, don't you?'

'If Ross turns up,' Alice promised, 'I shall make certain he is here when you return, if I have to sit on top of him!'

Sir Edward sighed. 'What is this world coming to? Women shooting and hunting, and now me own daughter talking about getting into a fight.' He shook his head. 'That's what comes of living in a country ruled by a Queen, I suppose.'

Sarah laughed. 'Cheer up,' she told him. 'You may grow to like it.' She turned to Bridewell. 'Please do as the Doctor suggests,' she begged. She wasn't sure why, but she had a definite suspicion that the Doctor was simply trying to get rid of Roger.

'Oh, very well,' Bridewell agreed with a sigh. He took Alice's hand. 'I wish I were coming along, though. It sounds like such sport.'

Alice laughed. 'I promise, Roger, you won't be bored in my company.'

'Time for you to change, Sarah,' the Doctor observed. 'Then meet us at the stables. By the time you're ready, we can set off for the moors.'

'I say,' exclaimed Doyle, draining his glass. 'This is jolly exciting, isn't it?'

'The best is yet to come,' the Doctor promised.

After she'd changed, Sarah hurried down to the stables. Sir Edward gave her an askance look but didn't comment on the trousers and jacket she was now wearing. Instead he simply handed her a rifle. 'You can really use this?' he asked.

'Want to see me try?' asked Sarah cheekily.

'No,' he answered, managing a slight smile. 'I suppose I am rather too hidebound, aren't I?'

'To be honest,' she told him, 'I think you're doing pretty well, all told.' She accepted the reins of a rather fine mare. 'She's beautiful. Aren't you, girl?' Sarah patted the mare's nose, and slipped the rifle into the boot on the saddle. She mounted the horse and rode over to where the Doctor was waiting. 'You didn't want Roger along, did you?' she asked softly.

'No,' he agreed, just as quietly. 'I think our friend Colonel Ross may turn up, and I'm not sure whose side our Mister Bridewell would take. I preferred not to have him make a choice. Besides,' he added with a grin, 'what could he do that you can't?'

'Not a lot,' laughed Sarah.

Sir Edward rode over, and one of the grooms handed them all dark lanterns and matches. 'Right,' the aristocrat said. 'I think we're ready. Now, stay close to me. The moors are considerably more dangerous than they might appear, and twice as bad at night. There are marshes and bogs that undoubtedly contain several bodies, and I'd be happy if we didn't add any more.'

'I'll drink to that,' Sarah muttered. The thought of being sucked to her death at the bottom of a bog was discomforting, but she intended to see this through.

Sir Edward nodded, then turned to the Doctor. 'As I promised, Doctor, I'll give you your chance to capture this beast alive. But if it looks like any of us are in danger, or that the creature will escape, I aim to shoot it down like the animal it is. I trust you can accept those terms?'

'You're being more than fair,' the Doctor answered. 'I am certain that we won't be in danger from this creature, but if there is trouble then I won't hesitate to kill it either.'

'Excellent.' Sir Edward gave them all a tight smile. 'Then let us be off.'

Sarah fell in behind him as they filed out of the stables and down the riding path. There was a slight queasiness in her stomach that she knew was nerves. While she'd faced greater troubles beside the Doctor – not least of which being the all-too-recent hunt for Morbius on the devasted surface of Karn – there was always something indescribably eerie about the unknown on Earth. She was fairly sure that the Doctor knew what he was doing, but there was always the knowledge that he also had a habit of messing up rather badly from time to time. She could only hope that this wasn't one of those times.

The ride was pleasant, with the setting sun tinting the woodland landscape in rich autumn colours. The wind was getting colder, however, as the sun paused on the horizon before bidding them all goodnight. Sarah shivered, and knew that only part of this was due to the chill.

The path led them out onto the moors proper, and it was as bleak and raw a landscape as any that even Karn could have offered. Grasses and stunted shrubs were littered haphazardly across the moors, but the soil over the base rocks was too thin to support much growth. What little that struggled to survive had to compete with the winds that seemed eager to hurl any growths away. In the gathering gloom, the pathside pools and swampy areas were little more than patches of black in the grey landscape.

Sarah could see why the locals so fervently believed that this was a landscape carved by the devil himself, and that the forces of evil walked about here when honest folks were warm and safe abed. Given her choice, that was where Sarah would have been by now. But she couldn't desert the Doctor when he might have need of her.

She glanced at Doyle, who seemed to be enjoying this adventure. It was a long time since she'd read his *Hound Of The Baskervilles*, but she recalled enough details to know that at least part of what he was experiencing this night would end up in the novel. Was the creature they were after the basis for the hound itself? Doyle had credited a local friend with the source of the legend, but perhaps that was to cover up his involvement in this strange hunt? She knew that none of his biographies had ever mentioned this stay-over in Devon. Nor had they mentioned his meeting with the young Kipling. But, as Sarah well knew, history was merely what posterity chose to record, and not necessarily what had actually occurred.

The night pressed in close about them. There was the sound of an owl hooting in the distance, but few other signs of life. Sarah knew that deer lived out on the moors, as well as the hardy local ponies. There were smaller animals too, like hares and foxes, and no doubt plenty of mice to temp the owls.

Plus there was the monster that they were after, whatever it might be.

They rode in silence. Sarah kept her eyes darting

127

about, but there was less and less to see. Bizarre rock formations melted into the darkness, and the weird, twisted stumps of trees ceased to stand out against the black sky. There was no moon again, probably because of clouds, since there were few stars glittering either. It was like riding on the far side of the moon, far from any life at all.

After a while, Sir Edward gestured to a side path. 'That should take us close to where we lost the creature last night,' he said softly. 'We'll have to camp out once we reach the bogs and wait. I daren't take us further.'

'It will come to us,' the Doctor informed him. 'The poor creature is most likely starving. It must take a great deal of fresh meat to keep a beast that size alive.'

'Good.' Sir Edward snapped his reins and his steed slowly took the side path.

Sarah's mare shied slightly, nickering a soft protest. It could probably smell the spoor of the creature they were after. Sarah gently insisted that it stay on the path, and the horse reluctantly obeyed. The feeling of oppression grew stronger in Sarah now, along with a horrible feeling that there were eyes out in the darkness, watching her. She tried to shrug the impression off as being just a case of the jitters, but it wouldn't leave. If there was any basis in fact to it, it had to be just some wary animal out there. It couldn't be the monster, could it?

After another ten minutes or so, Sir Edward halted. Sarah could barely see him on his steed now, the night was so dark. 'This is as far as I dare go,' he called softly. 'We'd better leave the horses here.'

Sarah slid off her mare and tied its reins to one of the twisted trees. The mare whinnied softly, then settled down as Sarah rubbed its nose. 'Easy, girl,' she murmured. 'Everything's fine.' She drew her rifle, though, and felt comforted holding it. Stepping out, she fell in with the

Doctor, Doyle and Fulbright. Together they moved further into the darkness. A minute or so later, the aristocrat signalled a halt.

The Doctor nodded and bent to examine the ground. There was the rasp of a match and the barest flicker of a flame in his cupped hands as he looked around. Then he blew out the light. 'It's not emerged yet,' he reported almost inaudibly. 'Positions.'

Sarah nodded. Ahead was the mire, and behind the pathway leading back to their mounts. Around were the tumbled remains of boulders. She moved to one of them, which was an outcropping of cold stone about ten feet tall. She settled down on a flattish portion and composed her mind to wait. There were soft sounds about her as the other three took their positions, and then silence.

How long would they be here? Sarah was very alert right now, but she knew that the edge would be taken off her wits if the wait was too long. Still, if the Doctor was right, their target would be out as soon as it felt safe. Would it sense them? At least the wind was such that it would carry their scent away from the creature, so it wouldn't have that as a warning.

To pass the time, Sarah tried making sense of what they had discovered so far. What connection could there be between grave-robbers, giant dogs, and monsters at sea that killed lone fishermen? What was Ross's role in all of this, and how did Breckinridge fit in? Or was he no more than an innocent party? What about the whaler, and the business its captain had in town? Try as she might, there was only one connection she could see – that this monster they hunted and the one that had killed Tolliver were hardly naturally occurring species for these parts.

The Doctor had mentioned something about their quarry being evolutionarily odd. Was it possible that someone here had brought creatures from the deep past or future into the local area? She and the Doctor had encountered examples of temporal interference before, so she couldn't rule out the idea completely. If the monsters weren't from some other time, then just what was their origin?

If she could only –

She froze, blanking out her mind. In the darkness, from the direction of the mire, she'd heard the sound of splashing water. Hardly daring to breathe, she concentrated all her attention on her hearing. Had it been some nocturnal bird? Or an animal? Or was it the hound?

For long seconds, she heard nothing more. Then came the rustle of something moving in the darkness. Her throat went dry and her palms went wet. She wiped her hand slowly and carefully on her trouser leg, and then gripped the rifle. It could well be the beast.

She tried to see something, anything, in the darkness, but there was no use. Aside from a few jumbled shapes of the rocks, she could make out nothing. There was the sound of another footfall, and then a vagueness in the rocks.

It was the creature.

Then there was sudden movement to one side. The beast was poised – to run? to attack? – and the Doctor's voice broke the stillness.

'SIT!'

His best Barbara Woodhouse impression! Sarah almost laughed with giddy relief and shock at the silliness of the command.

But the creature thumped to the ground.

There was the glare of a match, and then she saw the Doctor holding up his dark lantern, its soft light cast over the eerie scene. She gasped as she saw the beast, which hunched down, shaking, eyes darting about the clearing.

It was a dog, but not any kind of canine she'd ever

imagined. Her startled glimpse of the creature as it had jumped over her the previous night had not been incorrect, but it had been incomplete. Sitting, it was still as tall as she was, its massive head staring straight at the Doctor's grin-flecked face. It was covered in shaggy fur, tangled and matted, dark in colour. Teeth glittered in the glow of the Doctor's lantern, but the creature made no move to attack him.

But it was the eyes that captivated Sarah. Large, expressive and filled with pain, sorrow and fear. And, despite everything, not the eyes of some dumb animal. There were definite signs of intelligence within them.

'Lord!' breathed Doyle. 'That's a creature from the pits of hell itself!' His hand was shaking on the rifle he held.

'No,' said the Doctor softly. 'You're a good boy, aren't you, fellow?' He reached up and scratched the monster under the chin. Then he reached into his pocket and pulled out a large, cold pork cutlet. 'Here we are, then.' He held it out to the beast.

Sarah held her breath, expecting the creature to take the Doctor's arm with it. Instead, it gingerly set its teeth about the meat and then gulped the offering down. It looked at the Doctor, eager for more.

'As I said,' the Doctor told his companions without looking around, 'he's as gentle as a lamb if handled properly. There's no need to harm him, is there?'

'I wouldn't have believed it if I hadn't seen it,' said Sir Edward, still shaken by what he was witnessing. 'This is utterly extraordinary.'

It certainly was, Sarah reflected. They were all standing about the creature now, the Doctor having returned to scratching its head as if the thing were a lap-dog. 'What *is* it?' she demanded.

'I'm not entirely certain,' the Doctor replied. 'But it's no more a dog than I am.'

'It seems intelligent to me,' Sarah observed. She gave the beast an encouraging smile. 'Who's a good boy, then, eh?' She nervously reached out and patted its snout.

The animal used its huge tongue to gently lick her fingers.

Sarah couldn't help giggling as she shook her hand to get rid of the drool. 'He's a friendly chap,' she commented.

'Yes.' The Doctor stared at the creature darkly. 'I don't like its existence one little bit. There's something very odd about it.'

Then something changed. The beast suddenly sprang to its feet, its long snout twitching as if some scent had caught its attention. A low, savage growl seemed to roll out from the back of its throat, and its hackles started to rise. Sarah gasped and stepped back. The doctor whipped around, holding up his lantern.

The beast exploded into action. A huge paw slammed Sarah out of the way as it sprang past her. She whirled around, crashing painfully to the ground, and saw only a jumble of images. There was Colonel Ross, caught in the glare of the Doctor's lantern beam. There was the beast, fangs bared, snarling and leaping. A soft *phfft!*, and she was aware that something Ross had been holding had been dropped, and Ross was gone. The monster fell, the growl changing to a cry of agony that ended in the gurgling of blood and a choking sound. Then silence before a veritable storm of sound:

'I'll get the blackguard!' Doyle yelled, jumping forward.

'No, man!' cried Sir Edward, gripping his arm and dragging him back. 'You'll only get lost in the dark and stumble into some pit!'

There was the sound of the horses whinnying in fear and shock, and of Ross's footsteps fading into the night.

And there was the Doctor, kneeling beside the fallen beast, its head cradled in his arms. 'He didn't have to do this,' he said, his voice filled with anger and pain.

Doyle held out a hand and helped Sarah to her feet. 'Are you all right?' he asked, worried.

'Only bruised and winded,' Sarah assured him, grimacing as she flexed her foot and stood on it. 'I've felt better, but I've felt worse, too.' She limped over to the Doctor and the fallen monster. She could see that half of the creature's chest seemed to have exploded, and blood was oozing out over the dirty fur. Bubbles showed that the lungs and probably the heart had been punctured. It was quite clearly dead. Sarah felt a pang of sorrow, but she could see there was much more in the Doctor's hearts.

'There's nothing you can do,' she said softly.

'There's plenty I can do,' he replied grimly. He let the dead beast's head settle down to the ground and wiped its blood off onto the fur. His eyes held a dangerous glimmer in them as he stood up. 'I want to know what Ross was up to,' he said coldly. 'He came here specifically to kill the poor thing.'

'But what did he use?' asked Doyle, bewildered. 'I didn't hear a shot.'

'It was a rather powerful air rifle,' the Doctor answered. 'Virtually silent. The weapon of an assassin, not a hunter. He didn't count on my hearing him, and obviously expected to kill and escape before we knew what was happening.'

'Was it one of us he was aiming at?' asked Fulbright, shocked. 'I know he's a scoundrel, but I didn't think he'd stoop that low.'

'No,' the Doctor answered. 'He aimed at the creature. Ross is obviously too good a shot to have been after anything else. He hit it through the heart as it moved. A difficult shot in the daylight, but almost impossible in this light. If I didn't abhor what he's done so much, I'd have to admire his skill.'

Sarah couldn't quite grasp what the Doctor was talking about. 'You mean Ross came here to deliberately kill that monster?'

'Yes.' The Doctor stared at her thoughtfully. 'I think he knew exactly what this poor beast was, and this is why he was staying at Fulbright Hall. He's connected to this travesty of nature rather intimately. He's going to have some questions to answer when I catch up with him. And I'll take great delight in beating the replies out of him.'

Fulbright stared down at the dead creature. 'Well, Doctor, one way or the other, our work here is done. The poor thing is dead, and there will be no more killings.'

'Done?' The Doctor looked at him as if he were insane. 'It's hardly begun!' He gestured down at the body. 'We have something very solid to work on now. I aim to perform an autopsy in the morning to see what this actually is.'

'I'd be happy to help in any way I can,' Doyle said eagerly.

'Good.' The Doctor sat down on a rock. 'I think that the best thing that you can do right now is all go back to the Hall and get a good night's sleep. I'll stay here and keep watch over the body. First thing in the morning, Sir Edward, I'd appreciate your returning with a cart large enough to carry this back to the Hall. And then lending me somewhere I can dissect it.'

The aristocrat looked surprised, but then nodded. 'As you wish, Doctor. Your ideas have been good so far.'

'And what about me?' asked Sarah. 'What am I supposed to do while you're up to your armpits in monster intestines?'

'You have to go and see Breckinridge, remember?' the Doctor reminded her. 'I want you to take a good look at the factory of his. Make sure it really is manufacturing cables.'

'And not monsters, eh?' Sarah grinned. 'Should be a doddle.'

In the morning when Sarah went down to breakfast, she discovered Alice was feeling much better. Bridewell was very subdued, however, and Sarah realized he was probably trying to reconcile Ross's actions with their supposed friendship. Sarah was content to let him stew. She wasn't surprised to discover that Sir Edward and Doyle had both left at the crack of dawn with several servants and a cart to collect the slain monster.

As he had promised, Sir Alexander arrived after breakfast was over. He had his own carriage and horseman, and had secured access to Breckinridge, as he had promised. Sarah was very grateful, and happy to have his company for the grand tour of the factory. On the trip out, the magistrate spent the time talking about his family and the local gossip. Sarah was content to allow him to chatter on. She couldn't help wondering what might turn up at the factory.

There was a different man on the gate this morning, a heavier, duller-looking individual. As soon as he saw Sir Alexander Cromwell, he unlocked the gate and opened it. Very different from her last visit! It was amazing what money and influence could do.

The journey from the gate to the main door was a short one. The factory was one main building of several storeys, with a cluster of a dozen or so smaller box-shaped constructions about it. Sarah assumed that they were storage sheds. There was a side entrance, presumably for the local workers to enter by, and a rather impressive large front doorway. Its two huge oak doors were open, and Sarah could see a short entrance hall beyond.

Sir Alexander insisted on helping her from the carriage, and she linked arms with him to walk up the short flight of steps to the doors. As they entered the small hallway, Sarah saw that it was lined with glass cases showing the various forms of sizes of wires and cables the factory produced. To her surprise, the hallway was illuminated not by softly hissing gas lamps, such as were used at the Hall, but by glowing electrical lamps.

'I wasn't aware that electrical lighting was commercially feasible yet,' she commented to Sir Alexander.

'It isn't,' a voice said from a doorway. Sarah saw a tall, angular man emerge, his face illuminated by a wide smile. He was dressed conservatively but neatly, in a dark suit and with a dark tie over a white shirt. Small pince-nez glasses were perched on his thin nose, and mild blue eyes peered at her through them. His hair was dark, tinged with grey at the temples, thinning and swept back, showing a high forehead. 'I'm Tobias Breckinridge,' he said, extending a hand. 'You must be the Miss Smith who was so eager to visit me yesterday.'

'Sarah Jane,' Sarah replied, shaking his hand. 'I'm pleased you agreed to show me around.'

'I am very proud of what I have accomplished here,' he answered, 'Sir Alexander has been very supportive of my work, and I do believe that I have latched onto the wave of the future.'

'Like the lighting?' asked Sarah, gesturing at the lamps.

'Quite.' Breckinridge's eyes glimmered as he stared at the closest. 'Incandescent lamps. The invention just last year of the American Thomas Edison.' He blinked. 'Have you heard of him?'

'Thomas Alva Edison?' Sarah grinned. 'Who hasn't? A genius, they say.'

'I suspect they say it with great accuracy.' He waved his hand about. 'This factory would not have been possible without some of Edison's inventions. We are on the boundaries of science here, Miss Smith. I have an even dozen of his bipolar generators hard at work here. They power most of my machinery. Come, allow me to show you around.'

'I've seen this before, Tobias,' the magistrate interrupted. 'And my legs aren't as up to this as they used to be. Would you mind if I sat this out?'

'Of course not, Sir Alexander,' the factory owner said smoothly. 'I'll have my secretary bring you fresh tea.'

'Dashed decent of you.' Sir Alexander smiled at Sarah. 'I'm sure you'll learn a few things on this tour. Most interesting. Wish I were up to it myself.'

'Thanks.' Sarah turned to Breckinridge. 'I'm absolutely fascinated. Please, tell me all.'

'Certainly.' He gestured for her to walk with him down the short corridor. 'It's very gratifying to discover a person of your age and sex who is interested in such mundane matters as my humble factory.' He opened the door ahead of them and ushered her through.

'Don't be so modest, Mister Breckinridge,' she replied. 'This may be a factory, but it certainly isn't humble. You are, as you say, on the cutting edge of science here. And I'm fascinated by science. My colleague, the Doctor, is constantly teaching me about it.'

The noise level had increased here, and Sarah saw that they had emerged onto the main floor of the building. There were large vats with smoke and steam rising from them. Trolleys on wheels ran from these vats across the floor to what looked like large lathes and presses. Beyond those, other machines were whirring and chuffing away, spinning threads into cables. There were almost a hundred men hard at work down here, Sarah estimated. Apart from brief glances, none of them stopped working as they passed.

'The vats are where we load the raw materials,' Breckinridge explained. 'We import iron and other metals mostly from the Midlands. I'm thinking of installing a railway line out here to bring them faster than the ships and carriages can at the moment. We get through quite an amount of iron, as I'm sure you can imagine. It's melted down in the vats. Next, we check the purity of the mix, and add whatever small trace metals are needed for conductivity. Then the resultant mix is extruded through the next batch of machines. There it is pressed into wire of uniform thickness and purity before being cooled and wound onto those large spools that you see. Some of these are simply shipped off. We have a large storage area at the back, and we continually receive and send supplies.'

'And the rest of the machines?' asked Sarah, pointing to the far end of the floor.

'There we spin and weave cables, Miss Smith,' Breckinridge explained. 'They are corded together in bundles for carrying electrical impulses. I'd take you down on the floor, but it is important to maintain safety. Besides your own, I am, of course, concerned with that of my men.' He gave her a smile. 'A lady as pretty as yourself might distract them from their labours, and inattention can be dangerous, if not fatal.'

'I wouldn't want to cause trouble,' Sarah assured him.

'Thank you.' Breckinridge gestured to a door beside them. 'This leads to the stairs to the next level. If you'd care to?'

'Try and stop me,' Sarah said cheerfully. She opened the door and started off up the stairs. Breckinridge followed her up. They emerged into a short corridor, and when they closed the stairwell door behind them, the sound of the lower-level machinery was much diminished.

'This floor contains such dull but essential departments as the accountants, the shipping clerks and the laboratories,' the owner explained.

'Laboratories?' Sarah asked. 'You do research here, then?'

Breckinridge laughed. 'Don't I wish! I am certain that we English could duplicate and surpass the achievements of Edison, given half the chance. After all, scientific method was mostly born in this country. Davy, Boyle, Kelvin and so forth. No, the laboratories are mostly to check samples of the cable for accuracy and conductive properties, that kind of thing. You could take a look in if you wish, but you'd most likely find it rather boring.'

'I'll take your word for it, Mister Breckinridge.' Was he being honest, or simply trying to divert her attention? Sarah wasn't absolutely sure what to make of the man. He appeared to be open and honest, and he certainly had a winning way about him. But was this merely illusion, to cover some hidden depths? Or was she searching for clues to something that didn't in fact exist? 'Is this everything?'

'By no means!' Breckinridge's eyes sparkled. 'There is the final floor. I think you might well enjoy that. Come along.' He led her past the wooden and smoked-glass doors leading to the 'dull' areas, and to another door. As Sarah had expected, there was a further staircase beyond.

'Have you thought of installing elevators?' she asked.

'It had occurred to me,' he replied. 'But hydraulic elevators are not as efficient as they might be. I hear that our American cousins are experimenting with electrically powered models. I'm certain that they will soon become practical, and then I shall certainly install them. Until that time, alas, we have to endure the omnipresent stairs.'

Sarah nodded, and followed him up to another door. This was locked, and Breckinridge removed the key on a chain from his waistcoat pocket. 'This is my private part of the factory,' he explained. 'This is where I come when I wish to relax or to cogitate.' Throwing open the door,

139

he gestured her to precede him.

Inside, Sarah was impressed. It was a single large room that must have spanned about a third of the entire floor. There was a gentle hum of machinery and the sound of water splashing gently, but it was otherwise quite serene. Large aquarium tanks lined the walls everywhere except by the windows. Inside the tanks swam all manner of species of fish. Sarah recognized a few of the species, but many were strange to her. Some of them were clearly foreign. She stared at Breckinridge in respect. 'An impressive collection of species,' she observed, nodding at one tank. 'Is that a sand shark?'

'It is indeed.' His eyes lit up. 'You are an admirer of fish?' he asked hopefully.

'Mostly with chips, I'm afraid,' Sarah admitted. 'But I realize this is a most impressive collection. Is this your hobby?'

'More of an obsession, I'm afraid,' he admitted, like a boy with a guilty secret. 'And a fairly recent one, too. I began to study the oceans when I considered the laying of a telephonic cable to the continental United States. As I studied, marine life began to fascinate me. I've made a small fortune from my manufacturing plants here and in London, and was able to indulge my curiosity.' He gestured her over to the windows. 'I often stand here and simply stare out.'

Sarah emulated him, and saw that from this vantage point the bay was visible. She could see the waves on the surface of the grey waters, and from time to time spume flying as the waves crashed against rocks in the water. It really was very pleasant in this lofty perch. 'Is that why you met with Captain Gray?' she asked. 'Does he supply you with some of these samples?'

Breckinridge appeared surprised. 'You know about the captain?'

'His ship's surgeon, Doyle, is helping my friend, the Doctor,' Sarah explained. 'He mentioned that the captain had business with you, that's all.'

'Ah, I see.' Breckinridge shook his head. 'No, the captain does not bring live specimens back, I'm afraid. I met with him to offer him a job. I wish to finance my own cable-laying ship, and the good captain would be a perfect choice to skipper such a vessel. But, alas, I shall have to search elsewhere. Captain Gray is wedded to his love of whaling, it appears. I tried to convince him that whaling cannot last much longer, but he wouldn't listen. He knows that there are probably less than three hundred Greenland whales still in those waters, but seems impervious to suggestions that the whaling should at least pause for a while to allow their numbers to be replenished. A terrible shame.'

'Quite.' Sarah was amazed at his enlightened attitude. 'One day, I'm sure, more people will feel as you do. Perhaps then the whalers can be put out of action.'

'I only hope it's soon, Miss Smith.'

Sarah stared out of the window at the sea. So far, Breckinridge appeared to have been very honest and straightforward. She could see why men like Sir Alexander Cromwell and Sir Edward Fulbright were taken with him. This was the age of progress, and Breckinridge seemed poised to take advantage of it.

A movement in the yard some eighty feet below caught her eyes. Several small figures were moving about between the small outbuildings. 'Are they children down there?' she asked, unbelieving.

Breckinridge frowned at the tone in her voice. 'Yes. We have several dozen of them working here.' He gave Sarah a penetrating gaze. 'Ah, I take it that you're a supporter of Mundella's Act, and think that all children should be in school, not in work.'

'I am indeed,' said Sarah firmly.

'I can sympathize with that point of view, Miss Smith,' Breckinridge answered. 'But I don't actually agree with it, especially in these cases. You have to understand that the children you see down there are happy to work here.'

'I'll just bet they are,' Sarah said sarcastically.

That made him irritated. 'I see no cause for such animosity,' he snapped. 'Most of those children have lost their fathers at sea. They often have younger brothers and sisters dependent on them. Without the wages they earn here, they and their families might well all perish, and this nonsense about sending them to school wouldn't keep them alive. I feel that what I am doing here is helping them, not harming them.'

Sarah realized that she was projecting ideas a hundred years in advance of their time on Breckinridge. It was unfair to judge him by the light of her era when he was doing what he believed to be right. 'I'm sorry,' she apologized. 'It was rude of me to criticize you in that tone.' She stared down at the sad little figures in the courtyard below. 'Nevertheless, I do feel that they would be better off being educated than worked.'

'And if the law passes,' Breckinridge said, 'we may well get to discover which of us is correct. You believe they will be helped. I believe they will simply avoid going and many will become transients upon the city streets, as they were before I helped them. Until then, perhaps we could declare a truce?'

'Of course,' agreed Sarah. She smiled. 'I believe you're wrong, but I admit that you are sincere, and I have to admire you for doing what you believe is right.'

Breckinridge was mollified. 'Good. And I admire your outspokenness, Miss Smith, for a cause you obviously believe in. Now, would you like tea and sandwiches with our truce? Or would you prefer to see more?'

'A cup of tea would be marvellous.'

'Excellent.' He gestured toward the door. 'Shall we go?'

Thankfully, Sir Alexander didn't press her for details on the way back. Sarah was lost in her thoughts, unable to decide how she felt about Breckinridge, and whether he was merely a factory owner or something more sinister. She couldn't help wishing he'd seemed less idealistic and more exploitive. Then she'd have been happy to consider him the enemy. As it was, she simply couldn't decide.

He had apparently shown her everything at the factory. She'd peeked in at the laboratories on the way downstairs, but they had seemed to be exactly the kind of thing he'd described. He'd even allowed her to look around the yard and chat to a couple of the children without interference, which strongly suggested that he was hiding nothing. And the two young boys she'd spoken to had been grateful for their jobs as messengers and carriers at the factory. As Breckinridge had claimed, they were orphans who were supporting siblings with their wages.

Sarah sighed. It was so appealing to see the factory owner as a slave-driving villain, but the reality didn't resemble the prejudice much. He was enlightened and far-sighted. His schemes were all well within his grasp, and he showed a vivid certainty about the future that Sarah knew from experience was based in fact.

And yet – he was unknown in her age. She couldn't understand this. He should be dominating the field within five years, and yet he was destined for obscurity somehow. Why? How come he had never achieved his dreams of world-spanning communications? It was going to happen, and Breckinridge should have been there on the ground floor. He was prepared to seize the opportunity. Something obviously was going to go badly wrong for him? But what?

And could it be that she and the Doctor might be in a position to prevent it? She had often wondered what she would do if she were faced with the possibility of altering the past. Travelling in the TARDIS rendered such a thought more than academic. On her very first trip in the TARDIS, for example, she'd gone back to the Middle Ages. One change there could have affected the whole course of history. Now, here she was again, this time in Victorian England.

She had met and was interacting with two of the most famous English writers of their day – Arthur Conan Doyle and Rudyard Kipling. A little nudge from her, the wrong word even, and their lives could be altered. And while it might not change the entire course of history if Kipling never wrote *The Jungle Book*, say, something was bound to be affected.

It was a tremendous responsibility to rest on her shoulders. She could see why the Time Lords, the mysterious race behind the Doctor's past, strongly forbade interference in the history of other worlds. Though even they would meddle if they felt it was justified. They'd tried to destroy the Daleks at their birth, for example.

There was no use in looking for trouble, though. As far as she knew, there wasn't much chance that she and the Doctor would change history. None of what they were doing now had ever made it into any history she'd ever heard of. At the moment, it seemed that the most they were doing was influencing a couple of authors by providing them with plot materials. Hardly earth-shaking stuff!

On the other hand, there was something very wrong going on here. She'd bet her life on that. Sea-monsters and giant hounds were even more out of place here than she was. But was Breckinridge involved in this or not? He did have a fascination with the sea, but that wasn't necessarily an indicator of any kind. His own explanation for it was sufficient. However, she found his excuse for meeting Captain Gray to be a bit thin. Why offer the skipper of a whaling ship the job of running a cable-laying boat? Still, real life often did have thin threads of logic to it, and she might just be being a bit too suspicious there.

The problem was, she reflected, that life was never as tidy and neat as it tended to be on the telly or in a book. In fiction, all plot points were relevant and everything tied up neatly at the end to make sense. In real life, events often simply happened with no rhyme or reason, and resolutions either never came or passed so fast you could miss them if you blinked. Maybe Breckinridge was nothing more than he seemed: a man of vision and integrity. And maybe this was nothing but a mask that concealed a darker nature. She still had no real clue either way. All she could hope was that she and the Doctor could compare notes and that some enlightenment would come from it all.

The carriage drew up at Fulbright Hall, and Sir Alexander smiled at her. 'I trust you enjoyed your visit, my dear?'

'Very much, thank you.' Sarah shook his hand. 'You were super, Sir Alexander, and I really appreciate your help.'

'Any time, young lady.' He winked. 'It never hurts my reputation to be seen out driving with a pretty woman. Scandalizes the neighbourhood, you know. Let's be certain to set tongues wagging again, eh?'

'It's a date,' Sarah promised with a laugh. The groom helped her down from the carriage. 'Bye, Sir Alexander.'

'Goodbye, my dear.' He waved his driver on, and the carriage pulled away. Sarah went up to the door, which was opened by a footman. 'Any idea where the Doctor and Doctor Doyle are?' she asked him.

'I believe they're in one of the outhouses, ma'am,' the

groom answered. 'If you wish to find them, take the path to the rear of the house, and then ask one of the gardeners.'

'Thanks, Jeeves.' She gave him a grin and hurried to follow his instructions. At the rear of the house, one of the locals was raking leaves, and pointed her in the right direction. After a few minutes, she could smell the tang of formaldehyde in the air, and a sickly stench of decay. The rest of the journey was obvious.

The door to the small shed was open wide to provide some ventilation. One of the servants stood upwind of the shed, looking uncomfortable, while inside the hut were the Doctor and Doyle. 'So,' asked Sarah, 'made any great discoveries?'

'Indeed we have,' said the Doctor. His voice was tinged with anger and worry. 'It's been a most productive morning.' He gestured at the remains of the carcass on the trestle table behind him. 'Do you have any idea what that is?'

'Morbius's reject heap?' she guessed.

'You're very close, Sarah,' the Doctor replied. 'That isn't any known animal at all. In fact, it isn't even an animal.'

'Then what is it?'

The Doctor's eyes were haunted. 'Off the cuff, I'd say it's a ten-year-old boy.'

'What?' Sarah couldn't believe her ears. 'What do you mean?'

'I mean someone is tampering with the fabric of the human cell,' the Doctor said darkly, 'perverting its secrets to their own purposes.'

6

Swimming with the Sharks

Sarah gazed in shock and revulsion at the remains of the – the *whatever* on the table. 'I know some kids are ugly,' she said weakly, 'but that's a bit extreme, don't you think?'

'Extreme and extremely immoral,' agreed the Doctor. 'It's perversion of the natural order on a scale I've seen only once before.'

'But . . . there's no way that thing could be a ten-year-old child,' objected Sarah.

'It isn't. At least, it isn't any more.' The Doctor was very grim and she could detect the undercurrent of moral outrage below his surface. 'But that's how the poor creature began.'

Doyle, wiping his hands after having washed them thoroughly, walked over to join them. 'Even I don't understand how it has been accomplished,' he admitted. 'But there's no doubting the Doctor's core theory. That is not some animal.'

Sarah shook her head. 'Look, I know I'm not really up on the science stuff, but I'm no dummy either. It's impossible to create hybrids of humans and animals, isn't it?'

'Generally speaking, yes,' agreed the Doctor. 'But this isn't general. It's very specific. Without access to much more sophisticated analysis techniques, I can't be too sure what's happened, but the basics are fairly clear. The body structure of that creature is that of a normal human child.

Somehow, though, his genetic material has been melded with that of a canine – possibly a wolf, most likely a dog of some kind.'

Sarah frowned. 'Come off it,' she said. 'Are you telling me that thing's an honest-to-God werewolf?'

'It's not honest to anything, Sarah Jane,' the Doctor said hollowly. 'It's as dishonest as they come. And it's not a werewolf in the sense you imagine. This is a deliberately engineered monstrosity.'

'Somebody made a kid into that?' Sarah was appalled beyond any words.

'Yes.' The Doctor spoke quietly but firmly. 'The genetic match isn't too good, and the poor creature must have been in pain constantly, and probably more than half insane.'

'But that's not possible in this time period, is it, Doctor?' she insisted.

'Time period?' Doyle's eyes went wide. 'What the deuce are you talking about?'

'Later!' the Doctor snapped at him. To Sarah, he said, 'No, it isn't. Which means that we're dealing with something intrusive. That kind of genetic manipulation won't be possible on this planet for at least two hundred years.'

'Then what is happening here?' demanded Sarah.

'One possibility is that we have an intruder from the future.'

That sparked something in Sarah's mind. 'Wait a minute – I just met someone who seems to be a bit too aware of what the future might bring.' She told the Doctor and Doyle about her visit to the factory. 'Is it possible that Breckinridge is from the future, and that he's come back to this time to alter the course of history? That he aims to get rich when the communications boom comes in a couple of years?'

'It's possible,' agreed the Doctor. 'I don't know how

likely it is, though. Aside from his ideas — which a shrewd businessman of this time could still come up with — and this pitiful beast, there's nothing to suggest time travel.'

'That's it,' said Doyle firmly. 'I refuse to be shut out of this conversation any longer. Will you two please tell me what you are discussing here? Time travel?'

That had sunk it. Sarah sighed. 'Look,' she said. 'It's very complicated, and I know you won't believe it, so let it drop, okay?'

But Doyle was having none of that. 'Wait a moment,' he insisted. 'The only way that what you have both been saying makes any sense is if you claim to be from a different time period to this. The future, I assume, and you have somehow transferred back in time. Is that what you are claiming?'

'We're claiming nothing,' Sarah replied. 'Let it drop, please.'

'Oh, no,' Doyle said firmly. 'You can't just raise the idea and then walk away from it. The very concept is preposterous.'

'It is, is it?' asked the Doctor.

'Yes, of course it is.' Doyle waved his hands about his head. 'One cannot simply move freely back and forth between the ages. I'm a rational man, and I accept only those matters that science can demonstrate to a rational man.'

'Then heaven defend us from rational men!' the Doctor yelled. 'A pox on rationality! Has it never occurred to you that the human understanding of science is a small and pitiful thing? That there might exist vast areas outside of human knowledge that can still be explained scientifically, but not in terms of the puny knowledge that the human race possesses at this time? That there just might be realities undescribed by and unknown to your limited grasp of science? A rational man! Hah!'

149

'Well,' said Doyle, somewhat taken aback by this verbal assault, 'if you choose to put it like that – '

'I do so choose!' the Doctor replied.

'Then I have to say that you are correct, Doctor.' Doyle shook his head slowly. 'It is arrogant to assume that everything we know is everything there is to know.'

'Congratulations,' Sarah informed him. 'You've just made a huge step forward. Ignorance isn't so bad, but refusing to see ignorance is.'

'But I still find it hard to accept the notion of transference in time,' Doyle added honestly.

The Doctor gestured at the carcass on the table. 'Then merely accept it. You've seen it, you've touched it and you helped me to dissect it. Explain *that* in terms of nineteenth-century knowledge.'

'I cannot.'

'Good. I'd have called you a damned fool and a liar if you tried.' The Doctor patted him encouragingly on the back. 'Well, let's get a pot of tea and some scones, shall we? I do hope they have clotted cream and strawberry jam.'

'You're just leaving that where it is?' asked Sarah, jerking her thumb at the corpse.

'You're welcome to bury it if you wish,' the Doctor told her. 'But I thought we'd do better leaving that to the local vicar.' He set off back towards the Hall briskly.

Falling in beside him, Sarah asked, 'What's next on the agenda? After afternoon tea?'

'I wonder if we can hire a boat.'

'A boat?' asked Doyle, struggling to keep up. 'Whatever for?'

'I feel like a spot of fishing,' the Doctor replied.

Sarah grinned. 'Let me guess: you want to see what's out at sea.'

'You know me so well, Sarah Jane.'

'Here, I say,' objected Doyle. 'Isn't that likely to be a trifle dangerous, given what happened to old Tolliver?'

'No,' the Doctor replied. 'It's likely to be very dangerous. You needn't accompany me.'

'You'll need my help,' Doyle insisted. 'I'm a decent hand with a harpoon, you know, and a fair shot.'

'And you'd better not even dream about leaving me behind,' added Sarah.

The Doctor gave her a wide grin. 'There's no one I'd sooner have beside me,' he assured her. 'I knew you'd never stay behind.'

'You know me so well, Doctor.'

'That's a damned strange request, even for you, Doyle.' Captain John Gray stared at his ship's surgeon in surprise. 'The loan of a harpoon? There are no whales in these waters, man.'

Sarah rather liked the gruff old seaman. His receding hair was a wiry grey, matching his name, and his spade-like beard was full and thick. There was the tinge of a Scottish burr to his words, but no mistaking his puzzlement.

'I understand that, Captain,' agreed Doyle. 'But there is some kind of creature in the bay that killed a fisherman a couple of nights back.'

'Then what the blazes are you doing going out after it?' Gray gave a grim smile. 'Wait till the morning and half the crew would volunteer to accompany you on a hunt.'

'I suspect this beast only emerges at night, Captain,' the Doctor offered. 'And I doubt your men would be willing to indulge in a spot of night fishing.'

Gray snorted. 'After a day in port, they're in no shape to even stir this night.'

'Besides,' added Doyle, 'we may well not be attacked at all. The harpoon is merely for defence.'

151

'Oh, very well,' Gray agreed. 'I know you can use it, man. But be careful. You're a good shipmate, and I'd hate to have to bury you.'

'I assure you, we will take every precaution,' the Doctor replied. 'Incidentally, when do you sail?'

'Tomorrow morning, or the next,' Gray answered.

'Ah.' The Doctor nodded. 'Then your business transaction with Mister Breckinridge has concluded?'

Gray looked surprised again. 'Aye, that it has. What concern is it of yours?'

'Possibly none,' admitted the Doctor candidly. 'But might I presume to enquire as to the nature of the business?'

'You may not!' thundered Gray, getting to his feet. 'It is of a private concern, and no affair of yours, you impudent wretch!'

'Captain,' Doyle said hastily, moving between the two. 'The Doctor is from Scotland Yard, and is aiding the local police in solving two or three very mysterious cases. It is possible that Mister Breckinridge may have some connection with one or more of these cases.'

'A suspect?' growled Gray. 'Breckinridge has been an honourable man, and dealt fairly with me.'

'He may be innocent,' Sarah said gently. There was no point in clarifying Doyle's erroneous assumption of the Doctor's standing. 'But a little help from you could clear his name.'

Gray shook his head. 'I promised him that our transaction would remain our secret. Something to do with industrial espionage, or something.'

Sarah nodded. 'Not a job offer, then, piloting a cable-laying ship?'

'Good Lord, no!' Gray looked amused. 'Whoever told you that must be completely out of their heads. What would an old whaler like me do piloting a cable ship?'

'What indeed?' asked the Doctor cheerfully. He shook the Captain's hand. 'Thank you; you've been more than helpful.'

'My pleasure.' Gray shook his head in bemusement as they left his cabin. 'A cable layer,' he muttered. 'Me! These police chappies are all mad.'

As they passed onto the deck, Sarah smiled at the Doctor. 'So we know that Breckinridge lied about one thing at the very least.'

'But nothing more,' the Doctor chided her. 'Gray's story of Breckinridge being wary about industrial spying could well be true. There's a lot of it about, and their deal could well be honest.'

'I'm certain that it would have to be, from the captain's side at least,' Doyle offered as he selected a harpoon and began to coil the rope about his arm. 'Gray is one of the straightest, most decent men I've ever met.'

'I'm sure he must be.' The Doctor stared out over the gentle seas. 'A perfect night for a sail, isn't it? Hardly a swell in sight.'

'And where are we going to get a boat from?' asked Sarah.

'This is a fishing town,' the Doctor replied. 'The place is littered with them.'

'We can't just take one,' argued Sarah.

'I wasn't going to.' The Doctor led them off the *Hope* again and back along the quay. 'Tolliver's boat is still moored behind the Pig and Thistle,' he explained. 'He won't be having much use for it, seeing as they buried him today.'

'Constable Faversham might consider it stealing,' Sarah objected.

'Faversham is guarding the grave tonight,' the Doctor countered, 'in case the robbers show up again. I'm inclined to let him. I doubt the villains are stupid enough to strike on the night of the burial. They waited last time, and they will undoubtedly wait again.' He flashed Sarah a grin. 'And I aim to tell Mister Brackley that we're just borrowing the boat for the evening, and pay him to alert anyone who asks.'

'He'll just get blotted,' said Sarah.

'All the better. Then he's not likely to object, is he?'

He didn't. When the Doctor flipped him a shilling the one-armed sailor promised to keep a watch out for anyone asking after them. Sarah noticed that he was apparently aiming to spend the vigil warm and well lubricated, since he shot into the tavern before the three of them had even cast off the moorings of the small fishing boat.

'Are you familiar with these boats?' Doyle asked the Doctor.

'I'm familiar with all boats from coracles to catamarans,' the Doctor answered, slipping free the fore rope and jumping down to the deck. 'Or do I have to tie a sheath of sheepshanks to prove it?'

'I'll take your word for it.'

'Good.' The Doctor and Sarah raised the sail, while Doyle watched the wheel.

Sarah stared out across the bay. The main fishing fleet had departed earlier, to get well out to sea where the fishing would begin. That meant, at least, that there was no chance of a collision in the bay. Sarah was no great shakes on a boat; it hadn't been a terribly realistic option in South Croydon. She had done a little sailing, and did know that the pointy end of the boat went first, and that sailors insisted on port and starboard instead of left and right like normal human beings. After that she was lost.

At least it was looking like a calm night. That meant her stomach might well behave itself. She'd never actually been seasick in her life, but tonight would not have been a good time to start. Still, with the sun low on the horizon, it looked like being a calm and beautiful night. The wind that had nipped at her last night had died down, and there was just a light breeze to fill the sail and carry them slowly and gently along. The clouds were sporadic, and stars were already starting to twinkle. She wished that this were simply some pleasure cruise and that there was a packed picnic hamper and a bottle of some feisty plonk instead of harpoons, rifles and nets aboard.

Wouldn't it be lovely to actually be able to enjoy things for a change instead of having to fight or hide from things? Or would that just be normal and boring for her now?

Sarah glanced up at the Doctor, and saw the light of excitement in his eyes. How he must have been bored as one of those stuffy, legalistic Time Lords back on his home world of Gallifrey! No wonder he enjoyed meddling so much. He was making up for more lost time than Sarah could even begin to imagine. She began to sing softly: 'Blow the man down, bullies, blow the man down.'

'Heigh ho!' the Doctor agreed.

Standing on the headland close to Breckinridge's factory, Ross surveyed the bay through his collapsible binoculars. 'It's hard to see clearly in this light,' he commented, 'but that small fishing smack down there has three people aboard. One of them is definitely this Doctor, and the other two are probably Miss Smith and that Doctor Doyle from the whaler.'

'So what?' asked Abercrombie, munching on a cheese and chutney sandwich he'd liberated on the way there.

'I wonder how much they know about our business, that's what.'

Abercrombie shrugged. 'What's the difference?' he asked. 'If they're out there in the bleeding bay, they don't know much. And they won't be alive long enough to learn more, will they?'

Ross sighed. 'It's a pity, Abercrombie,' he said, 'but I fear you are quite correct. Sadly, the Doctor and his friends are likely to have a very lethal boating accident this evening.'

Once the Doctor decided that they were far enough out in the bay, he and Doyle dropped the sail and let out the water anchor. 'Now we just wait,' he said.

'So who brought the cards?' asked Sarah.

Doyle couldn't resist a smile at her easy manner. 'Do you two do this kind of thing often?' he enquired.

'Too blooming often,' Sarah answered.

'We do have a knack of walking into trouble,' the Doctor admitted.

'Walking?' Sarah laughed. 'Running headlong, more like.' She grinned at the medical man. 'You really wouldn't believe some of the adventures we've had.'

'Try me,' suggested Doyle.

Sarah shook her head. 'No, I mean it: you really wouldn't believe them. If you think the idea that we might be from another time is hard to accept, you should try taking the Doctor's pulse sometime.'

'I should?'

'No, you shouldn't,' the Doctor snapped. 'I'm in perfect health, as you can see. Sarah, stop trying to cause trouble.'

'Me cause trouble?' she asked in mock innocence. She simply couldn't resist baiting the Doctor at times. 'I suppose sitting out here in a tiny boat at night with an unknown killer is playing it safe?'

'It's as safe as I could make it,' the Doctor answered.

156

'But I need some answers to too many questions. And this is the only place to get them.'

Sarah stared over the surface of the sea. The sun had gone down now, and the Doctor had vetoed the idea of burning a lantern, wanting to stay out of sight of possible observers. Stars sprinkled across the blackness were also reflected choppily in the waters below. They were the only lights visible, and it was like being afloat in space.

And then –

'Doctor!' she hissed, not wanting to raise her voice too loudly. Both doctors joined her in the bows, and they all stared out into the depths.

Far below the boat, lights were visible in the water that were definitely not stars. There was a greenish tint to them, though that could be nothing more than the water casting a hue to white lights. There were hundreds of these lights, spread in a gigantic cartwheel-like shape. The hub of this wheel was several hundred yards to the left – port! – of the small boat. As Sarah stared in awe and astonishment at the shape, she could see that it was slowly turning.

'What is that?' she asked, spellbound.

'I've heard about phenomena like this,' Doyle answered her, just as gently. 'It's phosphorescence of some kind, as I understand it. There are minute sea creatures that glow in the night and live in colonies of thousands of individuals.'

'And they're all big fans of *Wagon Train*,' the Doctor scoffed. 'Doyle, those minute sea animals live in much warmer waters than these, and they certainly aren't organized in regular battalions. That's not a natural phenomenon.'

'Then what is it?' asked Doyle, somewhat peevishly.

'I'm not entirely sure,' the Doctor replied evasively.

'Then be a little uncertain!'

'Offhand, I'd say it was some kind of activity taking place on the sea bed.' The Doctor frowned. 'And one controlled by considerable intelligence.'

Sarah snorted. 'Oh, right. Davy Jones is a little restless tonight, so he's holding a dance.'

The Doctor shook his head. 'Sarah, Sarah,' he chided. 'I expect incredulity from Doyle; after all, he's a rational man. But I had hoped for better from you; after all, you're a journalist.'

'Thanks a heap.' Sarah couldn't take her eyes from the slow, majestic movement of lights. She couldn't even begin to imagine what it was. 'Are you suggesting that there's somebody down there right now doing that? In 1880?'

'Yes.'

'But how? The submarine hasn't been invented yet.'

'Actually, it has,' the Doctor contradicted her. 'Simply not developed yet. But I don't think that what we're seeing is native to this time. Or, perhaps, native to this world.'

Doyle gave an inarticulate cry. 'This is getting too preposterous,' he protested. 'That's the second time you've mentioned some kind of intrusion from another era, and now you also imply that this anomalous phenomenon might be the product of some other-worldly forces?'

'Forget your preconceived notions, Doyle!' thundered the Doctor. He gestured over the bows of the boat. 'Use your rationality to explain that if you can! If not, shut up and listen to wiser heads than yours.'

Doyle subsided, but Sarah could tell that he wasn't at all happy at whatever thoughts were passing through his mind. She could hardly blame them: the notion of time travel and alien intruders must be horribly far-fetched to him. Even his character of Professor Challenger hadn't faced quite this kind of puzzle, and he wouldn't create that irritable man of science for years yet.

Sarah stared out at the waters, and smiled. 'I don't know what is causing it,' she admitted, 'but it's very pretty.' There was also something vaguely familiar about the lights, but she couldn't quite put her finger on it.

' "Pretty" isn't a scientific term,' the Doctor said softly. Then he grinned. 'But it is accurate. It's like a Christmas tree underwater, isn't it?'

'Perhaps we should be a little more cautious,' Doyle suggested, 'in leaning out to observe those lights. After all, Tolliver was obviously looking over the side of the boat when he was attacked.'

The Doctor appeared astonished at the thought. 'My dear chap,' he cried. 'Of course! That's exactly what must have happened. He saw these lights, then leaned over for a better look and – '

Sarah and Doyle both dragged the Doctor away from the gunwale as he looked set to re-enact the accident. 'We may be safer here,' Sarah said, with a thankful nod at Doyle. 'Smart thinking.'

'I knew what I was doing,' the Doctor said peevishly. 'There was no need for that.'

'Whatever you say,' Sarah agreed. She could still see the wheel turning slowly below the water, though not as clearly. The surface of the water was starting to get choppy, breaking up the image.

'This is all very – ' Doyle began.

The boat gave a shudder as something slammed into it from below. It heaved in the water, and twisted, falling back with a crash. Sarah, caught completely off-guard, skidded across the small deck and into the gunwale. She barely had time to yelp from the pain to her shins when the boat was rammed a second time from underneath and it gave another lurch. Arms flailing wildly, Sarah attempted unsuccessfully to regain her balance. She heard the Doctor cry out, and then she was falling.

The water was cold and hard as she splashed down into it. The force of the impact stunned her, and she felt herself going under. At least she'd taken a gulp of air as she'd fallen, and she held her breath as she sank into the inky, frozen depths. As soon as she could move, she started to stroke with her hands, slowing her descent.

Her clothing was thoroughly wet. The Victorian dress, long and flowing, had been so impractical on the surface; here, waterlogged, she was afraid it would drag her down to her death. Frantically, she tried to stroke back toward the surface, but it was too hard. It felt as if an icy hand was dragging her down to her doom.

'My God!' exclaimed Doyle, badly shaken but managing to retain his grip on the mast, 'what the devil was that?'

'Something rammed us from below,' the Doctor growled, fighting to stay on his feet. 'Sarah! Sarah!'

Doyle's eyes whipped around. 'She must have gone overboard!' he exclaimed. He started to move toward the side.

'No!' the Doctor ordered. 'That's what those creatures want us to do! Then they'll attack.'

'Let them,' Doyle growled. He picked up his harpoon and hefted it. 'They'll get a taste of cold steel if they attack me. But what about your friend?'

The Doctor appeared ashen. 'They're most likely going after her.' He shucked off the cape coat and tossed the deerstalker on it. 'I'm going after her.'

'They'll kill you!' Doyle said in horror.

'They can try,' the Doctor growled. 'But I'm harder to kill than I look.' Before Doyle could say anything else, the Doctor sprang onto the gunwale, and then executed a clean dive into the darkness beyond.

Doyle shook his head, and staggered across to the side. The harpoon was cold and familiar in his hand. If any of those monsters came after him, they'd get a fight. And if, somehow, the Doctor or Miss Smith survived, Doyle could help them regain the boat.

Slowly sinking, Sarah struggled with her encumbering clothing, trying to either shed it or rip it free. But it was no use at all. She couldn't manage, and her lungs were almost bursting.

Then there was a sudden movement in the water. She felt something like a pressure wave slam into her. A dark shape grazed her, and she felt fire in her left hand as something raked across it. She could barely restrain a scream of pain, and the attacker was gone. She'd caught only a glimpse of it, but it had seemed to be some huge seal.

And it had to be coming back.

There was agony in her hand, and she knew that the beast had been toying with her. It could have killed her, but had instead just bitten her. The next time it might go for the kill, or for another wounding.

She saw movement again, as something approached her. It was hard to make out, between the darkness and the blotches in her eyes from the strain and pain, but this shape appeared to be very different. She could make out a tail, and what seemed to be hands. Struggling to get out of the way of this fresh attack, she flailed about without much effect. Then the creature came in closer.

It was incredible. This was not her attacker. It looked like a young girl, perhaps twelve or so, with long, light hair floating like a halo around her head. She smiled encouragingly, and gripped Sarah's uninjured arm. Sarah, struggling to stay conscious, was too astounded to know what to do. The girl seemed quite at ease – if she were

161

real, and not some nightmare of the deeps! — and she gripped Sarah's skirt. She bent her head, and bit at the fabric. Her teeth must have been made of steel or something similar because they cut through the skirt without effort, and the girl ripped the rest of it free.

A huge weight fell away from Sarah, and she stroked out with her hands. She felt herself rising at last, and then the gentle pressure of the girl's arms helping her. Sarah wondered what had happened to the monster that had attacked her, but concentrated on heading for the surface. As she did so, she saw another form close in suddenly. She had no energy left to fight it off, and then she felt the Doctor grab her arm tightly, and saw his face close beside hers. He smiled encouragingly.

The girl was gone in a flicker of motion. Sarah wasn't certain, but it looked like the girl had left by flicking a tail and charging away at an incredible speed. She had no strength left to wonder, though, and all she could concentrate on was reaching the surface once again.

And then she was there, bursting back out of the icy water into the cold night air. She emptied her lungs in a single burst and whooped in a fresh breath. She choked a little, but the fire in her head and chest started to die down.

The Doctor still supported her, and Sarah could see as she took another gulp of air that they were quite close to the boat. 'Chin up, Sarah,' the Doctor gasped encouragingly. 'Almost there.'

She nodded, and put her strength into stroking out toward the boat. The pain in her left hand was almost unbearable, but she had to get out of the water as soon as possible before —

There was a wake in the water as something threw itself toward her and the Doctor. It was the creature that had attacked her before, sleek, dark and deadly, coming in

162

for the kill. Sarah didn't have the strength to fight it off, but she freed herself from the Doctor's grip so that he might have a chance.

And something whipped past her head, missing her by only feet. Belatedly she realized it had been the harpoon. Doyle must have thrown it. The slim blade whipped through the air and slammed into the approaching creature. The beast's own speed helped drive the weapon home. Sarah heard a scream and a thrashing in the water, and the rope almost sang as it went taut.

'Got it!' she heard Doyle yell.

'And I've got Sarah,' the Doctor called up to Doyle. 'Haul that thing in!'

Sarah managed to make it back to the boat. The Doctor was floating there, holding onto a rope. She managed a small smile at him as he helped her up from the water to the side of the boat. It was a fight, but she managed to struggle aboard. She could barely use her left hand, and saw that it was badly skinned and still bleeding. Ignoring it, she turned to help the Doctor back aboard.

Doyle was concentrating on reeling in his catch. The harpoon was sticking up from the water at an angle, glittering in the light of a lantern Doyle had blazing. Sarah could see he had pierced some dark beast, very seal-like, but huge. As she bent to offer the Doctor her good hand to help him aboard, she saw an explosion of water close to the monster. A second creature leaped from the sea, and its large, teeth-packed snout ripped at the line to the harpoon.

Doyle gave a cry, falling backwards as the line parted. There was a splash as the second beast fell back into the cold waters, and the dead creature sank beneath the waves. Sarah felt the Doctor grab her hand and he hauled himself over the side.

There was another shock as something hit the boat right where he had been.

'Thank you, Sarah,' the Doctor gasped, regaining his feet. 'That thing almost had me.'

Doyle staggered across the small deck to them. 'It got away,' he howled angrily.

The Doctor grinned. 'I think you've lost your deposit on the harpoon,' he agreed. 'And I trust this attack is over. Would you mind taking a look at Sarah? I think she's injured her hand.'

Sarah was propped up against the side of the boat. She was shivering, partly from shock, partly from the soaking and partly from the fact that she had no clothing left from a foot below her waist. She looked at her left hand, which still bled very badly, and then up at Doyle.

'Oh dear,' she gasped, and lost consciousness completely.

Interlude 2

Lucy

The Guards ushered them all into the dormitory, then locked the door as they left. The children were all excited, scared and confused. They crowded about Lucy, all of them talking and asking questions.

'Settle down,' she ordered, taking control of them. 'Calm down. We have to be quiet, or the Guards may come back.'

'I doubt it,' Joshua said, his face split by a huge grin. 'They're too busy panicking.'

Vicki tugged at Lucy's arm. 'Are you gonna get into trouble for what you did?'

'That was very brave,' added Lizzy. 'I wish I had the courage you do.'

'It wasn't bravery,' Lucy replied. She swam over to help two of the younger ones into their sleeping berths. 'I just couldn't let them drown that lady.'

'She was from Topside, wasn't she?' asked Vicki.

'Yes,' Lucy answered. 'We were all from Topside once. But we can't ever go back now.'

'Do you want to go back?' asked Joshua.

'It doesn't matter what I want,' Lucy told him. 'We can't go back.'

'But would you, if you could?' he persisted.

'Would you leave us, Lucy?' asked Lizzy, worry in her voice.

165

'I'd never leave you,' she promised. 'Never. We belong to each other now. We're a family. All we have are each other. We have to all look out for one another.'

'Good,' said Vicki, satisfied again.

'Do you think the Guards will punish you for what you did?' Simon rarely spoke, but he couldn't stay quiet now. 'I won't let them hurt you. I'd sooner die!'

'I don't think they will.' Lucy ran her webbed fingers through his curly hair. 'And I know you'd defend me. But I don't think they really noticed what I did.'

'And,' added Joshua with a laugh, 'they're too busy burying the dead Guard and panicking. There's only three of them now. There are twenty of us.' He grinned. 'I'll bet we could take them out if we tried.'

Lucy didn't like that kind of talk. 'There may only be three Guards left,' she cautioned him, 'but they're faster and much stronger than we are.'

'Are you scared to fight them?' challenged Joshua.

'Of course I am!' Lucy snapped. She flicked her tail at him contemptuously. 'Calm down, Joshua. We may be twenty, but most of us are very young. If we try and attack the Guards, some of the younger children are bound to be killed. I won't endanger their lives.'

Joshua was still too new to understand fully. 'You'd rather stay here, cooped up like hens?' he exclaimed angrily. 'Doing what Ross tells us to do and waiting until the Guards get mad enough to kill us, like they killed Tim?'

'No,' Lucy replied. 'We all want to get away. But we need to pick the right time to do it. We need some advantage, some way to win. What we have to do is to keep our eyes open and watch for that chance.'

'We could be waiting forever,' grumbled Joshua, but he did seem to be getting the idea.

Lucy swam over to him and touched him on the

shoulder. 'Joshua, we won't be here forever, I promise. Haven't you noticed that the past few days the Guards have been very distracted by something? And today one of them was killed. They're not invincible, and even Ross can't foresee everything. I think that somebody Topside is on his trail. With a little luck, that may give us our chance. So, please, try and be patient for a little longer. You've only been here a short while. I've been here almost a year now. I hope none of us will have to endure this slavery for very much longer.' Lucy smiled at the younger ones. 'Now, it's time to get some rest.'

'Aw,' complained Lizzy, 'you promised to tell us the rest of your story.'

'It's very late,' Lucy replied. 'And the same thing happened to all of you. You already know the rest of it.'

'You promised!' complained Vicki.

Lucy could see that this was an argument she wasn't likely to win. 'All right,' she agreed. 'But it's going to be very short.'

'That's okay,' Lizzy answered. 'We just like the way you tell it.'

Lucy couldn't help smiling. 'Well, I was captured and knocked out by Raintree and Brogan. When I awoke, I was in a strange room with all kinds of machines and stuff. It was some kind of scientific laboratory, I suppose, but you've all been there. You've seen it. I didn't know what all the glass things were called, or the liquids and stuff bubbling away. I was on a sort of table, strapped down so that I couldn't move. And I didn't have any clothes on at all.'

'Were you scared?' asked Lizzy.

'I was absolutely terrified,' admitted Lucy, smiling. 'I didn't know where I was, or what was happening to me. All I knew was that Cherry was dead, but I wasn't free at all. If anything, I was worse off than before. I remembered rat-faced Raintree and the nasty Brogan, but they weren't around at least. I was afraid they'd brought me to this place just to kill me. Or, since they'd taken all my clothes, maybe other things first.

'Then Ross came in. He's quite good-looking, but I could tell that he wasn't a nice man. If he had been, he'd have set me free. Instead he came over and smiled down at me . . .'

'You're a very lucky young lady,' Ross said, his eyes shining with excitement.

'Please,' I begged him, 'let me go. I won't tell anyone anything. I promise!'

'Let you go?' He laughed cruelly. 'I can't do that. You have a wonderful destiny in front of you. You're about to become the first member of a new species.'

I didn't know what he was talking about, but I could tell he was going to do something to me. And he wasn't going to let me go, that was clear. 'What's a species?' I asked, hoping I could keep him talking long enough to escape from the straps. I was cold and scared, but he didn't care.

'A species, child,' he told me, 'is a distinct order of animals that can only interbreed with themselves and not with other creatures. A species is something distinct, with special adaptions that other creatures don't possess. A human being, for example, can breed with other human beings, but not with – oh, cats, shall we say? And cats are a species, which can't breed with dogs.'

'I don't understand you,' I told him. 'What are you going to do to me to make me different?'

Ross smiled, and I shuddered at the look on his face. He didn't see me as a person at all, just as some kind of experiment. 'Well, right now you're nothing,' he told me. 'Some dirty little girl who barely manages to survive on her wits. There are thousands like you, filthy creatures who'd be better off dead. And if it were not for me, I suppose Raintree or Brogan would have snapped your scrawny little neck or something. But you have been selected by destiny to become the forerunner of a new race, a new species. By the time I'm through with you, you will no longer be a dirty little girl. You'll be the shining star of a new kind of creature.'

'Don't hurt me!' I begged him. 'Please, let me go.'

'Stop whining,' he snapped, annoyed that I didn't seem to share his vision. 'You're on the verge of a wonderful experience. You are about to extend the threshold of science and become the first member of a new race.'

'What kind of race?' I asked him, still struggling with the straps. If he saw what I was doing, it didn't bother him. I don't think he saw me, really. He was so lost in his mad ideas.

'Have you heard stories about mermaids?' he asked me.

'Of course I have,' I replied. 'I've heard lots of stories.'

'Do you like the ones about mermaids?' Ross asked.

'Yes,' I said. 'I don't believe there really are such things, though.'

'There aren't,' he agreed. 'Not yet, anyway. But there will be, because you're going to be one.'

I couldn't believe what he was saying. 'That's stupid!' I cried. 'It's impossible! Nobody can do that, even with magic.'

'Magic?' Ross laughed at me. 'You stupid little girl, science is much more powerful than magic! I can do what I say and turn you into a mermaid.'

'I don't want to be half a fish!' I told him, crying at the thought. 'Don't cut me in half!' I thought that what he was going to do was to chop off my legs and sew on a fish's tail, and you can imagine how scared that made me feel.

'Stop that weeping,' he ordered, 'or I'll give you something to cry about.' He glared at me angrily. 'I'm not going to do anything like that. You're not going to be any part of a fish.'

'But isn't that what a mermaid is?'

'In stories, yes,' he agreed. 'But you can't mix people and fishes. They're completely incompatible. People are mammals, a separate class from fish. There's no common ground there.'

'Then what are you going to do to me?' I asked him. He wasn't making much sense, even for a lunatic.

'There are mammals that live in the sea,' he told me. 'Dolphins, seals and whales. What I am going to do with you is to change you into a hybrid creature, half-girl, half-dolphin.'

I didn't know then what a dolphin was, of course, but I still didn't like the sound of it. 'You can't do that!' I screamed.

He didn't understand what I meant. 'Nobody else can,' he told me. 'But I can do it.' He pointed to this big vat in the centre of the room. 'Look at that.'

I could see that it held a sort of thick, white jelly. It was a bit like ointment, I suppose, but that was all I could make out. 'What is it?' I asked.

'That's my transmogrifying fluid,' he replied. 'It enables me to combine two sorts of animal cultures, blending them into a single, viable whole.'

I still didn't know what he meant. 'You can't,' I protested again.

'I've already done it once, by accident,' he told me. 'When I discovered the fluid, I didn't know what it was, except it was some kind of medicine. Then a boy who'd been bitten by a rabid dog was brought to me. I could see he was going to die anyway, so I decided to try the fluid on him. It was incredible! Instead of dying, the boy began

170

to change. He started to get hairy, and grow teeth and eventually he changed into a hybrid – half-boy, half-dog. It was fascinating. Then I realized that this fluid enables two different forms of cells to join and become one, as long as they're of the same order – both mammals, for example. When I saw my boy-dog, I started to think about other possibilities. And you're my next experiment.'

He was really scaring me now, but I couldn't get free. All I could do was try to be brave. I wouldn't let him see me scream any more. 'You're going to use that stuff on me?' I asked.

'Yes,' he replied. 'And I'm going to mix into you some dolphin extracts. With luck, you should become a real live mermaid.' He shrugged. 'There's a chance you won't survive, true, but sometimes we have to make sacrifices for science.'

'I don't want to be a sacrifice for anything!' I yelled. I could see he was really much madder than I had thought. He didn't care if I died or not. I was just an experiment.

'Oh, shut up,' he told me. He pulled on a pair of gloves. Then he picked up a large, sharp knife.

'You said you weren't going to cut me in half!' I sobbed.

'I'm not,' he said impatiently. 'But I have to mix the fluid and extracts within your body. So I'm going to make a small incision, that's all. Stop whining, or I'll gag you.' Then he cut my arm open, just below the elbow. It started to bleed, and he put his hand into the vat and rubbed some of the fluid into the cut. After that, he picked up a bottle of some greyish liquid and poured that over the wound, too.

It hurt me terribly, like there was a fire burning inside my body. I wanted to be brave, but I couldn't stop myself from screaming. I could feel whatever the liquid was doing to me, like it was ripping me apart. Finally the pain was too much, and I couldn't take it any longer. I was knocked out.

When I woke up, I was still in the laboratory, but not on the table. I was inside a huge glass cylinder. I felt sick, but not as bad as I had before. I groaned, and then looked down at the cut on my arm. It was completely healed, and I couldn't believe it.

Then I realized what had happened to me. I stared down at where my legs had been. Now I didn't have legs – I had a tail! Ross had done what he'd said he could do. He'd made me into a mermaid. I had a tail, but not like a fish's. It was smooth and grey. I could move it and it seemed just like I'd always had it.

Then I saw that I was actually underwater, but I felt fine. I should have been drowning, but I wasn't. I felt perfectly normal. Ross was crazy and horrible, but he was right. I had been changed, made into something very new. I wasn't a normal person any more. I was the first mermaid.

Lucy looked around at the younger ones. 'And that's what he's done to you all,' she told them. 'You've all been through his laboratory and tank. You've all been given the powers to live and breathe and work underwater. We're all something new now. We're not human beings any longer. We're merpeople, something that's never existed before. I know Ross wants us to stay his slaves forever, but we'll get free some day. Then we can start a life for ourselves. Then we won't have to worry about being beaten, or hurt again. We can go somewhere where people will never find us, and we'll start a life together. We all love one another, and we'll take care of each other. One day, we'll be free. One day. I promise.'

She stared at them all, trusting and believing in her.

172

Even Joshua accepted what she said. And she was determined to make this promise of hers come true. One day they would be free, and they'd take care of one another.

Even if she didn't know how they could do it.

7

Grave Events

'To be perfectly frank, Doctor,' Fulbright declared, 'your story sounds utterly preposterous and like something that over-imaginative French author Jules Verne might have invented.'

'This is beyond anything that Verne might have imagined,' the Doctor snapped. 'Pass the kippers please, Doyle.'

Doyle complied, helping himself to more bacon. He was enjoying breakfast after the activities of the previous night. For one thing, he was glad to be still alive. 'I agree, Sir Edward,' he offered as he munched, 'it is a trifle difficult to accept, but – '

'A trifle?' Fulbright gave a sharp bark. 'It's completely impossible, man! Mermaids!'

'Did I mention that word?' asked the Doctor, annoyed. 'I simply said that there was a humanoid, sentient creature under the water last night. Plus, of course, the seal-like killers. I don't care what you want to call the creatures, but don't simply dismiss them out of hand.'

'After all, Sir Edward,' Doyle added, 'there's that poor boy-turned-hound in the shed out back. How difficult is it to accept a girl-turned-fish after that?'

'I only have the assertions of the Doctor and yourself that that monster was once a boy,' growled Fulbright. 'And frankly, at the moment I'd be inclined to doubt the pair of you if you told me the sun was going to rise again tomorrow morning.'

The Doctor glared at him, then speared his kipper. 'At least I know where we stand, then,' he commented. 'I take it that you are not willing to help me any longer.'

'I didn't say that,' Fulbright protested. 'But try and keep your requests rational.'

'Ah,' said the Doctor grimly, 'I should have known it: another rational man.' He made it sound like a swear-word.

There came a gentle knock at the dining room door, and one of the maids came in. 'Begging your pardon, Sir Edward,' she said meekly. 'I've been given a message for the Doctor.'

Fulbright grimaced. 'Then deliver it, Nan, and stop cluttering up the room.'

She curtsied. 'Miss Alice said to tell you that Miss Smith is awake and would like to see you at your convenience.'

The Doctor grinned. 'I see, Nan. And would those have been Miss Smith's words as well?'

Nan coloured. 'Umm . . . Not precisely, sir.'

'I imagine not,' the Doctor commented cheerfully. He nudged Doyle. 'Stop making such a pig of yourself and let's go and see Sarah, shall we?'

Doyle bolted the last of his bacon and took a quick swig of tea. 'By all means,' he agreed, patting his lips with the napkin. 'If you'll excuse us, Sir Edward?'

Fulbright waved dismissively. 'Out, out,' he growled. 'I've got some thinking to do.'

'Very wise,' the Doctor approved. He strode out of the dining room and followed Nan up the stairs to Sarah's room without pausing to check if Doyle was following. The maid tapped on the door, then opened it to let the men pass.

Sarah was sitting up in bed, her hand bandaged and her face scowling. It was clear that she didn't want to be there. Alice sat at the bedside, a grim expression on her face.

'Doctor,' Sarah started, but Alice broke in.

'Doctor, tell your friend that she must stay in bed and rest. She won't listen to me.'

The Doctor raised an eyebrow. 'And you think she listens to me either?' he asked. Then he smiled at Sarah. 'Try and be a good patient, please, Sarah Jane.'

Waving her bandaged hand, Sarah snapped, 'This is all that's wrong with me, and it'll heal just as well out of bed as in it.' She glared at Alice. 'Are you going to get me my dress, or do I have to walk around the house in my nightgown?'

Alice blushed, but didn't back down. 'You're an immoral girl, Sarah.'

There was no way that Sarah could scowl after a remark like that. She collapsed, laughing. 'If you'd seen some of the gear I wear,' she gasped, 'you'd be certain of that.'

'Why don't we compromise?' suggested Doyle. 'You stay in bed till lunchtime, then get up – but only if you promise to come back to bed if you don't feel well.'

Sighing, Sarah nodded. 'Deal,' she agreed. 'Now, will the pair of you tell us what's going on out in the bay? I gave Alice the gist of what I know, and neither of us is very enlightened.'

'I think she must have cracked her head, Doctor,' Alice explained. 'She claims that she was saved last night by a mermaid. And everyone knows that there are no such things.'

'Then everyone is wrong,' the Doctor replied. 'Because I caught a glimpse of one, too.' He looked vaguely puzzled. 'I'm not sure how it was created, but there definitely are mermaids living at the bottom of your garden, so to speak.'

176

'Told you so,' said Sarah smugly. She turned to the Doctor. 'Then what was it that attacked me?'

'There are two different kinds of creature down there,' he answered. 'The young – well, let's call her a mermaid for now, for want of a better word – is one, and that other creature looked more like some mutant seal.'

'Obviously the creature that killed old Ben Tolliver,' Doyle commented.

'Yes,' the Doctor agreed. 'Some kind of a guardian, I'd venture to say. It is supposed to kill or scare off anyone who gets too close to the lights we saw.' He slapped Doyle on the back. 'But you killed one, and its companion took it away to prevent us from getting a good look at it.'

'But it's got to be related to that hound in the out-house,' Sarah commented. 'Right?'

'Yes.' The Doctor frowned. 'It's certainly more than any seal born naturally on this world. The basic structure appeared to be a common grey seal, but it had been enhanced.'

Doyle nodded. 'You think, then, that it was another constructed beast, like that hound? A child mutated somehow into a seal?'

'Not exactly,' the Doctor answered. 'I think it was the other way around: a seal that had human characteristics like enhanced intelligence grafted onto it.'

Sarah was almost ahead of him. 'And that mermaid,' she said slowly. 'She was real, so she must have been a child merged somehow with a fish.'

'Not a fish,' the Doctor argued. 'More likely a dolphin or a porpoise. I only had a glimpse of the girl in poor light, but her tail was smooth, not scaled.' He snapped his fingers. 'Of course! Mammalian natures combined. Just like the boy and the dog.'

Doyle nodded. 'Something that occurs to me, Doctor,'

177

he offered, 'is that the *Hope* has plenty of mammalian matter aboard it in the form of whale and seal products. Perhaps Captain Gray's business with Breckinridge had something to do with those, do you think?'

'Right!' exclaimed Sarah. 'And Breckinridge is fascinated with the sea. Maybe he's behind these mermaids?'

'It's quite possible,' agreed the Doctor, holding up a hand. 'But this is mere supposition. We have no evidence linking him to the mermaids, do we?'

'We could get it,' said Sarah, 'if we sneak into the factory and have a good look-see.'

'Oh, no,' said Alice. 'You are staying here, Sarah.' She looked very crossly at the other woman. 'I can't follow everything that you've been saying, but this is obviously quite dangerous. It is no task for a woman.'

The Doctor grinned. 'She's right that it's dangerous, Sarah. You rest up, while Doyle and I check into it.' He winked at her. 'Maybe you could talk to Alice and explain a little about women's lib.'

'Darned right,' Sarah growled. 'If I have to stay here, I'm going to set her straight.'

'Women's lib?' asked Alice blankly.

The Doctor nudged Doyle. 'Come on,' he said. 'Want to wager that by the time we return Sarah will have turned the whole social order at the house upside down?'

'Good Lord!' exclaimed Doyle. 'She's not one of these militant females, is she?'

'Of course not,' the Doctor answered. 'Nothing that mild.'

The Doctor dismounted from the horse that Fulbright had loaned him before he reached Breckinridge's factory. Doyle, puzzled, reined in his own steed, but didn't dismount.

'We've still got a half mile or more to go, Doctor,' he said. 'Or were you planning a side trip?'

'Not exactly,' the Doctor answered. 'Just a thought that struck me.' He pointed ahead of them at the ugly brick building. 'That's Breckinridge's factory, right?'

'Indeed.'

The Doctor swung around about forty-five degrees until he was pointing out to sea. 'And that's the bay we were in last night, isn't it? I wonder if it's no more than coincidence that the factory overlooks the bay?' He rubbed his chin thoughtfully. 'I wonder if you can see the bay from the top floor of the factory? That's where Sarah said Breckinridge has his private retreat.'

Doyle shrugged. 'From the angle, I'd say it was quite likely. Why?'

'Because Breckinridge should have been able to see the wheel of light from up there, in that case. And yet he's never reported doing so. I wonder why?'

'Perhaps he never works late, Doctor,' suggested Doyle.

'He's a self-made man,' the Doctor snapped. 'You never get to be one unless you're prepared to work long hours. I think Sarah's right, and that he's mixed up in this affair somehow.'

Doyle frowned. 'Perhaps he is. Hadn't we better move on and see if we can get in to talk to him?'

'In a moment,' the Doctor answered. 'I was rather hoping that the boy hiding behind that tree over there would come out and talk to us before we left.'

'What?' Doyle stared at the trees, but could see nothing to indicate they were other than alone. 'Are you sure there's somebody there?'

'I'm sure.' The Doctor gave a large grin. 'Billy, isn't it?'

There was a stir of movement, then a thin, ragged boy stepped out from the trees. His face held a look a little way between annoyance and awe. 'How did ye know I was there?'

'It's my business to know things, Billy,' the Doctor replied evasively. 'How do you do. I'm the Doctor. I believe we have a mutual friend in Sarah Jane Smith.'

Doyle shook his head in amazement. 'Astounding, my dear Doctor.'

This was an opinion Billy evidently shared. He gave the Doctor a look of respect. 'Not many can spot me, mister. You be pretty clever.'

'Thank you, Billy. Now, did you just come here to tell me how brilliant I am, or do you have some news for me?'

The boy scowled slightly. 'It were for Miss Smith, really. But, seeing she ain't here, I suppose I could tell you. Early this morning, just after daybreak, there were a big wagon made a delivery at the factory.'

'That's hardly surprising,' Doyle commented. 'They must get supplies there all the time.'

The Doctor shook his head. 'Not that early,' he commented. 'The workers wouldn't have arrived. And it meant that the wagon must have been waiting nearby since yesterday to make a delivery at that time. It suggests they didn't want to be seen, doesn't it, Billy?'

'It do,' agreed Billy, smiling. 'And it weren't no supplies such as that factory needs.' He scuffed the dirt with his foot. 'I can't read, so I don't know what were in them, but it were barrels of some sort.'

'Excellent work, Billy,' the Doctor said approvingly. 'I doubt it was just floor polish, eh?' He took a shilling from his pocket and flipped it to the startled youth. 'Let me know if you hear or see anything further, will you?' Then he grinned at Doyle. 'This makes a foray into the factory more pressing, don't you think?'

Billy winked, and vanished into the woods again.

Doyle sighed and shook his head. 'This is all very peculiar,' he announced. 'I still don't comprehend it all.'

'Nor do I, yet,' admitted the Doctor, springing back up into the saddle. 'But some of the answers at least must lie within the factory. Come on. And follow my lead when we get there.' He urged on his steed and Doyle fell in behind him as they cantered the rest of the way to the factory gates.

As they approached, a rat-faced man jumped to his feet in the guard hut. 'Stay where you are!' he cried. 'There's no admittance.'

The Doctor glared down at him from his horse. 'Are you out of your mind, man?' he snapped. 'Didn't your master tell you to expect us?'

Rat-face looked surly and annoyed. 'I wasn't told to expect anybody.'

'Then someone has made a grave error,' the Doctor replied haughtily. 'We are with Lord Shaftesbury's committee. We have had reports that children are employed at this site, and are empowered to investigate and report on their working conditions. I am certain that Mister Breckinridge was notified of our arrival. Now let us in.'

The guard scowled. 'I wasn't told about no arrivals,' he replied sullenly. 'I can't let you in.'

'By thunder!' Doyle exclaimed, getting into the spirit of the masquerade. 'This is intolerable!'

'I'll say it is,' agreed the Doctor. 'Very well, we shall return with the local magistrate and a court order in fifteen minutes.' He glared at the guard. 'And the constable with a warrant for your arrest. Impeding an official enquiry is a serious charge. What's your name?'

Rat-face went pale. 'Here,' he protested weakly, 'there's no need for that.'

'Then announce us to Mister Breckinridge,' snapped the Doctor.

'I can't,' the guard answered. Before either visitor could protest, he added: 'Mister Breckinridge isn't here at the moment.'

'Then who is in charge, man?' demanded the Doctor.

'The factory manager, Mister Kinney,' the guard replied.

'Then we'll see him,' the Doctor said. 'Go and get him.' He leaned forward in the saddle. 'Now!'

The guard bolted across the open yard. Doyle moved slightly closer.

'Do you think this bluff will work?' he asked quietly.

'All the better for Breckinridge not being around,' the Doctor assured him. 'Flunkies are much easier to hood-wink than bosses. They're terrified of making mistakes that could get them fired later. Stay in character, and ask pertinent questions about the welfare of the child workers.'

The guard came rushing back, with a harried-looking man in tow. The newcomer appeared flustered and embarrassed. 'I'm Jack Kinney,' he said, panting slightly. 'I'm afraid Mister Breckinridge said nothing about any inspection.'

'That's not my fault,' the Doctor snapped. 'You'll have to do for now, I suppose. When will the owner be back?'

'Later today, sir,' Kinney answered, wringing his hands nervously together. 'I'm not certain precisely when. If you'd care to return then – '

'What?' Doyle thundered. 'And allow you the opportunity to cover up all your scandalous practices? Do you think we're feeble-minded, man?'

Kinney was practically wetting his trousers with fear. 'I assure you, there's nothing untoward happening here, and we have nothing to hide.'

'Then let us in,' the Doctor said coldly. 'We are the ones who will determine the truth of that, not you.' He dismounted and fished in his pocket. 'Here, you blithering idiot. My credentials. Don't you think to ask to see them?' He handed over a card and a bundle of papers through the gap in the gate.

Kinney took them as if they were booby-trapped. 'Ah . . .' he muttered, peering over the wad. 'Doctor John Smith of UNIT? I thought you said – '

'That I work at the moment for Lord Shaftesbury?' the Doctor snapped. 'I'm on loan as a specialist, man. Can't you see that for yourself? How can you be in charge of a factory when you can't even read plain English?'

Kinney, flustered, handed back the papers and card. 'Well, I expect it's all in order,' he agreed. To the guard, he said, 'Let them in, Raintree.' The guard, still scowling, unlocked the gate. The Doctor led his horse inside, followed by Doyle. The guard then ostentatiously locked the gate behind them. 'Now, what do you gentlemen need to see first?'

'Where, precisely, are the children employed?' asked Doyle. 'I must make a thorough inspection of their work area to ensure its compliance with all relevant legislation, you know.'

'Quite, quite,' agreed Kinney, wiping his hands on his trouser legs. 'Ah, over here, this way, this way.' He led his two difficult visitors on a whirlwind tour of the factory.

Doyle, quite relishing his role, really entered into the spirit of it, asking pointed questions and jotting down the replies in a small notepad. At one point he borrowed a tape measure, made several arcane determinations and scribbled down the results disapprovingly. Kinney was getting so agitated that he barely noticed that the Doctor was examining areas that were not included in the tour.

On the accounting floor, the Doctor suddenly barked, 'Where are the shipping logs? What chemicals do you use

183

here? Are any of them endangering the health of the children?' Kinney, white and trembling, pointed to the relevant accounting tomes. The Doctor scanned them and slammed them shut. 'And what's upstairs from here?' he growled.

'That's Mister Breckinridge's personal offices,' Kinney answered.

'Do any children work up there?' asked Doyle.

'None at all!' Kinney exclaimed. 'Nobody but Mister Breckinridge works there.'

'We'd like to see it to be certain of that,' snapped the Doctor.

'That's quite impossible,' the manager replied, shaking. 'Even I don't have a key to that floor. Only Mister Breckinridge does.'

'And he's conveniently absent,' growled Doyle. He made another mark in his book. 'This does not bode well, you know.'

'I think, in that case,' the Doctor announced haughtily, 'that we've seen all we care to for the moment.' He glared at Kinney. 'But tell your employer that we shall return tomorrow morning and expect to be met by him personally and shown around.' He leaned forward and said softly, 'And if there is any sign of alterations upstairs, we shall bring down the full force of the law on his – and your – head. Do you understand me?'

Kinney nodded until his head looked as if it would fall off. 'Oh, definitely. There'll be absolutely no problem, I'm certain of that.'

'There had better not be,' Doyle commented, closing his notepad with a snap and sliding it back into his pocket. 'I would hate to have to report further infractions.' Then he strode to the door, forcing Kinney to follow him. This allowed the Doctor a few seconds to scan the other open accounting books before following them.

184

As they left the factory and headed for the town, Doyle grinned at the Doctor. 'I was starting to rather enjoy the part,' he confessed. 'How did I do?'

'Rather admirably,' the Doctor replied. 'You distracted the poor chap perfectly, allowing me to make my own determinations.' His eyes sparkled. 'I am more convinced than ever that our missing friend Breckinridge is involved in this little business. Let's head along to the Pig and Thistle and grab a little lunch and liquid sustenance, and I'll tell you what I discovered.'

When they were suitably ensconced with a pint and a slice of pie, the Doctor started in on the food and his explanations. 'Young Billy was quite correct in his suspicions. There are signs of a burdened cart having arrived and departed this morning. About a dozen drums were unloaded and taken into one of the storage sheds.'

'You could tell that from the marks in the dirt?' asked Doyle. 'I saw no such drums in any of the sheds we examined.'

'They've been moved again already,' the Doctor answered. 'But there was the unmistakable scent of formaldehyde in the second shed we were shown.'

'And what possible use could that have for manufacturing wire?'

'None,' the Doctor said, grinning. 'But it's marvellous at preserving tissues, isn't it? There is something going on at that factory all right. And the shipping logs I examined don't have any entries concerning chemical deliveries.'

'Not entered yet, perhaps,' Doyle suggested, playing devil's advocate.

'Not even a shipping bill,' the Doctor replied. 'That delivery this morning didn't officially happen, which I find rather significant.'

'Then whatever answer there is to this mystery is to be found on the third floor?' asked Doyle eagerly.

'No.' The Doctor finished his pie, then looked up thoughtfully. 'Sarah's been shown that floor, and she didn't see anything significant. I suspect that the secrets are hidden below ground rather than above.'

'Below?'

The Doctor nodded. 'I was quite intrigued by the chips and grooves cut into the stone floor beside one of the lathes that doesn't appear to have been operated recently.'

Doyle's eyes lit up. 'Ah! You suspect a secret entrance to a cellar area.'

'I do indeed.' The Doctor grinned. 'I think Mister Breckinridge has a little more invested in the future of this village than he's let on to anyone.' He glanced around the half-empty pub. 'You know, this is rather a nice tavern, isn't it? I wonder if they have any rooms to let?'

Doyle frowned. 'I imagine so. Whatever for?'

'I'd like to stay in town this evening,' the Doctor replied. 'It'll be easier to slip into the factory that way.'

Doyle laughed. 'I like your manner of thinking, Doctor. I'm your man.'

'I rather thought I could rely on you to help.' The Doctor was abruptly serious. 'We may well be walking into grave danger, you know. These people would appear to have already killed to cover up their secrets. Do you possess a revolver? And would you be willing to use it if the need arises?'

'Yes and yes,' Doyle answered eagerly. 'I'm very keen to see this mystery through to the end.'

'Fine. Then you'd better settle matters with Captain Gray. I'll meet you back here at the stroke of midnight.' The Doctor stood up, and sang: 'Come, friends, who plough the sea / Truce to navigation / Take another station / Let's vary piracee / With a little burglaree!' With a grin, he added, 'Gilbert and Sullivan. Trust me, it'll be all the rage later this year.'

186

Doyle, puzzled, simply shook his head.

'I don't know how I let you talk me into doing this,' said Alice worriedly.

'Stop complaining,' Sarah answered as she saddled a horse. 'I thought you'd agreed that you had to know the truth about matters.'

'Yes,' agreed Alice, working on her own saddle. 'But going off alone like this – it could be very dangerous, you know.'

'Look,' said Sarah with a sigh, 'you can't hide behind men all your life, you know. Sometimes you've got to step out and face life full in the face. Otherwise what are you? A slave, a dish-rag or a wimp.'

'The Doctor will be annoyed,' Alice said, tightening the clinches. 'My father will be furious.'

'Let them be,' Sarah dismissed the problem. 'Look, if I'm right, we've got a good chance of getting a real lead on whoever's behind this whole plot. According to the Doctor, old Ben Tolliver was buried yesterday. Constable Faversham guarded the cemetery last night, but he can't pull night duty twice in a row. He has to sleep sometime. And the villains that nabbed Missus Bellaver's body took it on the second night last time. I'll bet that they'll try again tonight. All we have to do is follow them, then send for the authorities, who'll catch the gang red-handed. That's why I need a bit of help. I can't watch the crooks and go for help at the same time.' Her steed was ready, so she swung up into the saddle.

'I don't know that I'm up to this,' Alice confessed. 'I'm frightened.'

'You'd be daft if you weren't a bit scared.' Sarah patted her hand encouragingly. 'Honest, it won't be as bad as you think. And you'll be surpised how fast you can get used to this sort of escapade.'

'I'm sure you do it all the time,' agreed Alice, clambering onto her mount slowly. 'You're awfully brave, and I'm not.'

'It's just a matter of getting used to it,' Sarah assured her. 'Anything a man can do, a woman can do better. Believe me.'

'I'm starting to regret that I ever listened to you,' Alice commented.

Sarah grinned. 'Yeah, I know. I often wish I didn't listen to me, either. Let's get with the "Hi-ho, Silver" routine, shall we?'

'I'm afraid I don't understand you.'

'Let's ride.'

Ross examined the factory through his eyeglasses and then frowned down at Abercrombie. 'Eating again?' he chided. 'I'd ask where you got that sandwich, but I'm sure I probably don't want to hear the reply.'

'Likely not,' agreed his assistant, chomping down. 'It needs more bleeding chutney, mind you. Still, since I didn't pay for it, no sense in complaining.' He nodded his head toward the object of his boss's scrutiny. 'How's things?'

'Getting intriguing,' admitted Ross. He stroked his chin thoughtfully. 'The Doctor and his friends appear to have somehow survived their little expedition last night. He and that man Doyle have been in and out of the factory this morning. And I very much doubt that this will be their last planned excursion of the day.'

'Me too,' agreed Abercrombie, licking his fingers of the last drips of chutney. 'I had a few words with a barmaid named Jen. She says that the Doctor rented a room at the Pig for tonight.'

'For once, you seem to have been doing your job,' Ross commented. 'So it looks as if the Doctor plans to make an unheralded visit to the factory this evening. I think we'd better be prepared to intercept him, don't you?'

Abercrombie groaned. 'Have a heart,' he complained. 'I needs me beauty sleep.'

'Far be it from me to argue with that assessment of your looks,' Ross answered with a hint of a smile. 'But you'll have to catch up on it later. Tonight there will be plenty of work for you to do.'

'Bleeding hell,' muttered Abercrombie. 'All work and no play makes Jack a dull boy, as me mum used to say.'

'Then it's a good thing your name isn't Jack,' the colonel said. 'It isn't, is it?'

'You know it ain't.'

'Then stop complaining. Get a little rest now, so you'll be fresher tonight.'

Abercrombie just scowled and tried to settle down. It was clear he wasn't at all keen on roughing it. But it was equally apparent that Ross didn't care.

It was starting to get dark when Sarah and Alice arrived on the outskirts of Bodham. For the last fifteen minutes of the ride, Alice had been absolutely silent. Sarah glanced at her companion, seeing that the girl's hands were absolutely white, and that her pretty face was pinched and drawn. She started to feel guilty about what she'd put the girl through. It was hard for her to remember sometimes that not everyone was born brave.

'Listen, Alice,' she said, reining in her mount. 'I think you'd better go back home.'

'No, Sarah,' the other girl answered. Her voice was strained, and she was trying to put a brave face on it. 'I promised to help you, and I will not back down now.'

Sarah nodded. 'I know, but I bullied you into it. Look, I think you've done more than I should have asked. It's much harder for you to go through this than it is for me. We've had very different upbringings.' An idea struck her. 'Look, ride back to the Hall and make sure your father stays up for a few hours. Then tell him where I am and what I'm doing. If I read Sir Edward right, he'll insist on coming to my help with a rescue party. That way, if I get into trouble, he can help bail me out of it, can't he?'

'You think that's a good idea?' asked Alice eagerly.

Sarah could see that she was looking for an honourable way out of her dilemma. She really was terrified of spending the night in a cemetery, but she didn't want to let Sarah down. 'I'm sure it is,' she said gently.

'But what if you need help?'

'I'll get in touch with Billy, that boy I told you about,' Sarah replied. 'I'm sure one of the kids will be more than willing to bear messages for me. Someone will help me, I guarantee it.'

Alice hesitated, not wanting to look too eager to desert her friend. Then she nodded. 'You can count on me,' she vowed.

'I'm sure I can.' Sarah waved as Alice rode off. Then she sighed. 'Someone will help me,' she muttered to herself. 'Great line.'

'Luckily for you,' said a familiar voice, 'someone is more than willing to help out a maiden in distress.'

'Lord,' asked Sarah, her face turned toward the heavens. 'What have I ever done to deserve this?' Then she glared down at Kipling, who had crept out of hiding behind a wall to grin lecherously up at her. 'What happened to the other two Stooges?'

'McBee and Duns?' Kipling laughed. 'They were caught smoking behind the groundsman's sheds. They're in detention, silly buggers. But I'm here and eager to help.'

'Lucky me,' said Sarah with a sigh. Well, she supposed

it was her own fault. She had wanted to meet Kipling in the first place, hadn't she? And she could use someone to keep her awake and alert and to run for help if need be. 'Okay, you can come along. But you'd better behave. That means no lewd comments, understand?'

'Absolutely,' assured Kipling. 'The soul of honour, that's me.'

'Why do I find that so hard to believe?' asked Sarah, rolling her eyes. 'Don't answer that. And follow me.' She rode over to the Pig and Thistle, where she stabled her borrowed horse. Darkness was closing in on them now. Sarah took the dark lantern from her saddlebags and slipped it into one pocket of the jacket she wore. Then she led the way to the small graveyard.

As she'd expected, there was no sign of the portly Faversham. The poor, overworked man was probably at home right now, snoring his head off. She could sympathize with him. He had to be utterly out of his depth with the strange occurrences that were going on. On the other hand, she was right in her element here. In the failing light she examined the small burial ground. Tolliver had been buried near the entrance, in the poorer section of the cemetery. Several hundred yards further in, by one of the stone walls, there was a larger, more impressive monument. Some kind of a mausoleum, she assumed. She could barely make out the signs of a step well.

'Over there,' she decided. 'We'll be under cover, and we'll have a good view across at Tolliver's grave.' She grinned at Kipling. 'Not nervous, are you?'

'Me?' Kipling laughed scornfully. 'Not likely. But if you need a little comfort . . .'

'I won't,' Sarah assured him. 'Trust me on that one.'

Alice was feeling terrible as she rode back from Bodham. Despite everything, she was certain that she'd let Sarah down. This mission to get her father to help out was, she was certain, merely a sop to bolster her up. Sarah was doing all of the work and taking all of the risks, and she had done nothing but – what was that strange word that Sarah employed? – *wimp* out.

But she couldn't help herself. She was not by nature a brave person. The thought of spending the night in a graveyard, even with Sarah for company, terrified her. It was bad enough just thinking about being surrounded by mouldering corpses, but Sarah seemed to think there was a real chance of there being living people turning up, people that were desperate and despicable enough to rob the graves. She shuddered in horror at the idea.

This was not what she was supposed to do with her life. Her father had never intended that she should be adventurous. And she knew that Roger would have been appalled if he'd known what she had almost done. Roger loved her, of that she was certain, and he would always protect her. Even if he did seem to be a little odd when on the subject of that friend of his.

As if the thought of him had produced the reality, Edmund Ross stepped out suddenly into the road ahead of her, waving at her to stop. With a cry of shock, Alice reined in her steed. Ross marched over and grabbed the reins to prevent her from leaving.

'A little late to be out riding, isn't it?' he asked pleasantly.

'I'll do what I wish and when I wish it,' Alice replied, with as much courage and contempt in her voice as she could muster. 'I'll thank you to release those reins.'

Ross didn't remove his hands. 'Alice,' he said gently, 'there's no need to be so angry with me.'

'Is there not?' she asked him coldly. 'After what you did to me yesterday? Or is that of no consequence in your eyes?'

'You can hardly blame me for that,' Ross answered. 'You were trying to go through my luggage. The drug was merely a sleeping draught I use to protect my cases when I travel abroad. You'd be surprised how many foreigners have tried to rob me.'

'I find that a feeble excuse,' she snapped.

'Then I'll try and invent a better one,' Ross promised her. 'Please, Alice, don't be so harsh in judging me. I assure you that I bear neither you nor anyone dear to you any malice, nor intend to cause harm to them. But I have work to do, and that work must not suffer.'

'Work?' she asked, scornfully. 'Work that involves that thieving little friend of yours, no doubt.'

'Abercrombie, yes,' admitted Ross. 'I know he's not the most appealing person in the world, but he does have his good points.'

'Such as his skills at burglary?' suggested Alice, annoyed.

Ross didn't bother to deny her accusations. 'There are times when such skills do come in handy, yes.'

'At Fulbright Hall?'

Ross scowled. 'Alice, I resent the implication that I intend or intended to rob your family. Do you really think that little of me?'

'I don't know what to think of you!' she exclaimed, frustrated. 'You evade simple questions, you sneak about my home, and you ask me to trust you! How much of a fool do you think I am?'

'Obviously more of one than you may be,' he answered, equally annoyed. 'And not as great a fool as I am for thinking that you'd accept anything I had to say.'

She glared down at him. 'Then tell me what I want to know: what are you doing here, Edmund?'

He shook his head. 'I am not at liberty to tell anyone that right now. In a few days, perhaps, but not now.

There is too much happening, and too many people involved.' He sighed, and then looked up sharply. 'When you passed me earlier, Miss Smith was with you. Where is she now?'

'I don't see that that is any of your concern,' she replied imperiously. 'Let me pass.'

'She hasn't gone to the factory, has she?' he asked sharply.

Annoyed by his tone, Alice glared at him. 'I refuse to answer any more of your insufferably rude questions.'

Ross grimaced. 'I take it that means our enterprising friend is engaged in something most likely foolhardy and probably dangerous as well. Why won't any of you let well enough alone?'

'Why won't you let me alone?' cried Alice. In sudden rage she slapped at his hands. Startled, Ross allowed the reins to fall. Alice set her heels to her horse, and Ross barely had time to jump out of the way before the steed leapt past him and bore Alice away.

Ross was still staring ruefully after the vanishing horse and rider when Abercrombie emerged from the woods, a wide smirk on his face. 'Got a way with women, haven't you?' he asked slyly.

'Not one of my more useful traits, sadly,' Ross replied. 'Well, I think we may take it as read that Miss Smith has dealt herself a hand in this game. A pity. I was starting to like her.'

'So what does this mean for us?'

'It means that we'll be getting into the factory a trifle earlier than I had planned on.'

'Heigh-ho,' muttered Abercrombie. 'More bleeding work for me, that's what it means.'

Sarah found it difficult restraining her temper with Kipling. Not that he was exactly misbehaving, but he was trying to get as close to impropriety as he could without getting her completely furious. Now he was getting on her nerves by complaining about the darkness.

'If we had a light,' she hissed, 'then they'd be able to see us and wouldn't come, would they?'

'I know that,' Kipling agreed. 'But I resent being forced to act as a camping ground for so many dratted insects that can see me even in the night.'

Sarah was about to give him a sharp rejoinder when the nagging thought at the back of her mind finally crystallized. 'Light,' she muttered, smacking herself on the forehead. 'That's it.'

'That's what?' asked Kipling, puzzled.

'Last night I saw lights under the sea out there in the bay,' explained Sarah. 'At the time there was something that struck me as odd about them, but I couldn't place it. Now I have. What sort of lights will burn underwater?'

'I shouldn't think any would,' Kipling objected. 'The water would put them out. Unless they were covered with globes to prevent the water reaching them.'

'That's what I thought, too,' agreed Sarah. 'But wouldn't gas lights flicker? The ones I saw were quite even and steady, which suggests that they were electrical.'

Kipling frowned. 'I've heard about those devices,' he said, 'but there's none around here, are there?'

'Breckinridge has them installed in his factory,' Sarah told him.

'Ah!' Kipling caught on. 'So if there are lights under the bay, then they are most likely a part of his system.'

'Right,' agreed Sarah. 'Yet another probable connection between our friendly philanthrope and the mystery.'

'Evidence is absolutely piling up,' agreed Kipling. 'Why don't we just tell the police?'

'Because it's all circumstantial,' Sarah pointed out. 'There's nothing that definitely ties him to anything, much less to a crime. Even if those lights are his, there's no crime in lighting up the sea bed, is there?'

'But − ' Kipling started to say. Sarah suddenly clapped her hand over his mouth.

'Shush!' she hissed, and pointed through the darkness.

There was a movement by the far wall of the grave-yard, and the faintest of lights. It was sufficient to throw the strange shapes of decaying stones and figures into weird relief. Sarah shivered, partly from the cold. She wasn't superstitious, but after travelling with the Doctor for a while, you could never assume that even a graveyard was as still and safe as it appeared to be.

As they watched, a bulky figure slipped over the wall. The newcomer was carrying a dark lantern, slitted to allow only a tiny beam of light to escape. It sufficed to show his motion, but was not enough to allow Sarah to make out any details.

Kipling grinned excitedly. 'The grave-robbers!' he mouthed silently, and she nodded. At this time of the night, it certainly wasn't anyone taking a short-cut home through the graveyard on his way home from the pub.

The intruder moved slowly around among the tomb-stones, clearly looking for Tolliver's grave. Sarah watched intently, waiting to see what he would do. There was little doubt in her mind that they would have a longish wait while this person unearthed the casket, but it was exciting to see that she'd guessed correctly. Now they had a really good lead. All she had to do was follow him back to his base − she was certain it would be the factory − and then send Kipling to fetch help. The case would be sewn up, no thanks to the Doctor for once.

There was the faintest of sounds behind her. Belatedly she remembered that the Doctor had mentioned there being two grave robbers. As she turned, she caught a quick glimpse of a huge man towering over them. His upraised hands held a jar of some kind which he threw down at their feet. As Sarah started to rise, thick fumes enveloped her.

She gasped for breath as the fumes filled her lungs. She felt an icy chill, and then it was as if she were falling down an infinitely long tunnel into nothingness.

Explanations and Mutations

Billy was shaking with indecision as he saw the big man leaving the graveyard carrying two bodies. One of them was one of the three boys from the posh school. He couldn't care less about that little creep. But the other was Miss Smith, and she'd been fair and decent. For a second, as he hid behind the tree, Billy fingered his fish-gutting knife and considered the possibility of jumping out and plunging the blade into the big man's back. He knew, though, that it wouldn't be easy to make it a killing stroke in this light and with such a huge target – and that the man could move fast enough that he'd not have the chance for a second stroke.

Then the rat-faced man appeared beside his companion, and Billy dropped his plan of immediate attack. Instead, he decided, the best thing to do was to follow the men and see what they did with Miss Smith. He already knew that the Doctor was staying over at the Pig and Thistle. Once he was certain of the men's destination, he could call in help.

One thing he was certain of, even though he couldn't explain the conviction, was that the Doctor was the best possible person to have on his side in the looming battle.

Alice was almost shaking after her encounter with Ross. It was mostly anger, not fear. She couldn't believe the arrogance of the man. How could he demand so much and offer so little? And then appear to be annoyed with her simply because she refused to trust him? Hadn't he proven over and over again that any such trust would be sorely misplaced?

She couldn't understand how Roger could possibly be friends with the man, or fall for his claims. True, Ross was superficially charming, but what lay in his depths? But she knew that Roger was no fool, so what had possessed him to trust Ross? She simply couldn't work it out.

All she could do was to ride home and wait until near midnight, and then deliver the message she'd promised to her father.

He would know what to do. He always did.

Doyle had been unable to get any rest at all. He'd returned to the *Hope* to discover that Gray was firm about sailing the following forenoon. Uncertain whether or not he'd be finished with the mystery, Doyle had packed his few personal items and moved over to the tavern for the night. There he'd attempted to get some sleep, since it was likely to be a long evening. But rest had eluded him; excitement burned inside, and his mind was in a whirl.

He was still unable to make out too much of the mystery. The best he could say was that at least the various puzzles seemed linked by the factory. But how they could be linked was still way beyond his imagination. Maybe he'd be better off giving up the idea of becoming a writer. If he couldn't even make out the threads of reality, how could he ever hope to invent any?

Finally, at a little after ten, he gave up all attempts at resting and elected to take a stroll outside to clear his head. It was a bright but cold night, with the ever-present wind whipping up leaves and trash in the streets. The town was quietening down, with the patrons of the Pig and Thistle having left for home earlier. The fishermen were at sea and their families abed. He seemed to be the only one on the quiet streets.

Then he heard the pattering sound of bare feet on the cobbles, and around the corner flew a scarecrow of a boy. Doyle recognized him instantly.

'Billy!' he exclaimed. 'Whatever is the matter?'

The youngster skidded to a halt, looking at him warily before his identity penetrated. 'Oh, it's you,' he said, relieved. 'Quick, we got to warn the Doctor!'

'Warn him about what?' asked Doyle, alarmed.

'His friend – she were in the graveyard. Two men've took her to the factory.'

'Good Lord!' Doyle was shocked. 'She was supposed to be recuperating at Fulbright Hall. What the dickens was she thinking of? Still, no time to worry about that now.' He thought fast. 'Billy, are there any of your irregular friends you can rouse?'

'Aye,' the boy agreed, puzzled.

'If there's one who can ride a horse, the Doctor has one stabled here at the tavern. Send a message to Sir Alexander Cromwell and tell him what's happened. He'll have to organize the forces of the law.'

'Aye. What about the Doctor?'

'I'll rouse him myself.' Doyle gave him an encouraging smile. 'We were going to go to the factory tonight anyway. The game has just become a trifle more urgent, that's all. On your way, Billy.'

'Righto, sir.' Billy saluted in a ragged fashion and then ran off.

Excitement glowed within Doyle as he ran back inside the tavern and up the stairs to the Doctor's room. He hammered on the door and called his friend's name. A moment later the Doctor threw open the door.

'Whatever is the matter?' he growled.

Doyle was pleased to see the man was fully dressed and pulling on his deerstalker. 'It's Miss Smith,' he gasped. 'She's been taken by two ruffians to the factory. She was in the graveyard, apparently. And you told her to stay at the Hall!'

'Sarah never does what she's told,' complained the Doctor. 'She's almost as bad as me in that respect. Right, let's go.' He hurried past Doyle and down the stairs. The medical man whirled around and followed him.

'What was she thinking of?' complained Doyle as they came out into the street. He fingered the revolver he carried in his pocket, a trusty Adams .450 that constantly threatened to fall to the ground as he hurried to keep up with the Doctor.

'She realized that there was a good chance of the grave-robbers striking again,' the Doctor snapped. 'She must have been waiting for them and been captured.'

'Oh.' Doyle considered this a moment. 'Didn't you think there was a chance of them striking?'

'Of course I did,' the Doctor growled. 'That's why I left them to it. I figured that if they stole the body, we'd discover it at the factory when we arrived. That way there would be clear and conspicuous grounds for the arrests of all concerned. As usual, Sarah's jumped the gun and landed us all in serious trouble.'

It was beginning to dawn on Doyle how little he'd anticipated the Doctor's complex planning. 'It was a smart idea,' he approved.

'And now wasted,' the Doctor complained. He gestured ahead. 'There's the factory now.'

'Right.' Doyle drew his revolver. 'Do we storm the walls, break down the gate or what?'

'I'll go for the what,' the Doctor replied softly. 'We aren't the first people to arrive here tonight. Unless I'm very much mistaken, there goes a man I'm eager to have more than a few words with. Quickly, follow me, but don't shoot or make any untoward noise!'

He sprang forward, like a leopard after a gazelle. Doyle struggled to keep up with him as he dashed through the few remaining dark streets after the shadowy figures ahead of them. He and the Doctor were almost upon the two men when the leader whirled about with an exclamation. He lowered a walking stick as he saw who it was.

'Doctor!' exclaimed Colonel Ross, startled. 'I was not expecting you quite yet.'

'I didn't think you were,' the Doctor growled, coming to a halt a few feet from him and Abercrombie. The tubbier man looked shocked and worried. 'But it was a smart move to hold off using that air rifle of yours. As it is, you're a sight too free with it for my liking.'

'I had no option,' Ross protested.

'There are always options,' the Doctor snapped. 'But what I want right now are some explanations. You've played the man of mystery long enough.'

'Doctor,' exclaimed Doyle, gasping to catch his breath after their sprint, 'can't this wait until later? Miss Smith could be in grave danger inside there.'

'Nothing that a few moments now will affect,' the Doctor answered. 'And Colonel Ross's information may aid us considerably once we penetrate that lair.' He turned back to the man again. 'What have you been hiding? Aside from that scoundrel Breckinridge, who did you expect to find in there tonight?'

Ross hesitated, his face troubled. Finally he seemed to realize that he had no way out of this situation other than to provide the Doctor with what he wished to know. With a deep sigh, he admitted: 'My brother.'

A putrid stench in her nostrils shocked Sarah back to awareness. Gagging, she struggled to move her hands to cover her mouth, but was not able. As she coughed and choked, her mind started to focus once again. As she began to become aware of her surroundings, she wished she were still unconscious. 'Take it away,' she gasped, and the offensive odour was finally capped.

'Back in the land of the living, are we?' asked a cheery voice. 'At least for the time being, that is.'

Sarah struggled to free both her mind and body, but only the former worked. Her vision sharpened and she could make out only too clearly where she was. It had to be some kind of a laboratory, hewn out of base rock. Presumably deep underground, since there were signs of moisture on the wall and a constant dripping noise in the background. The air had that stale taste of caves or of old, musty books. The room was roughly twenty feet across in both directions and about ten high, but it was unfinished and none of the walls were terribly smooth. The floor, as a contrast, was almost polished to a shine. Though electric lights were scattered about the chamber at irregular intervals, the place was still dark and creepy.

That was without including the other trappings that made it even creepier.

She managed to straighten herself up, finding there was floor beneath her unsteady feet. Her hands were manacled together above her head, above a pipeline that had supported her while she was out. The circulation in her hands was barely adequate, but she doubted that an appeal for freedom would cut any ice around here.

The pipe she was chained over was one of about a dozen leading from the uncertain realms behind her into this room. Most of them led into a series of large glass tanks, but three of them led into a huge glass cylinder that stood in splendid isolation opposite her. The lights seemed to be concentrated about this tank, which was about five feet across and stretched almost to the ceiling.

A thick, bluish liquid filled the column almost to the top. Bubbles gently stirred the liquid.

Inside the glass cylinder was a mermaid.

Well, no, not exactly. It was male, for one thing, that much was clear. A young boy by the look of him, with curly black hair and haunted eyes. There were what looked like gill slits in the side of his neck which pulsed regularly, issuing some of the tiny streams of bubbles that rose within the column. The hands appeared webbed, the muscles of the shoulder abnormally strong.

From the waist down, any resemblance to a human being ceased. The skin there was greyer, and the legs fused to make a longer body that ended in a tail that gently thrashed from side to side, enabling the merperson to maintain a constant position in the tube.

Sarah was enthralled and sickened by the sight.

When she could drag her eyes away from the creature, she swept them quickly over the rest of the room. Stacked along one wall were open vats of chemicals. In the center of the room was a large pit. Within the pit and rising to about four feet above the hole was a large metal vat. Within it was some kind of gurgling, bubbling mess. It had the appearance of hand cream, but one that was pallid and unsettled, moving and venting constantly.

There were about a dozen tanks in the room that contained various forms of aquatic life. Sarah recognized a baby seal mewling in one tank. Another contained a dolphin that looked rather the worse for wear. Several others gave off the pungent aroma of formaldehyde and contained various organs and portions of internal anatomy.

There was one person in the room with her, regarding her with a mixture of amusement and interest. He was a tall, slightly chubby man with dark hair untidily brushed. He had piercing blue eyes and an almost cherubic face.

'I'd ask you to explain that comment,' Sarah finally answered him, her voice thick and still speckled with pain. 'But I doubt I'd like the explanation.'

'Probably not,' the man agreed readily. 'Dear me, Miss Smith, your inquisitive nature has really caused you trouble this time, hasn't it?'

'Oh, I'd say it was about par for the course,' she replied. The strength was returning to her tired muscles now. If she could just keep this man talking long . . . What? Maybe she could break the handcuffs with a mighty tug? Fat chance. She wondered what the time was, and whether Alice had managed to convince her father of the need for action. If she stalled long enough, maybe help could arrive. Besides that, there was always the Doctor. Sarah doubted he'd be too far away once the action began. But would he be close enough to do her any good? 'Speaking of which, just what is the course?'

Her captor gave her another of his happily innocent smiles. 'Miss Smith, you have a terrible habit of wanting answers to questions you shouldn't even be thinking about in the first place. Haven't you ever heard the old saying about a little knowledge being dangerous to your health?'

Sarah grunted. ' "If a little knowledge is dangerous",' she quoted, ' "where is the man who has so much as to be out of danger?" ' She gave him a thin smile. 'Thomas Henry Huxley.'

'Oh, very good!' the man approved. 'You have quite a wit about you.' He shrugged. 'Of course, it is about all you do have about you. And, speaking of danger, you are in it, and I am not. I suppose that makes me the man that you refer to.'

'And what makes you think I'm in danger and you aren't?' asked Sarah, putting on the most innocent expression she could muster. She didn't really expect it to fool him for a second, so she wasn't too disappointed when he laughed at her.

'Oh, you really are something special!' He shook his head sadly. 'Miss Smith – may I call you Sarah? "Miss Smith" sounds so formal.'

'Oh, by all means, let's dispense with formality,' Sarah answered. 'I'm not one to stand on etiquette. A step-ladder, maybe, but not etiquette. And what do I call you – that's polite in mixed company?'

'My name is Ross, Sarah.'

'Ross?' She narrowed her eyes and peered hard at him. 'You wouldn't happen to be related to a Colonel Edmund Ross, would you?'

'He is my brother.'

'Ah.' Some of this was starting to make a strange kind of sense to her now. 'And what do your friends call you? Assuming you have any, that is.'

'All men have friends, Sarah. Mister Breckinridge, for example, is a very good friend of mine. I allow him to call me Percival.' He smiled at her. 'I imagine I could extend that courtesy to you, too, while you are still with us.'

'Charmed,' Sarah replied. 'I'd shake hands, but it's a trifle difficult right at the moment.' She studied her captor with interest. This was definitely a man whose elevator didn't go all the way to the top floor. 'Percival, what are you up to here?'

'My, my, my,' he chided. 'Curiosity killed the cat, Sarah. And I'm afraid it's going to kill you, too.'

'Can we drop the corny literary allusions?' Sarah begged him. 'If you intend to kill me, where's the harm in telling me what I've got to die for?'

Ross shrugged. 'Why not? Immediately, you have to die because I sent those two blockheads after a dead body and they brought me back two live ones instead.'

Well, that was something. 'Kipling's still with us, I take it,' Sarah asked.

'For the time being, yes.' Ross gestured to the large cylinder at the end of the room. 'As soon as that chamber has been vacated, he'll probably end up in there. I'm not entirely certain that the process will work on someone who has so evidently passed the point of puberty as Master Kipling, but if it kills him then it saves me the bother of having to see to the task personally. And if it doesn't kill him, we'll have another worker.' He patted her gently on the arm. 'You, my dear, are obviously considerably past the age of puberty yourself. The process would definitely kill you – which is, I'm sad to report, your fate anyway. But it would also damage your internal organs, which would be a terrible waste.'

Sarah's mouth was definitely on the desert side of dry right now. 'Yes,' she agreed, trying to sound flippant. 'I'd hate to see my organs go to waste. You know what they say about a mind being a terrible thing to waste.'

Ross laughed, genuinely amused. 'Oh, you are a one, Sarah. It's a shame that you'll be staying with me, albeit in a number of small containers. I really would have liked the chance to spar with you a little more.'

'Well, you can't have everything,' Sarah managed to joke. 'You may have my body, but you'll never have my mind. Unless you intend to pickle that, too.' She was trying very hard to avoid thinking about his promises. 'But aside from the fascination of taking my liver out on a date, why do you want my body parts so badly, Percival?'

'For my work, Sarah,' Ross explained. He gestured toward the cylinder and the merboy within. 'As you can see, I've managed to create my own rather unique lifeforms. I believe you came face to face with a number of my creations over the past few days?'

'Yes.' She shuddered. 'Mutant hounds, killer seals and a rather pretty young mermaid.'

'The tip of the iceberg,' he assured her. 'Here in this laboratory, I have the means to achieve fusion of different animal species, combining their traits to form prototypical creatures that before now existed only in the imagination. Thanks to me, mermaids do exist.'

Sarah shook her head. 'I can't quite bring myself to believe this is just a hobby for you,' she said. 'I mean, most people just take up collecting butterflies or stamps for a pastime. Are you just doing all this because you can?'

Ross looked shocked. 'Sarah,' he chided, 'how petty you must think I am! Though I must admit that part of this is merely the desire to see what limits I can break. But my experiments do have a noble end: I am creating separate species of human beings that will take mankind beyond the oldest boundaries imposed on our species. My merfolk are the first – if we don't include that dreadful hound-boy, which was unplanned – but I hope to create more very shortly.' He waved his hands in the air like a comic-opera sorcerer. 'Imagine crossing human beings with cheetahs, for example, and creating a race with the endurance and cunning and prowess of the major cats. What warriors and athletes they might become! Or taking a simple bat and making from it winged beings that could ride the air currents and really fly! Isn't that a project worthy of great imagination?'

'It's certainly great something,' agreed Sarah. 'B.S., mostly. You can't be serious.'

He glared at her, his good humour vanishing in an instant. 'How can you say that after what you've witnessed?' he asked. 'My powers are quite real. The merfolk are alive, their bodies stable, and they are viable. Do you understand what that means?'

'Yes,' agreed Sarah, impressed despite herself. 'That they can have children when they mature. And that they will breed true.'

'Precisely. They can breed true. If I were to step aside now, the merfolk would continue to live and grow. I have done what no man has ever done before: I have created a new breed, a new genus, as my legacy. I have achieved what nobody has even dreamed of before – least of all that obnoxious, overbearing older brother of mine!'

'I suppose it's partly my fault from the beginning,' Colonel Ross admitted. 'Everything Percival has ever done in his miserable life was an attempt to either prove that he was better than me or else to try and hurt me for being what I am.'

'And what are you?' asked the Doctor carefully. 'If you're merely a military man, I'm a humbug. You remind me a little of a Brigadier chappie I know.'

Ross sighed. 'I've been attempting to avoid answering that question since I arrived here, Doctor. But in the interests that seem to have linked us, I have little choice left to me now, do I?'

'None at all,' the Doctor replied cheerfully. 'If I don't like or don't believe your replies, Doyle and I will truss the two of you up here and mark you "Do Not Open Till Christmas".'

Doyle privately wasn't sure that the Doctor's threat could be carried out quite that simply, but it appeared that Ross had already made his decision anyway.

'I am a special agent working directly under the command and authority of Her Majesty Queen Victoria,' he answered. 'It is my job to investigate those matters that lie outside of the conventional. Since the reports were first received about a monster hound on the loose on the moors down here, I've been working to track down the guilty parties.'

Doyle's eyes went wide. 'You can prove that claim, I take it?'

'Don't be an idiot, man,' replied Ross, his voice edged with weariness. 'In this line of work, how long do you think I'd last if I carried papers that proved I was under explicit orders of the Queen herself? Quite frequently I have to operate outside of both the law and this country.' He nodded at the Doctor. 'I think your friend knows I'm telling the truth.'

'I'm inclined to believe most of what you said,' the Doctor agreed. 'As I say, you have the same manner as the Brigadier about you.'

'Brigadier?' asked Doyle, out of his depth. 'What brigadier?'

'I'll explain later,' replied the Doctor. To Ross, he added, 'But I don't believe that shooting the hound was under explicit orders from anyone. There was no need to kill the poor creature.'

Ross shook his head. 'Doctor, you do not seem to understand what my brother is capable of. I am attempting to eradicate every last foul deed he has perpetrated.'

'Are you indeed?' asked the Doctor coldly. 'Well, let me give you fair warning, Colonel: if you attempt to eradicate a single one of those merpeople he has somehow managed to create, I shall take great delight in feeding you to his seals piece by bloody piece. Do I make myself perfectly clear?'

'Indubitably.'

'Good. I'm so glad we understand one another.' The Doctor abruptly smiled. 'Aside from those misguided attempts to cover your brother's tracks, you seem to be a reasonably decent sort of chappie.'

'Well, I'm still considerably in the dark here,' Doyle

protested. 'What has looking for your brother and his manufactured monstrosities got to do with staying at Fulbright Hall? The whole family seems convinced you were planning to loot the blasted place.'

Ross shrugged. 'A misunderstanding. Alice overheard me giving instructions to Abercrombie, and managed to misinterpret them. True, Abercrombie is a thief and a scoundrel, but in this line of work, it would be difficult to find a better partner.'

'Thanks a lot,' muttered Abercrombie. 'Talk about being damned with faint praise.'

'But what were you doing at the Hall?' persisted Doyle.

'I first latched onto these experiments of my brother's in London,' Ross explained. 'There he had set up an inhuman laboratory to experiment upon living creatures. He's long been fascinated with the concept of improving on the works of Nature. He read Darwin's *On The Origin Of Species* while in college, and decided that natural selection was an inefficient means of advancing change.'

'So he's elected to try unnatural selection,' muttered the Doctor.

'Precisely.'

'But how does he achieve this?' mused the Doctor. 'Technology on the Earth in this time period is certainly not up to anything on the order of change that he's managed. What is he doing?'

'I really have no idea how he works the technique,' admitted Ross with a shrug. 'Science is a background study for me. I know enough to get by on my missions, but little more. Percival is, in fact, the genius where that is concerned.'

'Genius my foot,' snapped the Doctor. 'What he's doing is beyond impossible.' He sighed. 'I suppose I shall have to ask him his laboratory methods myself. What else?'

'Well, his experiments cost a great deal of money,' explained Ross, 'and he was financing some from the proceeds of — ah, the production of extremely fine replications of the official currency.'

'Printed his own,' Abercrombie put in helpfully. 'Damned good queer it was, too.'

'Quite,' agreed Ross dryly. 'Well, we destroyed his presses, but by the time I was certain that was done, he had fled. I had seen his first experiment, that poor unfortunate hound, and when the reports of a gigantic beast on the loose reached me, I knew it had to mean that Percival had begun work again in this vicinity. The problem was deciding where.

'Since he needed a good deal of cash for his work, and there was no chance he could be printing it this soon, I knew he must have found someone to back his schemes. The only two people in this area with sufficient wealth were either Sir Edward Fulbright or Breckinridge.'

'Ah!' Doyle exclaimed with satisfaction. 'And you chose to investigate Sir Edward first.'

'Precisely. A foolish error, which has caused a good deal of trouble and inconvenience for me.'

'But why him?' asked Doyle. 'Surely Breckinridge was the most likely suspect?'

'Yes,' admitted Ross. 'And to my mind that made him less likely. You see, Percival employed a pair of assistants in London named Raintree and Brogan. Both men are currently employed as security officials at Breckinridge's factory. I reasoned that Percival planted them there as bait to lure me from the correct scent, since it was otherwise ludicrously obvious where he was.'

The Doctor couldn't restrain his laughter any longer. 'Oh, wonderful,' he said between gasps. 'Your devious little mind overlooked the obvious because it was obvious. I'll bet your brother is chuckling about that still.'

'He probably is,' agreed Ross shamefacedly. 'There was another reason, also. I could gain simple entry to Fulbright Hall because my old college chum Roger Bridewell had become engaged to Sir Edward's only daughter. I told him enough of my suspicions to make him willing to do anything to clear the suspicions against his future in-laws, so he managed to get me invited to the Hall. I'll admit that I was not the most popular guest they've ever entertained, but I did manage to confirm that Sir Edward was innocent of involvement. That left only Breckinridge.'

'And so you elected to break in here tonight to check on your suspicions,' the Doctor finished for him.

'Yes. I realized that you were going to come here eventually. I had to beat you to the mark, I knew, but you seem to have anticipated my moves.'

The Doctor grinned. 'Sheer dumb luck, if that's any consolation,' he admitted cheerfully. 'I had planned to be here later, but Sarah has managed to force my hand.'

'Sarah?' Ross frowned. 'What has she done?'

'Managed to get herself captured by your brother, at a guess,' the Doctor answered.

Ross went white. 'Then we had better end this conversation and get inside fast,' he said. 'My brother needs three things for his experiments: young children, who become the victims of his changes; animals, from which he makes the extracts to affect those changes; and third, he needs fresh corpses, from which he extracts human elements. These he uses on living animals, giving them humanoid speed and wits. I fear that Sarah is about to become the late Miss Smith – and that shortly afterwards, various portions of her will find their way into various other species of creatures.'

Interlude 3

Ross

'Have you ever been to Limehouse, Sarah?' asked Percival Ross.

'No more than I've been forced to,' she admitted.

'Understandable.' He seemed almost adrift in the sea of his memories. 'I always found it a loathsome place. Its name comes from the lime kilns that burn there, and you can really have no idea what a dreadful stench they produce. And the whores that patrol the streets there – painted Jezebels whose faces would fall apart if they washed off the layers of make-up they wear. And men who seem to be engaged in discovering the limits of human endurance when it comes to preserving their livers in alcohol. A disgusting place, the cesspit of the planet. I was there for three years.'

Sarah managed a cheeky smile. 'You can always tell a man by the company he keeps,' she quipped.

'Most droll,' Ross answered. 'I had little option, though. I needed a place where I could procure subjects for my experiments without too many questions, and a place to dispose of my failures without arousing too much concern. I founded what I liked to call a Charity Hospital – though the patients mainly contributed to me through their deaths. I used this as a cover for my experiments and probed the vast unknown areas of evolution, without notable success. Until, one day, the answer came to me in a flash.'

'Take up gardening instead?' suggested Sarah.

'No, I speak of a literal flash, Sarah.' He smiled at her. 'A star fell on Limehouse. The locals called on me, since they were terrified that the heavens were visiting divine vengeance on them. If God Almighty had done so, I wouldn't have been too surprised, but it was nothing quite like that . . .'

As my carriage arrived at the place where the so-called star had fallen, I immediately realized that I was in the presence of something from vastly outside my limited sphere. The star had descended amidst some old warehouses that had been abandoned down by the river. Flames illuminated the night, burning with preternatural splendour and defying all efforts by the terrified residents to douse them. The women were gone and the men were panicking. They were ready to believe that the flames were the product of Old Nick himself, I think. Several wounded people had crawled out of the area, where vagabonds spent their miserable nights waiting for the dawn of bleak days.

It fascinated me, because I had never seen anything quite like this before. Despite the fears of the locals, I could see that what I was confronted by was certainly not celestial in nature – at least, not in the sense of the word that they chose. But there was something inside the broken buildings that lived, because I could hear a strange screaming. It was a little like the cry that an animal in mortal pain makes shortly before it expires, a sound I've heard many times in the past.

Steeling myself, I walked carefully into the damaged area. Fires burnt all about me, consuming even the bricks themselves. Yet there was surprisingly little physical heat, and I possessed barely more than a faint sheen on my skin as I entered the area. The greenish glow of the flames made everything appear supernatural, but I felt that at the heart of this mystery lurked something considerably more mundane.

I was, in fact, utterly wrong. Oh, I admit it freely: I was out of my depth at the start. I came across shattered and blazing chunks of metallic substances, and strange, broken instrumentation of a kind and order that I could not even begin to comprehend. It started to dawn upon me that I was in the presence of some kind of transportation device. A flying cab, if you like. It had suffered some calamity and come crashing down to the Earth. I realized that I was dealing with neither demon nor angel, then, for neither such creature could require a conveyance to move across the heavens. Excitement mounted within me as I pressed forward.

In the centre of the area of destruction lay the core of this conveyance. It had once been large and circular, like a flying dish of some sort. Little of the outer shell was intact, however. That was clearly the source of the strange metals and instruments that blazed about me. The interior of the craft had suffered no less damage, but it was still in one piece. After a moment in which I fought off the noxious smoke fumes from the craft, I began to make sense of what I was witnessing.

Do you recall the line from the Book of Revelations: 'There was war in Heaven'? The evidence that this was true lay before me. The star cab that lay there had been damaged in some great battle fought way above our world. In its death-throes it had crashed to the Earth and lay there before me, burning with a strange fire. There had been a war and here was the loser, a broken conveyance, along with its expiring driver.

I had never seen any creature like this before. It resembled a jellyfish somewhat, being almost shapeless and gelatinous, but it was far too large for any such beast.

216

It was some four feet across, and the source of the screaming sound I had followed to this spot. That this was no mere animal was apparent, because it was as burnt and damaged as the cab itself, yet it was moving with volition and purpose. Its – not skin, but whatever held the being together – was blackened from the crash, and it had to be in grave pain. Yet it had somehow formed a portion of its body into some kind of tentacle, and it was tearing apart a portion of its craft in search of something it desired badly.

This monster had no eyes, and yet it seemed to sense me nonetheless. I cannot say that it turned, but somehow I knew that its attention was focused on me now, while it had not been aware of me before. The tentacle that it had been using wavered, and then gestured toward a portion of the craft as yet untouched by the fires.

I was torn by indecision. This hideous creature was obviously asking me to risk my life to get it something from the craft. I saw no need to endanger myself to do anything for a being so repulsive. Then again, had the creature been the archangel Michael himself and asking the same thing, I'd have been as little inclined to aid him. The only thing that prevented me from leaving the thing to die was a single thought: if, in its dying moments, the being desired something brought to it from its ship, it must be something of immense value.

In which case, I could use it better.

Protecting myself as best I could from the flames, I plunged into the wreckage. The vile creature had indicated some kind of a cupboard inside its conveyance. I wouldn't have known how to open it, so I was fortunate that it had sprung apart in the crash. Inside the compartments was a single container. This was obviously what the being desired, so I snatched it up and fled the star cab. Behind me, as I ran, the flames engulfed the craft, and explosions began to rack the area.

The foul creature attempted to make me stop as I rushed past it. Somehow it extruded a tentacle in my direction. I succeeded in evading its foul grip and made my way out of the blazing warehouse. Behind me the shattered roof collapsed and the horrendous screams of the dying creature were cut off at last. I brushed past the spectators and hurried back to my laboratory with my treasure, still uncertain of what I had found. Yet it had come from a craft that had never been constructed by human hands. Whatever I had salvaged, I reasoned, must be worth a fortune if I could only deduce its purpose.

In the safety and peace of my laboratory I opened the container, to discover it filled with a gooey semi-liquid. At first I couldn't comprehend what it was, and then it finally came to me in a moment of inspiration: this was some kind of healing gel for the dying creature. It had wished to cover the burnt sections of its skin with this material. I had suffered a number of small burns in the fire, and so I hesitantly applied a small amount of the gel to my skin. I knew that I could be making a terrible mistake: the creature had not been human by any stretch of the imagination, and perhaps its metabolism was vastly different from my own. What might cure the shapeless creature might serve only to kill me. But I had to know the answer.

It came within seconds, as the burns healed over, leaving pinkish, fresh skin in their wake. I could hardly believe my luck! This was some kind of miracle cure-all, it seemed. But I needed to do further experimentation to see what its limits were.

As I mentioned, I was working in the area under the guise of a Mercy Hospital. One of the patients that had been brought to me was a young boy who had been bitten by a hydrophobic dog. There had never been any chance that he would recover, but I was fascinated to study the effects that rabies had on his body as he slowly died. Now a thought came to me: no matter what effect the cream I now possessed had, it could hardly do more than kill the boy, which the rabies was already well in the course of achieving. So I applied some of the salve to the bitten areas, and waited to see what would occur.

Within hours I was witness to the most astounding of changes. The symptoms of the disease had vanished almost entirely, and he appeared to be recovering well. I had visions of being the first man to announce a cure for rabies – which would surely have brought me fame and fortune, towards neither of which am I averse. However, as I watched, something even more astounding began to take place. The boy, I realized, was growing hair on his exposed skin. Now this was a boy of perhaps ten years of age, no more. How could this be happening? As I watched, his body became more and more distorted, and I realized that he was gradually taking on the characteristics of a dog, which were becoming admixed with his human characteristics.

This was utterly unforeseen and unheard of. I knew that I was on the verge of the major discovery of my life here. The gelatinous mess was somehow fusing the boy's human characteristics to those of a canine!

You can imagine how excited this made me. I stayed up three days in a row, watching and waiting to see and record every small change, to note every detail. It was fascinating, watching this gel change the boy into a viable hybrid. It had somehow picked up on the canine elements present in the boy's wounds and fused them into his own structure. As I watched, I puzzled over how this could have come about. Then, finally, I realized that the gel was more than simply some kind of healing cream for that unearthly creature that had perished in the blaze. I had noted that the being had possessed a kind of amorphous structure. Presumably on the cellular level, the creature had been similarly uncertain. The salve, in order to heal, must have therefore needed to somehow analyse what was to be repaired and then accomplish the deed.

Naturally, when I had applied it to myself, it had healed me with no strange effects. But when the boy's bodily structure had been invaded by the cells of the rabid dog, the salve had then latched onto both patterns and somehow fused them into a single viable entity. It was staggering – the mechanism I had sought had been literally delivered into my hands from the sky!

As I watched, I worked feverishly. I had a good supply of the salve, but it would hardly last forever. I experimented in various ways, and finally came up with a method that enabled me to reproduce the gel if I supplied it with the raw elements it needed to reproduce itself. This left me with a self-regenerating supply of the gel, which now rests in the large vat within my current laboratory.

I was forced to flee London in somewhat hurried circumstances before my researches were quite concluded. I did bring with me the vat of gel and my hound-boy. On the way here, however, the hybrid managed to escape the carriage bearing it, and roamed free on the moors until it was slain a few nights ago. I didn't really care whether it lived or died, for my studies of the beast had enabled me to formulate my plans, and to work on achieving my goal.

Financed by Breckinridge, this laboratory area was hollowed out of old caves in the rocky cliffs and connected to his factory above. Here I was able to plan my next step: the creation not of an individual but an entire race! Breckinridge was fired with a similar vision to mine, and the concept of the human/dolphin hybrid was one that seemed natural to us both. I managed to get samples of the marine creatures I needed, and Raintree and Brogan supplied me with a prime subject, a young street urchin.

Breckinridge wanted a species that could live and work underwater, which was a ticklish proposition. Dolphins, as you know, possess lungs and breathe air. I didn't feel that the merfolk could be kept secret if they constantly had to surface to breathe, nor could their work levels be terribly high. In the end, I managed to create a dolphin-like creature that possessed gills. This I then grafted into my test subject. To my delight the grafting took instantly, and I was able to monitor her changes. She came through it perfectly, and is the proud leader of my new super-human race.

Changing the children was one thing, but training them quite another. Like so many children, they did not wish to work to repay us for our efforts. We were therefore left with no option but to compel them by force to do as we wished. For that, we needed guards. I took several immature harbour seals and grafted human elements into them. These elements are taken from the fluids extracted from recently deceased humans. This increased both their intelligence and their aggression level. It rendered them perfect for their tasks. They guard the merfolk and ensure that they work as required. They also patrol the area to keep out intruders and spies.

I have achieved my dream, and even as we speak the new race that I envisioned and formed is working on the sea bed. I have achieved the greatest possible triumph for a man of science – I have turned my dreams into reality!

9

Survival of the Fittest

Sarah stared at Ross in anger and pity. The guy was a total nut-case, apparently oblivious to the incredible pain and suffering he had caused in the pursuit of this insane dream of his. He had detailed without any shame or remorse crime after crime against human – and non-human – species. And he seemed to think that she should be pleased to die so he could use her for spare parts! 'You're mad, you know that?' she asked him. She tried to sound cheerful and brave, but she was terrified of him.

He didn't seem at all bothered by her comment. 'Sadly,' he informed her, 'one of the guards was slain last night, and I need to produce a replacement. This is where you will provide me with the help I need, Sarah. Your fluids will enable me to mutate a new guard and allow my work to continue. You should be very proud of your contribution to science.'

'Thanks a lot, but I could skip the honour,' she answered. 'Couldn't I just leave you my body in my will?'

'Come now,' he admonished her. 'Don't be so reactionary. You have to die anyway, since you persisted in investigating matters that were none of your concern. Raintree and Brogan would happily murder you for an evening's entertainment if I allowed it, but they would be unlikely to return your corpse to me in a state I could use. This way, I promise you a painless death and some achievement once you have expired. Wouldn't you prefer that?'

'Can I sleep on it and let you know in the morning?' she asked.

Ross laughed, genuinely amused. It was scary how he could divorce his conscience and his mind like that. 'Oh, I'm rather sorry to lose you, Sarah. You do provide me with such amusement.'

'Court jester extraordinaire, that's me,' Sarah said. 'Look, why don't you just buy me a nice fool's costume, and I'll be happy to hang around and entertain you.'

'I'm sorry,' he replied, and he did sound genuinely sad. 'But that's not a viable option.' He picked up a scalpel from the table beside him. 'Goodbye, Sarah. It's been a pleasure chatting with you, but I'm afraid that it has to end now. I'm on a rather tight schedule, you know, and business is business.'

Sarah's eyes focused in horror on the sharp tip of the instrument as he moved towards her. Her heart was pounding, and she wanted to scream. Terror welled up within her as he moved slowly and relentlessly across the room to murder her.

As the small party reached the locked gates to the factory, Ross turned to Abercrombie. 'Time for you to earn your pay,' he said.

Abercrombie sighed, and moved to the padlock. 'I've been meaning to speak to you about that,' he said. 'I think I deserve danger money for these here jobs. I'm in grave danger of being murdered once we get inside here.'

'You'll need it even more if you don't hurry,' Ross informed him. 'I'm likely to murder you here and now.'

'Is that what you call an incentive?' grumbled Abercrombie. As he complained, he worked on the lock using a piece of bent wire and a nail-file. After a second there was a soft snick and the padlock sprang open. 'You may applaud if you wish.'

'We don't,' Ross answered, helping to remove the chain that held the two gates together. One by one they filed through the gate, leaving it slightly ajar as they passed on towards the main building.

'I believe the route we have to take is through the main working area,' the Doctor informed Ross. The colonel nodded, leading the way to the side entrance. There was a large oaken door here, sturdy and padlocked. During the day it would be opened to allow the delivery of supplies to the work floor. In the corner of the larger door was a smaller one, also equipped with a strong-looking lock.

'Can you open that up quickly?' Ross asked Abercrombie.

His assistant examined the lock carefully under a tight beam from his dark lantern, then shook his head. 'No way,' he replied. 'It's too modern for that. I could be here all night fiddling with that.'

'What do we do now?' asked Doyle, frustration tinge-ing his voice.

'Use the other option,' replied the little thief. 'Here, hold this.' He gave Doyle the lantern, and then removed a small hammer and spike from his pocket. Using the spike, he gestured at the hinges. 'Typical dumb mistake,' he pointed out. 'Put on a big lock and think the door's imprega-blooming-ble.' He grinned, and then used the spike to tap out the rod from the hinges. Ross and the Doctor then pulled the door apart. 'Easy when you know how,' Abercrombie said, grinning.

'We'll send you a thank-you later,' the Doctor informed him. He peered cautiously inside the factory floor. 'It appears deserted. Come on.'

The small group hurried after him to the lathe he'd spotted earlier. Now that Doyle looked closely, he could see that there were indeed scratch marks in the floor in a

224

quarter-circle, starting at the lathe's left corner.

'Now ain't that corny,' sighed Abercrombie. 'You think they'd be more bleeding inventive, wouldn't you?'

'It appears to work,' the Doctor answered. 'There's probably a release catch somewhere on the base that prevents it from moving accidentally.'

Ross nodded, and bent to examine the bottom rim of the heavy base with his own lantern. After a second, they all heard a click. 'I think that's it,' Ross announced, straightening up. 'Shall we?'

The four of them pushed on the right-hand side of the lathe. Silently it swung about on a pivot, revealing a dark pit below. The top five or six steps of a flight of stairs leading down into the ground were visible in the dim light cast by their lanterns.

'Will you step into my parlour?' intoned the Doctor.

'What other choice do we have?' asked Ross. 'I'll go first.' Using his walking stick to probe the darkness ahead of him, he led the way down. The Doctor and then Doyle followed.

'I'll just wait for you here,' suggested Abercrombie. 'A rear guard, if you like.'

'You'd better guard your rear if you don't come on,' growled Ross. 'Else I'll deliver a swift kick up it.'

Abercrombie sighed and started down the steps after them.

Ross and Doyle had their dark lanterns opened partway, allowing only trickles of light out. As a result, their descent of the stairs was carried on in a small, dull circle of illumination. Ten steps down and it was as if they were in another world entirely. There was the soft sound of dripping water from ahead of them. In silence, they slowly descended the stairs.

After about a hundred steps, the stairs ended in a short passage that sloped gently forward. Ross risked opening the aperture of his lantern slightly so that they could see down the passageway. It culminated in a large iron doorway about twenty feet ahead of them. Turning down the light, he led the way to the bulkhead door. In the centre of this was a wheel.

'In case of trouble,' the Doctor murmured. 'We must be below sea-level now. This can be locked in case of leaks.'

'Yeah,' muttered Abercrombie. 'Plumbers must be hard to come by down here.'

Ross gestured for the others to stand back, and then gripped the wheel. Slowly he turned it anti-clockwise. Soundlessly, it moved, and then the door swung open. Beyond it lay another dark area. Silent again, they filed forward, while Ross started to close the door behind them.

Doyle used his lantern to examine the room that they were in. It was hewn from the rough bedrock, and only about six feet across. It was completely empty, but an identical door to the one they had just passed through stood slightly ajar opposite them. The Doctor nodded to indicate their way forward. Doyle started to push the door open when it was suddenly yanked from his grasp and swung wide.

Two almost intolerably bright lights snapped on, dazzling the four adventurers. Doyle cried out in pain and surprise.

'Good evening, gentlemen,' Breckinridge said amiably from beyond the glare. 'I fear you're a trifle late for the daily guided tour, but please do come inside.'

Shielding his eyes from the brightness, Doyle staggered forward as the Doctor shoved him from behind. He stumbled across the threshold and past the two glowing lights. Beyond them he saw the factory owner and two nasty-looking customers carrying side-arms that were

226

pointed in the direction of the four of them.

Breckinridge pulled a pocket watch from his waistcoat and glanced at it. 'Almost midnight already. Dear me, if you'd simply made an appointment earlier with my secretary, all of this tedious waiting could have been avoided.'

'I shall remember that,' the Doctor promised, 'the next time I plan a secret mission to stop the grandiose schemes of a deluded megalomaniac.' He grinned at Breckinridge. 'No offence meant.'

'And none taken, Doctor Smith.' Breckinridge's smile seemed quite genuine and unforced.

'Doctor who?' asked Abercrombie of his master. Ross stomped on his foot, making the tubby thief wince.

'If you've all quite finished?' asked Breckinridge. 'I think you've kept me up quite late enough as it is. Shall we get this over with so that I can get a little rest? I have a busy day ahead of me tomorrow, you know. You really can't imagine how hard it is to run a factory.'

'You scoundrel!' exclaimed Doyle. 'Do you expect us to sympathize with you?'

'No, Doctor,' Breckinridge answered. 'I expect you to die. Then I expect the little fishies outside will have a feast. Beyond that, I couldn't care less what you do.' He gestured with one hand, and the two men with him raised their guns.

'Excuse me,' said the Doctor, politely raising his hand. 'Could I ask for a teensy little favour first?'

Breckinridge sighed. 'Really, Doctor, you do try my patience, you know. I do so hate late nights. Early to bed, early to rise and all that.'

'I always preferred Thurber myself,' the Doctor replied. ' "Early to rise and early to bed, makes a man healthy, wealthy and dead." '

'Well,' Breckinridge told him, 'you're about to prove

the truth of that saying. Now, what is this favour of yours?'

The Doctor glanced at the floor. 'It's a failing of mine,' he confessed, 'but I'd really hate to be killed without knowing exactly why I'm being murdered. I mean, I can see that you're a busy man, things to do, worlds to conquer, infinitives to split and all that. But could you spare just a little time to enlighten me on a few points?'

The businessman smiled. 'I suppose I do owe you that, at the very least.' He considered the matter for a moment. 'Very well,' he agreed. 'I'll illuminate you concerning my plans. Then Raintree and Brogan will kill you. Happier now?'

'Absolutely ecstatic,' the Doctor assured him. 'So, what's it all about, Alfie?'

'I'm sorry?'

'Ah, this whole scheme,' the Doctor said, gesturing about. 'Hiding in slimy little tunnels, killing poor innocent fishermen, snatching bodies, breeding dogs that Crufts wouldn't even think of giving a blue ribbon to. That sort of thing.'

Breckinridge nodded. 'You're wondering what the point of all this activity is, I take it?'

'Exactly!' The Doctor beamed. 'How succinct. So tell me: what's the point of all this activity?'

'Progress, Doctor, progress!' Breckinridge smiled happily, and waved his hands around. 'This is the wave of the future, Doctor.'

'Really?' asked Ross, mildly amused. 'Humanity is going to start living in leaky subterranean tunnels? Doesn't sound like much of a future to me.'

Breckinridge glared at him. 'Mock me if you choose,' he said coldly, 'but remember who holds the power here.' He turned to the Doctor. 'Really, how could you ally yourself with such a crass individual?'

The Doctor shrugged. 'Necessity makes for strange bedfellows,' he suggested. 'Now, what was that you said about progress?'

Breckinridge nodded. 'Come with me, Doctor, and I will show you more wonders than any man has ever imagined.' He glared at Raintree. 'Watch them all. If any of them makes a false move, shoot him. Otherwise, don't harm them until I'm finished.' With a charming smile, he said, 'Gentlemen, if you'd care to follow me?'

'I think I speak for us all,' the Doctor murmured, 'when I say that we're a captive audience. Lead on, Macduff.'

Holding the scalpel in front of him, Ross moved slowly across the laboratory towards Sarah. 'I promise you,' he said, 'this will be as swift and painless as I can manage. I have no desire to hurt you.'

'Well, I've plenty of desire to hurt you,' snapped Sarah. Her pain and fear had built within her to almost fever pitch, but she wasn't about to let him get away with his insane plans. She gripped the pipe over her head with her hands, and waited for him to move closer. As he stepped within four feet of her, she exploded into action.

She whipped up her right foot with as much force as she could muster. Her toe slammed into his wrist with bone-shattering impact. The scalpel flew from his nerve-less fingers, clattering to the ground in the distance. Ross screamed and used his good hand to grip his smashed right wrist. Suspending herself from her hands, Sarah whipped up her legs, hooking her right foot behind his neck and pulling him toward her. Then she slammed down her left foot on his back. She felt the heel of her shoe crunch down hard on his ribs, and heard the distinct sound of a bone breaking.

Ross screamed wordlessly as he fell to the cold floor. Panting, Sarah twisted about to try and use her feet on him again. But though Ross was wounded and in pain, he wasn't stupid enough to stay still. Crab-like, he scuttled out of her reach, then tried to straighten up. He winced, and his skin turned a sickly shade of white as he succeeded in regaining his feet.

'My hand!' he screamed. 'You've broken my hand!'

Sarah glared at him through her fringe. 'What a wimp,' she mocked him. 'You don't care how much pain and misery you've inflicted on others, do you? But break one little bone in your hand and you start blubbering like a baby.'

'You'll pay for that,' he hissed, glaring in anger and agony at her. He was still nursing his broken wrist, and was slightly hunched over as a result of the blow from her heel. 'Oh, you'll pay for that.'

'It'll be worth it,' she told him. She wanted him mad enough to attack her again. Despite appearances, she was actually at an advantage here. Ross had been expecting some meek Victorian maid who'd faint at the thought of what he'd do to her. He probably still didn't realize how much she was capable of – but he'd find out if he gave her half a chance. 'Come on,' she encouraged him. 'I'm not going anywhere, am I? Almost as easy as kidnapping helpless children, isn't it?'

He cast his eyes around the laboratory, clutching his hand. 'I've got to get this seen to,' he muttered, refusing to be baited.

'Stick it in your healing jelly,' she suggested. 'That should do the trick.' She grinned. 'As long as there's nothing else in there, of course. You didn't swat a fly, did you? Maybe you'll grow compound eyes if there's a fly in your ointment.'

That taunt hit home. Ross stared uncertainly at the container of the salve. He was obviously a basically weak and insecure man, prey to nightmares and massive feelings of inferiority. Sarah was certain that she could get him worked up enough to become reckless, if she had the time alone with him.

She didn't.

The door to the laboratory opened and the Doctor walked in.

'Doctor!' she exclaimed happily. 'Am I glad to see you! It's a bit tiring, all this hanging around.'

The Doctor shook his head and pointed to Breckinridge, who had followed him in. One by one, Doyle, Colonel Ross, Abercrombie, Brogan and Raintree filed into the room.

'This isn't a rescue, I'm afraid, Miss Smith,' Breckinridge said pleasantly.

'It's not even a party,' agreed the Doctor. 'I forgot to bring the cake.' He peered at Ross. 'Ah, you must be the mad scientist, I assume.' He held out a hand. Ross whimpered.

'Sorry,' Sarah apologized. 'He's not going to be shaking hands for a while. I'm afraid I broke it. Careless of me, I know.'

'Very,' agreed the Doctor.

Colonel Ross stepped forward and glared at his younger brother in disgust. 'Percival,' he growled, 'you've certainly disgraced the family name.'

'*Percival?*' echoed the Doctor in mock horror. 'This whole insane scheme was dreamed up by a man named Percival? Oh, that's too dreadful for words.' His eyes darted about the laboratory, intrigued, and came to rest on the vat of gelatin. 'Ah! So that is what is behind all this.' He wandered across to it.

Brogan raised his revolver, lining up on the Doctor's back, but Breckinridge shook his head. 'There's no need for that – yet,' he said. 'So, Doctor, what do you think that is?'

231

His face almost in the goo, the Doctor replied, 'It's obvious: Rutan healing salve. The store brand, too, by the stench of it.' He dipped his finger in and examined the glob. Then he sucked it off his finger. 'Cherry – my favourite flavour.'

Breckinridge stared at him in shock. 'Don't you know what that can do to you?' he gasped, appalled at what he'd just witnessed.

'I know what it can do to *you*,' the Doctor countered. 'It won't affect me.'

'It affects any human being,' croaked Ross, ashen at the thought of what the Doctor had done.

'Precisely,' agreed the Doctor. He wandered over to the closest aquarium tank and stared down at the baby seal inside. 'Hello, little fellow. Lost your mummy?'

'Doctor,' Doyle asked, 'what the blazes is going on here? Do you really know what that stuff is?'

'Yes,' the Doctor replied, spinning about on the balls of his feet. 'It's Rutan healing salve. The Rutans are a species of amorphous nature that live – ' he gestured vaguely in the air ' – in a galaxy far, far away. They have the ability to alter their appearance because their cellular structure is unstable. As a result, when one of them is injured, they need a medication that's pretty unstable too. Like this goo. The problem is that the salve works on the basis of reforming the amorphous cells. When it comes in contact with some non-Rutan tissue, it causes genetic fusion.'

'Which we witnessed in the hound-boy and the mermaids,' finished Sarah.

'Precisely.'

Colonel Ross raised an eyebrow. 'And these "Rutans" of which you speak; they are of other-worldly origin?'

'Very.' The Doctor grinned at the agent. 'Do you find that rather incredible?'

232

'No,' Ross replied. 'I've seen too many strange things during the course of my life to balk at the thought of a non-Earthly lifeform.' A thought seemed to dawn on him. 'Ah! Doctor, am I to take it that *you* are another?'

The Doctor's smile grew even wider. 'I knew it would dawn on someone sooner or later.'

Doyle shook his head. 'This is all getting far too preposterous for me,' he opined.

'Me too,' agreed Abercrombie. 'Non-humans. I hate non-humans. I've had enough bleeding non-humans to last me several lifetimes.'

Sarah realized that the Doctor had obviously learned something about Colonel Ross's past that was still hidden from her, but it was obvious that Ross was on their side – at least for now. Which definitely made matters interesting. Counting Ross's brother, there were four of the villains here; not counting her, since she was manacled and hardly free to move, there were four on the other side. Even forces, if Brogan and Raintree had not been armed. She decided that the best thing she could do was to keep attention focused on her and trust the Doctor to improvise something as usual. 'Junior Ross here,' she said, nodding at the scientist, 'mentioned finding the stuff on a flying saucer that had crashed in Limehouse.'

'Part of their almost eternal war with the Sontarans, Sarah,' the Doctor answered. 'They've been fighting in this sector for a while. The Rutan must have been a casualty and come down in flames.' He glared at the tub. 'Which is where that stuff belongs.'

'No, Doctor,' Breckinridge broke in. 'That stuff belongs with me. Ross and I have a great deal more use for it yet.'

'I don't get it,' Sarah said, puzzled. 'I can see what Frankenstein-hopeful here gets out of all this. He's just wild about breeding his own lifeforms, like the poor kid in the bottle over there. But what's in it for you? Just the pleasure of hurting little kids, robbing graves and killing people?'

Breckinridge was stung by this. 'Miss Smith!' he protested. 'You do me a grave injustice. I am not some mindlessly sadistic monster. Surely that is obvious?'

'What is obvious,' Colonel Ross said coldly, 'is that you are a depraved human being who has no thought for the consequences of his actions.'

Oh, well done! thought Sarah. Ross's accusation had really wounded Breckinridge's pride. The factory owner went almost purple with rage, and then managed to gather his wits together.

'Very well,' he said, frost dripping from his voice. 'No thought for the consequences of my action, indeed? Well, I'll show you just how wrong you are.'

'Breckinridge,' the scientist said, the pain still twisting his voice, 'he's taunting you. He does this all the time. Kill him now. Better yet, let me kill him.'

'Brotherly love,' murmured the Doctor dreamily.

'How much of a fool do you think I am?' growled Breckinridge. 'I know what he's trying to do. And if you want to murder him, you can be my guest. But not until after he's seen what I am creating here.' He glared at the colonel. 'I am not having him die thinking I'm a savage.'

'Oi,' put in Sarah. 'What about me?'

Breckinridge studied her for a moment, then he nodded at Ross. 'Get her down from there. I want her to see this as well.'

Ross shook his head. 'I don't trust her,' he protested. 'She's already broken my hand and – '

'And I'll break the other one for you if you don't do as you're told!' screamed Breckinridge. He raised his hand, on the verge of slapping Ross. It was clear to Sarah that

Breckinridge didn't like his orders questioned – even when they were quite idiotic.

Ross, terrified of further pain, ducked and scuttled across to where Sarah was hanging from the pipes. It took him a minute to fish the key to the handcuffs from his pocket, and even longer to manage to unlock them one-handed. Sarah sighed happily as she could finally lower her arms. They'd felt like the joints were about to break at any moment. Rubbing her wrists, she joined the other captives.

Breckinridge smiled at her. 'And, lest you think that my decision to allow you to join us shows evidence of any favour in your direction, or weakness on my part . . .' His hand whipped around in a savage blow to her cheek that threw her backwards across the floor. 'Think again, please.'

Sarah cried out in pain and stumbled backwards into the tanks, smacking down hard on the floor. Her backside stung, and there was the taste of blood in her mouth.

'There was no need for that,' the Doctor growled at Breckinridge.

'On the contrary,' the businessman purred. 'Or would you prefer me to have Brogan shoot someone so that you understand the situation here? Brogan would happily do that; he likes to kill people.' Breckinridge sighed theatrically. 'He does have such simple tastes, but he's a dedicated worker.'

'It's okay,' Sarah said. She wiped at her mouth with the back of her right hand. Blood smeared across it, which she wiped off rather obviously on to her skirt. 'I'm not badly damaged.' She groaned as she started to rise, but for effect and not from pain.

The scalpel she'd knocked out of Ross's hand earlier now lay inside her left sleeve. Her ostentatious mannerisms with the blood had been to distract attention while she'd palmed the fallen weapon. Simply having it gave her more courage. Breckinridge and his minions might aim to kill them all, but she would go down fighting, if she went down at all.

'Very well,' Breckinridge announced. 'Let's be moving out of here. Ross – *Doctor* Ross,' he added with stress, 'lead the way to the viewing room.' He turned to the Doctor. 'I'm sure Miss Smith informed you that the ocean is something of a passion with me?'

'It's nice to see that you have a few innocent passions,' the Doctor answered as he fell in beside his adversary.

'Oh, I have lots of them,' the man laughed. 'Though you may not believe it.'

'You're right,' agreed the Doctor, just as cheerfully, 'I don't.' He glanced around as Sarah joined him. Doyle, Colonel Ross and Abercrombie – muttering gloomily under his breath – followed them, and the two thugs brought up the rear as they paraded out of the laboratory. Sarah realized that the rest of the subterranean passageways and rooms that had been added to the factory were all in roughly the same shape as the laboratory. The passageway bent at odd angles several times, showing that it had been cut to follow the pathway of an old cave system. The rooms that they passed were closed, and presumably had been cut from larger openings. The walls were rough and unfinished, with electric lights at set intervals, linked by thick cables that snaked along the passageway. The sound of dripping water increased, and the floor shone in spots where puddles gathered in the uneven surface. She had the distinct impression that they had now travelled under the sea bed.

At one of the doors they passed, the Doctor halted, frowning. 'What's in there?' he demanded. There was the sound of movement within the room.

'Precautions, Doctor,' answered Doctor Ross. 'The

seals aren't the only guards I've bred for this place. Thus far, though, the guardians in there haven't been needed.'

'More abominations,' muttered Doyle.

'My brother has a fertile mind when it comes to such matters,' Colonel Ross said, quietly but audibly. 'What he lacks in intelligence he makes up for in depravity.'

His brother whirled to glare furiously at him. 'I've been in your shadow all my life,' he snarled. 'It was always "you're not half the man your brother is, Percival" and "look how well Edmund is doing at Oxford, Percival". Well I've had enough! Today I shall prove to everyone that I'm the more intelligent Ross, because I'll be alive and creating a new world, and you'll be dead.'

'So there,' added the Doctor. 'Talk about an inferiority complex.'

'I've never seen a more complex complex,' Sarah offered.

Breckinridge shook his head sadly. 'Please can we dispense with the silly jokes? I'd hate to have to dispense with either of you before you see our triumph. Through the next door, if you please, Doctor.' He stood aside to allow the Doctor and Sarah to precede him.

Sarah dutifully followed the Doctor into the indicated room, and then stood just inside, staring in wonder at what she could see.

The far wall was almost entirely glass. It was about twenty feet long and half that in height. She couldn't guess its depth, but it had to be pretty thick to hold out the pressure of the water beyond. As a result, the glass wasn't crystal clear. Patches had a smoky appearance and some parts were not quite level. But it was enough to show what lay outside.

Outside lay the ocean. Rows of lights led away from the gigantic window, set into the sea bed and glowing faintly. The illumination was low-level, but sufficient to show them what lay out there. Sarah took several steps forward as the others crowded into the room behind her. She heard Doyle gasp in amazement at the view.

'Quite staggering, isn't it?' asked Breckinridge proudly.

Sarah didn't want to admit that it was, so she continued moving. There was only one piece of furniture in the room, a table of sorts. Strapped to it, unconscious, was Kipling. She spared him a quick glance to be certain he was still breathing, then moved until she was touching the huge window.

The sea bed looked marvellous. Rocks, pebbles and sand were illuminated gently. In the distance – probably only a few hundred yards away in the dark waters – was a large wheel, set in a spool. Attached to the wheel were more lights. This was clearly the source of the mysterious lighting that they had witnessed from their boat the previous night.

Closer to the window was a garden of sorts. There were seaweeds there, and other plants, all in neat, short rows. They were obviously being cultivated, and Sarah gasped as she saw the workers in these strange fields. There were almost two dozen of them – merfolk, all children. Each of them was naked, their upper torsos human, their lower sections dolphinine. They moved slowly along the rows, weeding and checking the growing plants. Sarah stared at them, and recognized one of them as the girl who had saved her life. She looked as if she were the oldest one among them, and seemed to be in some kind of charge over them.

Beyond the workers, though, were three dark shapes that moved continually: the seal guards.

'Dear Lord!' said Doyle fervently, from behind her.

'They're bleeding real,' muttered Abercrombie. He glanced uncertainly at his boss. 'I guess your warped brother ain't entirely mad.'

'On the contrary,' the Doctor said, in a soft, dangerous voice that Sarah knew too well, 'he's criminally insane.' The Doctor whirled around to glower at Breckinridge and Ross. 'Those are children out there that you've mutilated.'

'Mutilated?' Breckinridge sounded incredulous. 'Doctor, they're not mutilated at all! They're magnificent! They can stay out there indefinitely, harvesting the sea, and they are viable, the nucleus of a brand new race. I assure you, they are not ill-treated.'

'They're slaves,' the Doctor thundered. 'That's why you need those guards: to prevent your slave army from escaping!'

'They're useful, for the first time in their miserable little lives,' protested Breckinridge. 'Doctor, every one of those children out there was doomed to die if they stayed here on the land. They're all from the docks and wharves and gutters. Parasites, scavengers and worse. Now, thanks to Ross and myself, they have useful, productive lives.'

'Useful to you,' the Doctor countered. 'Production for you. None of them was given the chance to decide whether they wanted that life or not. You made that choice for them.'

'They were hardly in a position to make rational judgements, Doctor,' Breckinridge argued. 'Dirty, ill-educated, disgusting little urchins from the dregs of the street. Now look at them – they're magnificent!'

'Not all of them,' Sarah said quietly. 'One of them is a boy named Anders, from the same school as Kipling. He's got parents that care for him, and he wouldn't have been a parasite.'

'True,' agreed Breckinridge. 'But he stumbled across us one night when certain supplies were being delivered. It was either change him or kill him.' He nodded at the glass. 'I assume you approve of the choice I made?'

'I approve of nothing you do,' she answered. 'It's inhuman, disgusting and perverted.'

Breckinridge flushed. 'I should have known you wouldn't understand,' he snapped. 'Can't you see that those children are better out there than they would be if this asinine Government of ours had their way? All this talk of educating the street brats. What a waste! They don't have the minds or the imaginations to take advantage of an education. And who would pay for their waste of time? Businessmen like myself, that's who! Well, out there —' he gestured savagely out of the window again '— is my response to the unwanted children. We can transform them, put them to useful work, to extend Man's dominion.'

'To enslave them,' the Doctor added coldly. 'To make them work for you. That's the real reason, isn't it?' He pointed to the garden. 'That's pathetic, a sham. What you really have in mind is to make the children work for you, isn't that it? That wheel of light of yours has no real point, does it?'

'It has its reasons, Doctor,' Breckinridge responded. 'I'm training those children because, as you rightly observe, they will have to work to repay me for all I've done for them. I foresee a future, Doctor, where the world is linked by communication. The telegraph is outmoded, and the telephone is just beginning. I see a day when pictures as well as words can be transmitted through such cables. And he who has the network in place will be the master of this new world.'

'So that's it,' said Colonel Ross. 'Those children are being trained to work so they can lay your cables.'

'Precisely,' agreed Breckinridge. 'Do you have any idea how expensive it is to lay cables from ships? And if one breaks, there's no way to repair it. You have to start over again, laying a new sea-bed cable. But with my race of merfolk out there, those problems cease. They can lay the cables and even repair them, if needed, at any depths. They're the perfect workers, and they will help me to become the leader in a new world order.'

'I pity you,' the Doctor said, in that icy, dangerous tone of his. 'Ross, at least, is doing his filthy work as a perversion of science. But you are doing it simply to make more money.'

'And what's wrong with making money?' cried Breckinridge. 'Without men like me, this world would grind to a sorry halt in days. It is my money that gives the people here in town work. It's my money that funds research, and brings on the future!'

'It's your money that bastardizes everything that we hold holy and just,' snapped Colonel Ross. 'This perversion is sickening, and must be destroyed.'

'No!' snapped the Doctor. 'Ross, try and control that indignation of yours.' He pointed out of the window. 'Those are children out there. They never asked for the fate they've been given, and they're innocent of any blame.'

'Whatever they may once have been,' countered Ross, 'they are abominations now.'

'If you touch one of those children,' the Doctor vowed, 'I shall personally take great pleasure in breaking every bone in your body – commencing with those in your inner ears.'

Breckinridge laughed. 'Come now, gentlemen,' he said. 'Please don't argue about this. After all, you seem to forget who is in charge here. It is I, not you, who decides what shall happen. You are both powerless.' He smirked at all his captives. 'The future belongs to me, not to any of you, because none of you has a future.'

'You're wrong,' said Sarah flatly. 'You don't have a future. I know, because I'm from it.'

'What?' Breckinridge stared at her, his face a twisted mass of emotions. It was clear that he didn't quite believe that claim, but also that he wasn't certain what she was up to. His eyes narrowed. 'You expect me to believe that? You're just trying to – '

'Believe it,' Sarah told him. 'I'm not due to be born for over sixty years yet. I'm from that future you're talking about, and I can tell you that nowhere are you mentioned. Oh, everything you've talked about is there, and more. But there's no genius named Breckinridge anywhere in it.' She gestured towards Kipling. 'In fact, he's going to become far more famous than you could ever be. He's going to become a great writer.'

'That snotty-nosed little schoolboy?' sneered Breckinridge. 'You're trying to say that he will be known and I won't?'

'Yes.' Sarah glared at him. 'So believe me: you may think you're winning, but you're doomed. Your insane plan can't succeed, because I'm from the future where it hasn't succeeded.'

Anger and disbelief waged war for the businessman's features. Anger finally won. 'I'm still not sure that I believe you, Miss Smith, even though you are like no other woman I've ever met. But I can disprove your little theory quite simply.' He glared at Ross. 'Take Kipling there to your laboratory now, and give him a dose of the salve.' He smiled tightly at Sarah. 'Let's see if he can still become a great writer when he has to spend the rest of his life underwater. His paper is liable to get a trifle damp, I fear.'

Sarah gasped with shock. 'No,' she said. 'You can't do that. You can't change history.'

'Your history, Miss Smith, not mine.' Breckinridge smiled, self-assured again. 'And if I change that small detail, then everything else will change as well, won't it?'

'Yes,' agreed the Doctor darkly. 'If you can change one brick, the wall of recorded human history will tumble down.'

Breckinridge nodded happily. 'Then do it,' he ordered Ross.

Sarah watched in horror as the scientist crossed to the unconscious schoolboy and started to unfasten him from the table. She'd really done it this time! She'd hoped to convince Breckinridge to give up, but all she'd managed to do was to make him grimly determined to change the course of history as she knew it.

Was it possible? Could he somehow succeed? The Doctor seemed to believe it could happen. Was Sarah about to be the unwitting pivot about which history would shift and change?

Lucy pulled another strand of seaweed from the vegetable patch and slipped it into the collecting bag that she carried slung across her shoulders. As she did so, she glanced at the observation room in front of her. Sometimes she had seen Ross in there, watching his 'creations'. At others, Breckinridge would be there, staring out at the empire he was hoping to create for himself. Lucy stared in astonishment as she saw that the viewing room was almost overflowing with people.

And she recognized two of them. One of them was definitely the young woman she'd prevented from drowning. The other one was the man who had helped the woman back to the surface.

What were they doing here? She swam closer to the glass wall to get a better look. Then she saw that Brogan and Raintree were there, the two men who'd captured her in the first place, and three other men that she didn't recognize. And there was another person strapped down to a table. Brogan and Raintree had guns, so the two people she knew and the other three had to be prisoners. What was going on?

'Joshua,' she called to the newcomer. He'd been with them only a little while, but he seemed to be filled with fire and intelligence. She liked him, and felt that she could rely on him. 'Look at the viewing room.'

Joshua swam slowly to join her. His eyes narrowed and he frowned. 'What's going on?' he asked softly.

'It looks like the woman I helped last night is in trouble again,' Lucy explained. 'I think she and her friends are trying to stop Ross and Breckinridge.'

'It does look like that,' Joshua agreed. 'In fact . . .' He gave a little jump of shock. 'That boy on the table! I know him! That's Gigger!'

'Who?'

'Someone from my school,' Joshua explained, excited. 'He must have been looking for me. These people are trying to fight those villains, I'll bet!'

'Then they're not doing very well,' Lucy observed. 'They're in serious trouble, by the looks of things.'

'Then we have to try and help them, Lucy,' said Joshua eagerly. 'If they can manage to stop Ross and Breckinridge, then we'll be free.'

'Do you think so?' She wanted so desperately to believe that. But –

One of the Guards swam swiftly over, squealing a warning at them. Lucy knew that it meant *return to work*. The seal's mouth opened to show its cruel fangs. She knew that it was hoping for some excuse to attack. It loved to maim and kill, and with the slightest excuse it would rip into them all. ·

'We'd better do as it says,' she told Joshua.

'No!' he yelled. 'I won't! You said that you were waiting for the best time to break free. Well, this is it! There are only three Guards left, and it looks like Ross has his own troubles.'

'Joshua!' she yelled, but it was too late. He ripped the collecting bag from his shoulders, and threw it in slow-motion to the sea bed.

'I'm *not* going back to work!' he yelled at the Guard. 'What are you going to do about that?'

Horrified, Lucy saw exactly what the Guard intended to do. It swam away slightly, and then whipped around, teeth bared.

It was going to kill Joshua!

Without hesitation, she snatched up Joshua's discarded bag. As the Guard shot past her, she threw the strap from the bag about its neck and then hung on grimly. The strap tightened about the Guard's throat, cutting deeply into its windpipe. Unlike the merfolk, the Guards still needed to breathe air from time to time. Even though the Guard could go for half an hour between breaths, its instincts told it that it was being strangled, and it panicked. The raking teeth missed Joshua entirely as the Guard twisted, trying to get Lucy off its back. She held tight to the straps, twisting them in her hands to get more leverage.

She'd almost forgotten that the Change had increased her strength until she heard the snap of the Guard's neck, and felt its death throes. In shock, Lucy let go of the straps. The broken body of the dead Guard sank slowly to the sea bed. She could do nothing but stare at it, hardly able to understand what she had done.

'Lucy!' cried Joshua happily. 'You did it! You killed the Guard!' He whirled about to face the other children. They had stopped working to watch what they had felt certain would be Joshua getting killed. Instead they had witnessed the unexpected − a miracle.

'They're vulnerable!' Joshua yelled, pointing to the fallen Guard. 'And there are only two of them left!'

The children needed no further urging. As one, they

went for the two remaining Guards. The seals had been bred to be killers, but even they couldn't stand against this force. One of them fastened its teeth onto Patrick's arm and tore the limb apart in a spray of blood that clouded the water. Patrick screamed and went rigid in death. The Guard didn't even have the time to spit out the arm before six of the children, wielding stones torn from the sea bed, battered it into pulp.

The final Guard tried to flee, but the children were faster. Two of them grabbed the Guard's flukes and the rest of them descended on it like locusts, hammering away at it, not letting up until it was a bloody smear in the dark sand.

'We did it!' Joshua cried triumphantly. 'We're free!'

Sarah watched numbly as Ross loosened the straps on Kipling. The boy, thankfully, was still unconscious and thus unaware of what was in store for him.

'Are you still so certain that I cannot change the future?' asked Breckinridge.

'Yes,' the Doctor broke in. 'I think you'd better take a look behind you.'

Breckinridge laughed. 'Come, Doctor! How naïve do you think I am?'

The Doctor shrugged. 'What are my choices? But this is no bluff. Your undersea slaves are revolting. And they appear to be winning.'

With a cry, Breckinridge glanced over his shoulder. He saw in horror what Sarah saw in hope: the merchildren had turned on the Guards and were beating the living daylights out of them. Ross stared at the scene too, transfixed, supporting Kipling with his one good hand.

The Doctor moved slowly, uncurling several lengths of his scarf. Then, while even Brogan and Raintree were distracted by the battle beyond the glass, he whipped out

246

a length of the scarf, looping it neatly about Raintree's gun hand, and jerked the thug off-balance.

'Now would be a good time to use that stick,' he snapped at Colonel Ross.

Ross smiled and whipped up his walking stick. Sarah recalled his use of the stick during the hunt, and that it was actually a single-shot air rifle. There was a loud hiss of the compressed gas going off. Ross had aimed at Breckinridge, but the industrialist – either through luck or some preternatural instinct – had moved slightly. The bullet missed him and slammed into the glass wall beyond.

Instantly, spider-webbed cracks started to form in the glass.

'Dear God!' cried Doctor Ross. 'The pressure outside!'

It was obvious what he meant: they were way down below the water level here, and the crack in the glass gave it a terrible weak spot. In seconds, the wall could collapse.

Sarah slipped the scalpel she'd hidden into her hand and stabbed at Ross with it, striking his good hand. Ross screamed as blood bubbled up, and let Kipling fall. Sarah grabbed for the boy, managing to hold onto him. As she tried to straighten up, the room degenerated into mad confusion.

Raintree had staggered aside as the Doctor jerked him off-balance. Panicking, he fired. The bullet slammed into the glass wall, creating another series of growing cracks before the Doctor could wrest the gun from his hand. Brogan whirled around and brought his gun up, centring on the back of the Doctor's skull. Sarah cried out, but there was nothing she could do.

The revolver that had somehow appeared in Doyle's hand spat fire. Brogan was thrown backwards, his chest a mass of blood. He was either dead or dying. Colonel Ross spun about and reversed his grip on his walking stick. He whirled it in a lethal arc that finished in Raintree's skull, splattering blood and bone about.

'You've got to stop this habit of killing,' the Doctor snapped.

'We've got to get out of here,' Ross countered. 'That glass won't hold for much longer. Abercrombie!' he yelled. 'The boy!'

Sarah was still trying to get Kipling up when Abercrombie gently but firmly pushed her aside and scooped the boy up. He flung Kipling over one shoulder, giving her a quick grin. 'Time for the better part of valour,' he grunted, scuttling off under his burden. Sarah didn't need any further encouragement. Over the groans and yells she could hear the sound of cracking, and that meant that the water was about to break through.

As she sprinted out of the room, she saw she was behind Abercrombie and Doyle, who were both haring down the dank corridor ahead of her. Despite his load, Abercrombie was managing a respectable speed. Sarah glanced back and saw that Ross and the Doctor were hard on her heels.

How far did they have to get to be safe? She had no idea. And how long did they have before the glass wall gave way and the sea rushed in? It couldn't be more than minutes, and possibly not even that long. Once the water came through, it would flood the corridors in next to no time. She tried to remember her hydrodynamics, but science had never been her strong point. Didn't water speed up when faced with a constriction? If so, then as soon as the ocean broke into the corridor, it would send a killer wave after them all.

Talk about encouragement for speed! Sarah's ribs ached, and her lungs felt as if they were on fire as she ran for her life.

* * *

248

Breckinridge glared about the viewing room, fury eclips-
ing every other emotion, even his drive for self-preserva-
tion. His prisoners had escaped – at least for the moment
– and his world was crumbling. Raintree lay dead on the
floor, his blood and brains leaking from his shattered
skull. Ross had vanished with the others. His slaves
outside in the ocean had finished killing the guards and
had vanished into the darkness beyond.

Cold rage building inside him, he started for the door.
As he passed Brogan, the injured man reached out a
trembling hand.

'Help me,' he gasped. Blood was frothing up in his
chest wound, and he was desperate.

'Go to hell,' Breckinridge growled, kicking away the
groping hand. Ignoring the weakening pleas of the dying
thug, he left the viewing room and ran up the corridor to
where the final Guards were kept. He unlocked the door
and threw it open.

Snarling, the four enhanced dogs strained at their
chains. They were monsters of their kind, taken from
attack dogs bred in Europe and given extra cunning and a
drive to kill by Ross's salve and human fluid implants. All
four were ready to do his bidding, desiring nothing more
than to kill. Breckinridge crossed to the main link of the
chain and unlocked it. As the heavy chains fell away, he
gestured at the door.

'After them!' he screamed. 'Instruments of my vengeance! Kill!'

Three of the beasts leaped to obey him instantly,
dashing through the door.

The fourth whipped around and bared its teeth.
Breckinridge barely had the time to realize that Ross had
made these dogs too well. Their only drive was to kill,
and they didn't care who their victims were. He backed
away as the hound jumped. Teeth raked through his

upraised arm, shredding flesh and bone alike.

He had time for one last scream before the dog's teeth fastened onto his throat.

Doctor Ross, whimpering and racked with pain from his injured hands, staggered into his laboratory. Everything had gone wrong! Breckinridge had ruined it all, insisting on boasting and playing games with his captives. The man's ego had brought everything crashing down about them – and in seconds that could become more than just a metaphor. Ross saw that his plans were finished, and everything had crumbled. Once again, his accursed brother had beaten him.

He whimpered from the agony in his hands, caused by Sarah. One hand was broken, the other ripped apart from the scalpel she'd wielded. He couldn't bear the pain any more, and he staggered across to plunge his hands into the healing salve. In seconds, most of the pain was gone and he felt the gel soaking into his body.

And then the world exploded. He heard the shattering of the glass in the viewing room even from this distance. Blindly he looked around, wondering where he could run or hide, but there was nowhere left. A roaring sound filled the corridors as the waters crashed in, flooding through in a wave of tidal fury.

It slammed into the laboratory like a hammer, shattering equipment, splintering the tables, and then soaking him, throwing him back against the wall. It felt as if his spine had been crushed, and pain and fire filled his ravaged body.

The gel was still working, however. Even as he fought against the rising water, struggling for breath, he felt the burning within his limbs as the salve took control of his body. Would he drown, or would the cream cause some mutation that might enable him to somehow survive?

There was no way to tell, and no time left. As he lost consciousness, his body burned about him.

Sarah ran as fast as she could, trusting that Doyle and Abercrombie knew the route back. She'd not seen it, of course, as she'd been insensate when she was brought here. Dimly, in the distance behind her, down the twists and turns of the passageway, she could hear something. Even over the pounding of blood in her ears, there was no mistaking the howl of a dog. Several dogs.

The guardians are out! she realized desperately. There was no doubt that they'd be coming down the passageway after them – to get away from the water, if nothing else. And they had been bred to kill . . .

She simply couldn't move any faster. As it was, she didn't know how much longer she could keep up her current pace. She ached terribly, her lungs felt like they were burning inside her, and her legs were almost ready to seize up.

'We're here!' Doyle gasped back to her as they came to the bottom of a flight of steps that appeared suddenly from the gloom. He was still holding his revolver, and he stopped, waving her on with it. 'I've got a couple of bullets left,' he panted. 'Go on. I'll cover us.'

Sarah didn't waste time or breath arguing. Instead she started up the stairs, every step jarring and painful. After what felt like minutes she saw Abercrombie shoot out of sight at the top, and then Sarah plunged onto the factory floor right behind him.

'Out the door,' he gasped, leading the way. She saw that he was almost on the verge of collapse, so she went to offer him help with Kipling. 'Move it,' he sighed. Together they half-carried, half-dragged the boy to the doorway. Behind them they heard rapid footsteps, and then the Doctor, Ross and Doyle were with them. The

Doctor wasted no time or words, but simply kicked open the factory door.

And then the dogs bounded out of the gap in the floor. There were three of them, and in the dim light all Sarah could make out was powerful bodies and rows of sharp, drooling fangs.

Suddenly there were hands helping her through the doorway. Through the red haze that had settled over her eyes she could make out several people.

'Get them out of the way!' Sir Edward Fulbright snapped. He had a rifle at his shoulder, and was poised to fire.

Sarah accepted the help without question, and she was dragged aside by two people. She fell against one, and realized that it was Alice.

'Thank God we got here in time!' exclaimed the girl.

'Indubitably,' agreed Sarah, as she sucked in the fresh night air. Then there was a barrage of firing as Fulbright and his men let the three attacking dogs have the full force of their guns. The animals howled in pain, but went down.

The Doctor dropped to the ground beside Sarah. For once he looked as if he had been through the wars, too. There was a gash down one cheek, and his deerstalker was missing. His scarf fluttered in the breeze, and there was a happy gleam in his eyes. 'Three cheers for the Seventh Cavalry,' he joked.

'Is it over?' Sarah asked. There was a ringing in her ears as Fulbright and his men fired a second time. All sounds and movements from the dogs ceased.

'No,' the Doctor informed her. 'It's far from over. But the war is done. Now we have the peace to negotiate. I have to stop Ross from doing anything foolish – which isn't likely to be very easy.'

Coda

Sarah stood on the stony beach as the sun began to rise. There was a chill in the air, but less of one in her heart now. It had been a long night, but the dawn promised to wipe a great deal of the pain and loss away. She glanced around as Alice came to join her in staring out over the choppy waters.

'Father says that the underground passageways have flooded,' she said softly. 'They found the body of the last dog in the water there.'

'But not Doctor Ross or Breckinridge?'

'No,' Alice sighed. 'But Edmund – Colonel Ross – has finally explained everything to my father.' She shook her head. 'If only he'd told us some of this earlier.'

Sarah couldn't resist a smile. 'What did your father say when Ross told him he'd been the chief suspect for a while?'

Alice laughed. 'He was about ready to challenge him to a duel, I think. Then he saw the funny side of things, and they're getting along rather well now.'

'He's not such a bad person, is he?'

'Edmund?' Alice shook her head. 'Only he's so secretive, even when it's not needed.'

'I guess it comes with the job,' Sarah replied. 'He's a little like the Doctor in some ways, you know. They both keep secrets, sometimes too well.'

'I've been meaning to ask you,' Alice said, 'where is your friend? Nobody's seen him for a while, and everyone has questions that they want answered.'

Laughing, Sarah said, 'That's why he's not around. He hates explaining things. Besides, he's gone to fetch the TARDIS.'

'The TARDIS?' Alice frowned. 'Is that your carriage?'

'Something like that,' Sarah agreed. She just hoped that the Doctor was right, and that he really could make the short hop from Dartmoor to the beach. He'd probably have to go via Mars to make it, though. She'd had to trust him, because she had been too worn out from her adventures to accompany him back to the ship.

Another figure stumbled down the path from the town towards them. Sarah winced as she realized it was Kipling. She couldn't help liking the boy, but sometimes he could be such a nuisance. 'How are you feeling?' she asked him.

'Like I've got a hangover,' he admitted. 'I missed out on all the fun, I gather.'

'You were almost a part of it,' she told him. 'Breckinridge had a change in mind for you. Luckily, it didn't come about.' She smiled at him. 'Do you recall anything about last night?'

'After the graveyard?' He shrugged. 'All I know is that I dreamed of wolves, howling all about me.' He shook his head. 'Odd. Oh well.' He looked up at her. 'Will you be going now?'

'Soon,' Sarah admitted.

'Pity.' Kipling suddenly leaned forward and kissed her cheek. 'It's been fun, though. I won't forget you, Sarah Jane Smith.'

'Nor I you, Rudyard Kipling.' She laughed. 'You're going to make lots of people proud of you.'

He waved, nodded at Alice and then started back up the path. 'School's going to be ruddy dull after this,' he muttered. 'Wolves, graveyards, mermaids . . .' He disappeared, still muttering to himself.

'Not a bad sort, really,' Sarah said. She glanced at Alice. 'You're going to hear a lot more about him, you know. I'm glad I got to know him.'

Alice stared at her uncertainly. 'Are you . . .' she began. Then she screwed up her courage: 'Are you really from the future? The others were talking, and . . .' She gave a quick gesture of uncertainty with her hands.

'Yes,' Sarah admitted. 'I am.'

'Then you know what becomes of us all?' asked Alice.

'Not all,' Sarah admitted. 'Just a few of you, the ones I happen to have heard about for one reason or another in my time.'

'Oh.' Alice stood quietly beside Sarah, staring out to sea.

It was pleasant, standing here, with nothing much to think about. Sarah felt happy, just watching the sun rise and hearing the sound of the seagulls wheeling overhead. In the distance she could see several small boats. 'The fishing fleet's coming back,' she murmured.

There was a roaring, crashing, grinding sound that slowly began to fill the air. It appeared to be coming from a spot about ten feet down the beach. Alice went white and clutched at Sarah's arm.

'It's okay,' Sarah reassured her. 'I think that's my cab arriving.'

The air shimmered as the familiar outlines of the TARDIS formed and then solidified. There was a final thump and the sound died away, then the door was flung open and the Doctor stormed out. He was back in his usual costume, his hat rammed down over his curls, and the scarf trailing free once more instead of being tucked inside a cape coat.

'Right,' he said briskly. 'Time to finish things. Come along, Sarah, don't dawdle.'

Pulling a face at his retreating back, Sarah followed

him up the pathway and back to the factory. Alice, fighting down the questions she obviously wanted to ask, struggled to keep up with them.

The factory had been closed for the time being, until decisions could be made about its future. There was a small knot of men there, talking in animated fashion. Sarah recognized most of them: Colonel Ross and Abercrombie, Sir Edward Fulbright and Roger Bridewell, Arthur Conan Doyle and Sir Alexander Cromwell, Constable Faversham and Doctor Martinson, and the one-armed fisherman, Brackley.

'Ah,' Fulbright growled as they joined the party. 'Glad you're back.'

'So am I.' The Doctor turned to Ross. 'Now, I assume the main problem left is the children?'

'Yes,' he agreed. 'We've agreed that everything else can be kept quiet. There's certainly no need for any of this to come out. The salve is destroyed, I hope?'

'I believe so,' the Doctor answered. 'It doesn't mix too well with salt water. Even if it's not gone, it's so diluted now as to be useless.'

'Splendid.' Ross nodded briskly. It was obvious that he'd taken charge by virtue of his office as special agent to the Queen. 'But the children are a distinct problem.'

'Why can't we just leave them alone?' asked Doyle. 'They didn't ask for this, and they're harmless, surely?'

'No,' replied Ross and the Doctor, almost as one. The Doctor glared at him, and then amplified his response.

'The human race isn't ready to share this world with another species, Doyle.' The Doctor looked grim. 'And that's what those children have become. They can't stay here.' He glanced at Ross. 'There are always people who wouldn't rest until they were destroyed – or worse. I've a friend called the Brigadier who's a bit like that. He means well, but sometimes jumps the wrong way.' He stared at

256

Ross. 'One of your failings,' he added candidly.

'Possibly,' agreed Ross. 'But this is a real problem, and unless you have a better solution, I'm going to have to have those merbeings hunted down and killed.'

Doyle frowned. 'A brigadier who means well . . .' he mused. Then he blinked and stared at Ross. 'What you propose is nothing short of murder,' he snapped.

'Don't you think I'm aware of that?' asked Ross. He looked very pained. 'But I cannot allow those creatures to exist. They may be children now, but one day they will grow up and breed. Then we will have a nasty mess on our hands. Who knows how their minds will work?'

'Those creatures are, as you say, children.' The Doctor frowned. 'And I cannot condone your solution. I propose instead that I remove them from this planet and take them to another where they can set up their own society in peace.'

'Another world?' spluttered Sir Alexander. 'Are you out of your mind?'

'No,' Ross answered. 'He isn't.' He nodded to the Doctor. 'An admirable solution. As I say, I've no wish to harm them. Do you think they'll agree to this?'

'Given their options,' the Doctor answered, 'how can they refuse?'

'Quite.' Ross held out his hand. 'Well, Doctor, I wish you luck. As soon as everything is tidied up here, I'll be returning to London. Then who knows where?'

The Doctor considered for a moment, then shook the offered hand. 'Try to restrain that itchy trigger finger of yours,' he advised.

Doyle pulled his watch from his pocket. 'Well,' he said, reluctantly, 'Captain Gray sails within the hour. I'm sorry to miss out on the last bit, but I think I've done as much as I can.'

'You've been a marvellous help,' the Doctor replied.

'And I'm sure you'll have no problem with the writing.'

Doyle smiled. 'If nothing else, I've had a few ideas for stories from all of this.'

Ross glared at him. 'You'd better be certain that the incidents are very much disguised if you use any of this.'

'Otherwise,' the Doctor explained solemnly, 'her Majesty will not be amused. Take care, Doyle. I'd hate to think they'd reopen the Tower just for you.'

With a cheery wave, Doyle headed back towards the docks and the waiting *Hope*. Sarah turned back to the Doctor.

'These mermaids,' she said. 'You think you can talk to them? Can they still speak English?'

'I doubt it,' the Doctor informed her. 'I suspect they use a modified sonar method for speech, derived from the dolphin base. Fortunately I speak dolphin fluently.' He strode off towards the beach.

'Is he joking?' asked Alice.

'Haven't the vaguest idea,' Sarah answered. She wouldn't be too surprised if he were telling the truth. On the other hand, it could have been one of his jokes. 'Well, I guess it's time for me to say goodbye. Take care, Alice. It's been fun.'

'That's one word for it,' replied Alice. 'But it's not the first one that springs to my mind. Take care, Sarah. Shall we see you again?'

Sarah gave her a grin. 'Save me a slice of the wedding cake,' she suggested. 'I'll see if I can't pop round to eat it. Cheerio.'

'Are you coming, Sarah?' called the Doctor, without looking around.

With a final wave, Sarah dashed after him.

Back in her room in the TARDIS, Sarah changed into her borrowed swim-suit. The iridescent fabric moulded itself to her body again. Then she grabbed a towel and set off down the corridor towards the bathroom.

The TARDIS was in flight once again. Soft hums filled the corridor, just on the threshold of audibility. The Doctor had set the co-ordinates and vanished off in one of his mysterious mood swings again. Sarah didn't care how long the flight took, or even really where they were going. Some water planet in Andromeda was all the Doctor had bothered to explain.

She pushed open the door to the bathroom and walked in. A large beach-ball bounced off the tiles in front of her. High-pitched squeaks came from the pool. Laughing, Sarah chased the errant ball and tossed it back.

In the pool, twenty merchildren were romping and enjoying themselves. They were splashing, mock-fighting and laughing in squeaky voices. It was self-evident that they were happy. They had accepted the Doctor's offer of a new home without hesitation.

Sarah slipped into the water to join them. It was warm and there was the tang of salt. The Doctor had tipped in a bucketful to enable the merchildren to survive in the pool. Sarah pushed off from the side and swam out to join her new friends. The leader, Lucy, came to join her with a nimble flick of her tail. She held up her hand, palm forward, and piped a happy greeting.

Holding her own palm flat against Lucy's, Sarah smiled. 'Hello, friend,' she replied.

It didn't matter how long this voyage lasted. It was going to be a lot of fun.

Semi-Historical Notes

Sir Arthur Conan Doyle went on to become the writer he'd always dreamed he'd be. Aside from creating the bad-tempered man of science known as Professor Challenger (who the Doctor insists is not based on him), he also became the scribe of choice for a private consulting detective who preferred to be referred to as Sherlock Holmes. To further aid in this mysterious man's quest for obscurity, Doyle had his illustrators depict the detective in a deerstalker and cape coat.

Alice Bridewell went on to become one of the founders of the Women's Suffrage Movement, backed by her husband Roger and her ageing father.

Rudyard Kipling turned his hand to writing; first as a journalist and later as a novelist. Some of his tales dealt with time travel, and others with a child brought up with wolves.

Colonel Edmund Ross and his man Abercrombie continued in service to the Queen, having further strange adventures that may perhaps be safely related at a future date.

Lucy, Joshua and the others moved to a small world whose star is hardly even visible from the Earth.

The Doctor continues to travel.

Author's Note

Many of the details in this story are reasonably accurate. For help with information on the early life of Arthur Conan Doyle, I'd especially like to thank Bill vande Water, B.S.I., who came through with just the right material, as always. Some historical facts have been tampered with to better suit the plot, so please don't blame Bill for that.

Thanks are due to Rebecca Levene, Peter Darvill-Evans and Andy Bodle at Virgin for their patience and understanding, despite extreme provocation. And, finally, thanks to Alister Pearson for another stunning cover, and for allowing me to see the painting in advance.

Available in the Doctor Who – New Adventures series:

The next Missing Adventure, to be published in October 1994, is *Venusian Lullaby* by Paul Leonard, which will feature the first Doctor, Ian and Barbara.